DEAD ON THE TRACKS

It did seem as though we were traveling at a snail's pace, although this wasn't a sudden phenomenon. I'd noticed since leaving North Vancouver that the Whistler Northwind was not about to set any speed records. But that was the whole point—wasn't it?—a leisurely three-day journey on a classic train with every possible comfort, much like a luxury cruise ship, taking in the beauty and majesty of British Columbia. To go any faster would violate the very premise of the trip. And there were other passengers in the coaches up front, passengers who were unaware of the tragedy that had taken place in the car reserved for the members of the Track and Rail Club. Speed wouldn't help Al Blevin, not anymore. Still, I knew what Callie was feeling. I'm sure we all shared her desire to reach Whistler and get away from the train, away from the dead body in the club car. . . .

DESTINATION MURDER

A *Murder, She Wrote* Mystery

A Novel by Jessica Fletcher
and Donald Bain
based on the Universal television series
created by Peter S. Fischer,
Richard Levinson & William Link

A SIGNET BOOK

SIGNET
Published by New American Library, a division of
Penguin Group (USA) Inc., 375 Hudson Street,
New York, New York 10014, USA
Penguin Group (Canada), 90 Eglinton Avenue East, Suite 700, Toronto,
Ontario M4P 2Y3, Canada (a division of Pearson Penguin Canada Inc.)
Penguin Books Ltd., 80 Strand, London WC2R 0RL, England
Penguin Ireland, 25 St. Stephen's Green, Dublin 2,
Ireland (a division of Penguin Books Ltd.)
Penguin Group (Australia), 250 Camberwell Road, Camberwell, Victoria 3124,
Australia (a division of Pearson Australia Group Pty. Ltd.)
Penguin Books India Pvt. Ltd., 11 Community Centre, Panchsheel Park,
New Delhi - 110 017, India
Penguin Group (NZ), cnr Airborne and Rosedale Roads, Albany,
Auckland 1310, New Zealand (a division of Pearson New Zealand Ltd.)
Penguin Books (South Africa) (Pty) Ltd., 24 Sturdee Avenue,
Rosebank, Johannesburg 2196, South Africa

Penguin Books Ltd., Registered Offices:
80 Strand, London WC2R 0RL, England

Published by Signet, an imprint of New American Library, a division of Penguin Group (USA) Inc. Previously published in a New American Library
edition.

First Signet Printing, September 2004
10 9 8 7 6

For Abigail Kathryn Paley Brown

ACKNOWLEDGMENTS

Thanks to naturaltraveler.com's founder, and friend, **Tony Tedeschi**, for suggesting that the story be set in Vancouver and on a train into British Columbia, and for paving the way.

And our gratitude to:

   Cathy Thomson and **Bruce Stephen**, and their top-notch staff, at Vancouver's wonderful Sutton Place Hotel.

   BCRail's **Jean Cullen** and **Elaine Drever** and PR counsel **Nora Weber**.

   Annabel Hawksworth, publicist for the splendid Top Table Restaurant Group.

   Detectives **Rob Faoro** and **Sean Trowski** and Sergeant **Bob Cooper** of the Vancouver Police Department's Homicide Squad.

   The Vancouver Tourist Board's **Laura Serena** and **Kate Colley Lo**.

   BC Tourism's **Mika Ryan**.

   Whistler's **Danielle Saindon** and **Michelle Comeau**, and **Monica Hayes** for her courtesies at the ski resort's spectacular Westin Resort and Spa.

   Patrick Corbett, owner of Hills Health Ranch.

   Some liberties were taken for the sake of the story. All errors are ours.

Chapter One

Vancouver guidebooks claim that the corner of Robson and Burrard Streets has more foot traffic than any other intersection in Canada. From what I observed, that isn't an overstatement. The streets were chock-ablock with people, overwhelmingly young. The city's large Asian population was very much in evidence, although every ethnic group was abundantly visible in the shops that lined both sides of the street and in the mix of eateries with outdoor dining patios. There seemed to be a Starbucks on every corner, testimony to the Pacific Northwest's love affair with coffee, and lots of candy shops, too.

Vancouver, British Columbia, is one of my favorite cities in the world. Poised on the tip of a peninsula, with the Coast Mountains smiling down on the advancing spires of skyscrapers under construction, it has all the eagerness and energy of a frontier town, which it was once and in a sense still is. It's the launching port for myriad cruise ships that ply the inland waterways leading to an even newer frontier in Alaska. And it's both the terminus and departure point for locomotives chugging their way through the mountain passes, exposing millions of tourists to the rugged beauty of Canada's western provinces. I'd fallen in love with the city and its citizens' sense of adventure and pleasure in nature two years earlier while on a book promotion tour and kept trying to find the time, and an excuse, to revisit it. Reggie Weems gave me that excuse.

Reggie had a successful insurance agency back home in Cabot Cove. He also had a hobby—trains. The large basement in his home was devoted to an elaborate model train layout, considered the finest in all of New England, and he was an active member of the Track and Rail Club, an organization of railroad buffs that held its annual meeting in different cities around the world. This year's site was Vancouver, and when Reggie invited me to join the group on its journey, I readily accepted.

But it wasn't just the lure of Vancouver that made up my mind. Each of Track and Rail's annual meetings centered around a trip on a historic train. The highlight of the week would be a three-day journey on the famed Whistler Northwind from Vancouver up into the British Columbia interior, passing through and over glacier-carved canyons to the famous Whistler resort, then following the Cariboo Gold Rush Trail and Fraser River Canyon to a town called 100 Mile House, and finally arriving at Prince George, with overnight stays in hotels at each stop. I've always loved traveling by rail and am dismayed at how we've allowed train travel to founder in our country.

I walked for an hour along Robson Street, taking it all in, occasionally popping into a store to browse but leaving empty-handed. I was to meet Reggie shortly at the chocolate buffet in the Sutton Place Hotel, where we were staying. I considered pausing for a snack. It was six-thirty local time, nine-thirty back home according to my circadian clock. But I'd had a big meal on the plane, and the contemplation of facing twenty types of chocolate desserts in an hour was enough to stifle that urge.

I was on my way back to the hotel when the only unpleasant moment of the afternoon occurred. As I turned into the driveway, following a small group of people, a limo—black windows concealing its occupants—came around the corner and drew up to the hotel's entrance. An elegant couple emerged from the car's darkened interior, and the woman peered in my direction. A man walking in front of me did an abrupt about-face and slammed into me, almost knocking me off my feet. I kept myself from falling by grabbing the shoulder of a woman standing nearby. I had a brief glimpse of the man's face because our collision caused him to come to a momentary halt. He was deeply tanned, with piercing, almost black eyes, sharp features, and shaggy, shoulder-length coal-black hair hanging over his ears. If I expected an apology, I was to be disappointed. He hurried away; all I saw was the back of him as he pushed through people coming out of a side door to the bar and disappeared around a corner.

"Jerk!" said the woman whose shoulder had kept me from falling.

"An inconsiderate one at that," I said, brushing the skirt of my black-and-white shirtwaist dress. "Thanks for the shoulder to lean on."

"No problem."

By the time I walked into the hotel, I'd put the incident out of my mind. Rude, inconsiderate people could be found everywhere in the world, even in a friendly, courteous city like Vancouver.

"Jessica! There you are."

Reggie Weems bounded across the beige granite floor. The Sutton Place lobby was a handsome space, with its graceful chandeliers, huge vases of freshly cut flowers, and European artwork—which included magnificent large, original oils behind the front desk by French Impressionist Bernard Cathelin, who'd studied with Matisse. I'd commented on the paintings when I'd checked in and had received their provenance from the clerk along with my room key.

We'd flown in together from Boston that morning. Reggie had worn what he called his flying outfit: chino pants, multipocketed safari shirt—"My answer to a woman's purse," he'd told me—and loafers that could be slipped off and on easily, should security people at the airport wish to inspect them. For the buffet, he'd changed into a blue double-breasted blazer, a white shirt, a burgundy tie with tiny locomotives in gold emblazoned on it, crisply pressed gray slacks, and two-tone shoes. Reggie was a short man of slender build with a narrow face and a prominent nose on which oversized eyeglasses rested. He walked with a perpetual spring in his step. He was considered a bit of a dandy in Cabot Cove and was well liked throughout the community, although the fact that he'd never married occasionally raised inevitable but unwarranted speculation about his sexual orientation. Aside from an insurance client complaining over the terms of a claim settlement every once in a while, no one seemed to have a bad word to say about him.

"Ah, Jessica, how was your shopping expedition? I see you're empty-handed."

"I had a lovely walk, Reggie. How was your meeting?"

He scowled. "Not especially pleasant. The club's board's been having its differences and . . . well, that's not of interest to you. Ready for a trip to chocolate heaven?"

I followed him to the hotel's famed chocolate buffet,

located in the elegant Fleuri Restaurant, its walls covered in rich damask, the tables graced with floral-print skirts. Three tables were laden with a variety of chocolate desserts waiting to be sampled and were presided over by a female chef in a white uniform, who described the delicacies on offer. It had sounded absolutely decadent to me when Reggie suggested it, but once I stood before the incredible array of artistic creations concocted by Sutton Place's chocolate chef, I decided I was ready for a taste of decadence. I placed tiny portions of Sacher torte, hot chocolate soufflé, chocolate mousse made with Jack Daniel's, and a chocolate crème brûlée on my plate—saving the chocolate pie, chocolate sorbet, and crêpes with chocolate sauce for another time—and carried it back to a table where Reggie, his selections already on the table in front of him, sat with four people to whom I'd been introduced earlier. Hank and Deedee Crocker were from Pittsburgh. Hank was an accountant; his wife was a florist—"I used to sell flowers but now I specialize in exotic plants. All the decorators love my shop." Junior and Maeve Pinckney of Atlanta were, respectively, an auto parts dealer and a part-time real estate broker.

"Ah'm quite a fan of your books, Mrs. Fletcher," Maeve said in a pronounced drawl. She was clothed like the quintessential southern belle, her dress a frilly white and yellow number that came up high on her neck. A pretty woman with a creamy complexion, wide hazel eyes, and full sensuous lips, she had a deft hand at makeup and an enviable metabolism, if the pile of sweets on her plate was any indication. "When ah heard you would be joining us on this trip, ah became absolutely excited," she said, digging into a slice of chocolate mousse cake heaped high with whipped cream.

"Thank you," I said. "I wouldn't have missed it. I understand the train we're taking in the morning has quite a history."

That was a cue for Maeve's husband to launch into a lecture on the Whistler Northwind and historic trains in general. Junior was a pudgy man with red hair, a ruddy face, and large, moist eyes. Like Reggie, he wore a blue blazer, but with a pink golf shirt and no tie. His plate was overflowing with chocolate goodies from the buffet, and his accent was decidedly south of the Mason-Dixon Line.

"We'll be in the Summit Coach," he said. "The Pavilion club car next to it was built back in '39 for the Florida East Coast Railroad. Only stainless steel car on the train, built by the Budd Company. Was known as the Bay Biscayne car when it was runnin' between New York and Florida. BC Rail picked it up in 2000 after Amtrak sold it to a company in Nashville. They ran it as the Broadway Dinner Train."

"How interesting," I said.

"Junior's quite an expert on old trains, Mrs. Fletcher," said his wife.

"Please call me Jessica."

"Hank and Deedee know a lot about historic trains, too," Reggie said; I had a feeling he'd offered it to head off another of Junior's speeches.

"How many trips have you taken on old trains?" I asked the Crockers.

"We've lost track," Hank replied, interrupting whatever his wife was about to say. He was a nondescript middle-aged man with grayish skin and a hangdog expression that I would go on to observe seldom left his face. He spoke in a monotone, the barest hint of irony coloring his voice. "At least I have."

"I think we've taken every trip since the organization was formed," Deedee put in. She was a small, birdlike woman with sharp features and a cap of fine brown hair. Both of them were dressed informally, in navy slacks and matching Hawaiian shirts.

"Nineteen years ago," Reggie offered.

"Are there that many historic railroads running?" I asked.

"Oh, sure," Junior cut in, resuming his animated lesson on railroad history.

We all listened politely until he stopped in midsentence and looked at a striking man and woman poised to enter the restaurant. It was the couple I'd seen getting out of the limo.

"Look who's here," Hank Crocker muttered, his tone not friendly.

"Is *she* coming with us?" Deedee Crocker asked in a whisper.

"Seems so," Reggie said, adding a small laugh. "How about that?"

I leaned close to Reggie and asked, "Who are they?"

He said into my ear, "Alvin Blevin and his wife, Theodora."

"Some people are just so brazen," Maeve Pinckney said with a sigh.

"Fraud," Hank mumbled to himself. But I heard it, and it caused me to straighten in my chair.

"Alvin Blevin's our club president, Jess," Reggie whispered to me. "It gets a little complicated. His wife, Theodora, used to be married to a man named Elliott Vail. Elliott was active in the club until he disappeared three years ago."

"Disappeared?"

"Yup. Just like that. He's never been found."

"Oh, my. No indication of what happened to him?"

Reggie shook his head. "Well, there are rumors . . ."

"I wouldn't be surprised if she killed him," Maeve drawled.

"Oh, come on, Maeve," Reggie said.

"She may be right," Hank said. "No one knows for sure what happened."

I said to Reggie, "You say she's married to that man she's with?"

"Right."

"But her missing husband can't have been declared legally dead. It's too soon. It generally takes seven years."

"Not if you have a powerful, well-connected lawyer like Alvin Blevin," said Hank from Pittsburgh. "He handled her case and got a judge to declare Elliott legally dead after only three years."

"She must have inherited a lot of money," Maeve said, "because he divorced his wife right away and married her. Caused quite a scandal here in Vancouver, or so I've been told."

I watched Blevin and his wife as they chatted with one of the restaurant's hostesses before smoothly moving to the chocolate buffet. Alvin Blevin was a tall, broad-shouldered man with the bearing of a successful attorney or United States senator. A full head of silver-gray hair was carefully coifed, and he sported a deep tan. His gray suit looked English cut to me, possibly from one of London's exclusive custom tailors. His wife, Theodora, was as impressive as her husband in stature and bearing. Tall, with an exquisite figure sheathed in an aqua silk pants suit, she had what's generally called classic features: chiseled cheekbones, a nose of appropriate size and shape, and thin lips made to appear slightly larger with lipstick. Her hair was silver-blond and meticulously arranged. A power couple to be certain, commanding attention whenever entering a room, as they had with us.

"Hank sued Alvin," Deedee Crocker said of her husband.

Reggie quickly said, "I don't think Jessica is interested in the club's dirty laundry, Deedee." To me: "Are you, Jess?"

"Well, I—"

"Ah imagine Mrs. Fletcher is always interested in people's dirty laundry," said Maeve, "bein' a mystery writer and all."

"Please, it's Jessica."

Hank Crocker said, "I sued him because he was misusing the club's money."

"Oh?"

"Here they come."

The Blevins approached the table, their small plates of chocolate delicacies carried by a uniformed waiter.

"How's everyone doing?" Blevin asked as they paused tableside. His voice was deep and well modulated, no surprise, his light blue eyes piercing. He had a cleft in his chin, and a jaw that jutted forward determinedly.

"Just fine, Al," Reggie said, standing. "Say hello to my friend Jessica Fletcher."

"The famous murder mystery writer," Blevin said, taking my hand. "I heard you were joining us. Delighted, I'm sure. This is my wife, Theodora."

"Pleased to meet you," I said.

She gave forth with what she considered a smile, I suppose.

"Death by chocolate," Blevin said, his grin exposing a staunch set of teeth, their whiteness rendered more so against the tan of his handsome, rugged face. "Enjoy. See everyone on the train in the morning."

When they were gone, Junior Pinckney said, "He's too damn slick for my taste."

"He's a thief," Hank muttered, focusing on the plate in front of him.

"I still say she must have murdered her first husband, that dear man, Elliott," Maeve said softly. "And Alvin, taken in by her." She shook her head. "I thought he was more discerning than that."

I ate my chocolate treats, thankful when the conversation about the Blevins ended.

Later, I joined Reggie for a drink in the hotel's Gerard Lounge, an English club–style room that I was told was Vancouver's favorite celebrity-spotting venue. He seemed distressed.

"You look as though you need that drink, Reggie," I said, referring to a large perfect Manhattan in front of him. I opted for a club soda with lime.

"Everything would be so simple if it weren't for people," he said glumly.

I laughed. "Someone giving you a hard time?"

"Seems like everyone is. Hank Crocker is just waiting to make a scene. I dread it."

"Mr. Crocker said something about having sued Mr. Blevin. What was that all about?"

"He wasn't entirely in the wrong—understand?—but Hank doesn't know how to handle anything with subtlety, much less diplomacy. He just rams ahead like a bull."

"What happened?"

Reggie sighed. "Blevin decided to build himself the world's biggest and best model railroad layout."

"That doesn't sound unreasonable," I said.

"It would have been fine if he hadn't done it with club funds. Crocker voted against it, but Blevin sold the rest of the board on allowing him to do it, and he went ahead."

"So he had the board's approval."

Reggie raised a finger. "He was supposed to create the layout in modules so that it could be transported around the country for display by different regional chapters."

"He didn't do that?"

"Unfortunately not, Jess, although whether it was on purpose or not, I won't venture to guess. Blevin owns a big office building here in Vancouver. He donated one of the floors as club headquarters; it's huge, plenty of space for meetings, even has a plush conference room for the board of directors."

"That sounds very generous."

"Oh, sure, it is. But he designed the model layout to fill up three-quarters of that floor. It's got both O and HO gauge running on five different levels, a complete set of Micro-Metakit—the engine alone cost over two thousand—plus I don't know how many miles of track. He's got most of British Columbia's rail lines represented, even duplicated the Fraser Canyon down to the muddy river, which rises with rainfall."

"That sounds expensive."

"That's putting it mildly. It's got to have close to a million invested in it, and he says it's not done yet."

"Was all of that the club's money?"

"A good portion, but he must have sunk a lot of his own into it, too. Still, once it was finished, it was supposed to go on tour. But when they tried to break it down, they discovered the modules had been made too large; they wouldn't fit through the door. Instead of a source of pride and joy which all the club members could share in, it ended up Alvin's own personal toy. Hank is convinced he made it that way on purpose."

"I see. But if people are angry with him about it, why not simply elect another president?"

Reggie finished his drink and motioned for the waitress to bring him another. "I ran for president against Alvin two years ago and got trounced. No matter how much members complain about his high-handed tactics, they realize he owns the building, and they like having such posh headquarters. Not many clubs have anything like it. Besides, he's put some of his own money into club programs. He's loaded. Nobody likes him, but they're not about to get rid of him."

With his fresh drink before him, Reggie opened a folder he'd been carrying and said, "Let me run through the train trip itinerary with you."

The itinerary had been mailed to me in Cabot Cove and I'd already gone over it, but Reggie seemed determined to explain it to me. We would be three days on the Whistler Northwind and three days in Vancouver. A trip to a local railroad museum was scheduled for the day after our return, as was a club dinner at a local restaurant.

"Oh, almost forgot," Reggie said. "We'll be taking BC Rail's Pacific Starlight Dinner Train our last night in Vancouver. It was up in the air, but I got a call this evening confirming. It's not on your itinerary."

"Another train, another meal," I said. "I hope they don't have a chocolate buffet on it. It was absolutely delicious, but—"

"A chocolate a day keeps the doctor away."

I laughed. "I think you mean an apple."

"Do I? I'll take chocolate any day."

We soon left the bar and he escorted me to my tenth-floor suite.

"Sleep tight," he said.

"I'm sure I will," I said. "It's well after midnight on my Cabot Cove clock."

I dressed for bed and curled up with a bestselling

mystery on the couch in the large living room of the suite. But my mind was too active to read. What a shame, I thought, closing the book, that people who share so much, a love of trains and traveling by rail, would have such acrimony within their ranks. I hoped they'd be able to put aside their differences and simply enjoy the three-day journey.

I got into bed and turned off the light. Various images came and went as my eyes began to close, including a fleeting image of the man who'd collided with me outside the hotel. "Jerk," I said softly, repeating what the person with the helpful shoulder had said. I smiled and turned my thoughts to the excitement of the excursion ahead. Nothing, not rude pedestrians nor squabbling club members, would spoil my enjoyment of the Whistler Northwind, I promised myself before allowing sleep to engulf me.

Had I known, however, that the Northwind would soon be the scene of a grisly murder, I might not have been so eager to take that trip.

Chapter Two

"All aboard!"

I hadn't heard that nostalgic summons to board a train in many years, aside from scenes from old black-and-white movies where a conductor calls out in his best baritone. This day it was announced in stentorian tones by Bruce, the Whistler Northwind's guest services supervisor. He'd made the rounds of passengers in the small, pleasant station house in North Vancouver prior to our leaving, happily welcoming us, fielding last-minute questions, and distributing souvenir pins: a circle with a W over an N, divided by an arrow. There was a large group clustered around a coffee and pastry bar for those who hadn't had time for breakfast before leaving the hotel and who couldn't wait until we were served brunch on the train. Others waited eagerly on the platform outside or wandered through a picnic area where a striking young man, presumably another passenger, sat alone at a table. While I watched, a young woman in uniform came over and sat down with him. She offered him a doughnut.

Eventually, Bruce and his staff rounded us up and we were led to our cars on the Whistler Northwind, where the onboard serving staff stood at attention as we approached, the attractive young men and women smartly dressed in black slacks, white shirts, silver-patterned vests, and straight ties. Hands were extended to help us step up onto the train and into the Summit Coach, which had been reserved for our group, a luxury domed car with tinted glass on the upper portion to mitigate the sun's rays. Seating was two abreast on each side of the aisle, and we were instructed to choose any of the large, comfortable seats. It was surprisingly modern, considering it was part of a historic train, but the cars that flanked it were of an older vintage. While we waited for last-minute stragglers to arrive, I took the opportunity to explore them. On one end of the Summit was the club car, the Pavilion, which Junior had talked about. It had stainless steel walls and casual seating served by a bar. It was the oldest car on the train, Bruce proudly told me.

"All our cars have seen service around North America and beyond. Your dining car, for instance, was once part of the City of Denver, which ran from Chicago to Denver."

When I poked my head into the Strathnaver, the original name of our dining car, it was already set for our brunch with immaculate white table linens, gleaming glass and silverware, and vases of colorful fresh flowers. An art deco–style mural depicting scenes from British Columbia, through which the train would travel, was painted in a panel over the windows and ran down one length of the car and up the other. Permanently coupled to it was the D'Arcy kitchen car, a full-service galley with the latest in commercial cooking equipment.

"Mind if ah join you?" Maeve Pinckney asked after I'd returned to the Summit Coach and settled into a window seat near the front.

"Please," I said.

After she was seated, I asked, "Where's your husband?"

"Junior? Probably out takin' pictures of the train with some of the other foamers."

"Foamers?"

"Railroad buffs. You know, they foam at the mouth over choo-choo trains." She laughed, shook her head, and pulled out needlepoint she'd already started. "Won't see much o' Junior for the next three days. He'll be hangin' out the door between cars the whole trip. I guess you could say ah'm a train widow."

"You don't seem to mind," I said.

"Ah'm used to it by now, Jessica. I've been on more damn trains over the past twenty years than I can keep count of." She turned to her needlepoint, leaving me to observe other passengers as they chose their seats. Hank and Deedee Crocker, the couple from Pittsburgh I'd met the night before, sat a few rows back, across the aisle from us. I noticed that Theodora Blevin, whose entrance had sparked heated comment at the chocolate buffet, had taken a window seat and piled hand luggage on the seat next to her, perhaps to keep anyone else from joining her. Her husband sat in a seat behind her. Next to him was the handsome young man I'd seen at the picnic table, who I judged to be in his mid twenties.

There were three long blasts on the whistle, and as the train shuddered and started moving forward, those passengers who'd been taking pictures and exploring the adjoining cars spilled through the door to find their seats. The club had reserved the entire car, but with only half the seats taken, there was plenty of room to move around.

After safety instructions were read, much like on an aircraft prior to takeoff, we were truly on our way, and people began to leave their seats and mingle in the aisle. I excused myself to Maeve and went to the opposite side of the car to take in the passing scenery from that vantage point. The train moved through a busy rail yard with multiple tracks, emerging into an industrial area with a view of the city across Burrard Inlet, a body of water that separates North Vancouver from the municipal center.

Reggie joined me. "All settled in, Jess?" he asked.

"Oh, yes. The seats are very comfortable."

Even though the places around us were empty, Reggie glanced left and right to ensure we were alone before nodding toward where the Blevins sat and saying softly, "See the young guy next to Alvin?"

"Yes?"

"Theodora's son by her marriage to Elliott Vail. Name's Benjamin."

I kept a smile to myself. Reggie was known back home in Cabot Cove to be an inveterate gossip. If you wanted to know what was going on in town—what was *really* going on—ask Reggie.

"I noticed him at the station before we left," I said. "He sat outside at one of the picnic tables."

"He's one of those brooding types," Reggie said conspiratorially. "You know, like all the young male models you see in magazines and catalogues."

I sighed. "I suppose knowing that your father disappeared and has never been found can take a toll on a young man."

Our conversation was interrupted as the staff arrived carrying trays of champagne flutes and glasses of orange juice. Once everyone had been served, Bruce proposed a toast: "To each of you and your journey on the famed Whistler Northwind." With that, the staff passed through the car clinking glasses with us, creat-

ing a festive atmosphere as the engineer gave another
sharp blast of the train's whistle.

I went to the vestibule linking the coach and dining
cars. The top half of the exterior door on either side
was open, allowing people to lean out and take in the
scenery from that windy perspective. Maeve's husband, Junior, was where she said he would be, head
and shoulders jutting out through the opening, camera
in hand, an Atlanta Braves baseball hat worn backwards on his head. I didn't want to disturb his reverie,
and when I turned away, I found myself face-to-face
with Alvin Blevin.

"Enjoying yourself, Mrs. Fletcher?" he asked. Unlike
everyone else on the train, who'd dressed in casual
clothing, Blevin wore an expensively tailored single-
breasted tan blazer, white shirt, and club tie.

"Very much," I said. "And it's Jessica."

"Lovely old train, isn't it, Jessica?"

"Old, but nicely refurbished. Our coach looks
brand-new inside."

"That's because it is. They've mixed old and new
cars on the Whistler Northwind. But the dining car
goes back to nineteen fifty-three."

"I have a lot to learn about trains."

He flashed a big smile. "Don't get caught up in it
like us, Jessica. A simple hobby can become an obses-
sion. Say, they'll be serving brunch soon. I'd be pleased
if you'd join our table."

"I'd be delighted."

I stood just inside the coach car and did a fast mental count of the number of people in our party. I esti-
mated I was one of thirty people, which didn't fill even
half the car. According to Reggie, vacationers occupy-
ing other cars on the train had no connection to the
Track and Rail Club.

"A shame," a man from behind said.

I turned to the voice.

"What's a shame?" I asked.

"The number of people with us this trip," he said in an unmistakable British accent, extending his hand. "Winston Rendell," he said, "and no need for you to introduce yourself. I'm well aware of who you are, Mrs. Fletcher. One can hardly escape your name. Your reputation as a writer of popular mysteries is as firmly entrenched in England as it is here and in the States."

"I'm flattered," I said, not entirely sure I should be. "Rendell? Any relation to Ruth Rendell, one of your famous mystery writers?"

"Afraid not. Frankly, I prefer the crime novels of Baroness P. D. James, but they both have such command of the language—so literary, almost not like genre writing at all, don't you think?"

"I love their books," I said, wondering if his intention was to insult me by grouping me with "genre" writers.

"Researching your next whodunit, *Murder on the Whistler Northwind*?"

"Oh my, no." Ignoring my suspicion that Mr. Rendell was not exactly a fan, I changed the subject and explained why I was with the group. "Is this a smaller turnout than usual?"

"So I'm told. The numbers on these trips have been dwindling year after year. Of course, that doesn't reflect interest in trains. The club membership continues to grow. But—" He looked past me to where Blevin stood next to his wife's seat and lowered his voice. "There are rumbles of bad leadership, I'm afraid," he said. "T and R used to be a democratic organization, as it should be. But some felt it belonged to them and took a rather dictatorial approach to leading it."

"But here *you* are," I said, "all the way from England."

"Ah, but for reasons other than communing with fellow railroad buffs."

"Other foamers?"

"You're learning fast. Yes, quite right. I'm here on business."

"Are you in the railroad business back in England, Mr. Rendell?"

"In a manner of speaking. I'm researching a book. You see, I'm an author as well, Mrs. Fletcher, perhaps not as celebrated as you, but with a measure of respect in my field." He again looked past me. "You'll excuse me, I'm sure. There's someone I must speak with. I hope we have another opportunity to converse. Perhaps you'll join me for the brunch?"

"Thank you, but someone else has already invited me," I said, grateful I could decline.

"My loss, then. Another time, I hope."

I watched him move up the aisle, deftly navigating the train's slight swaying movement, and disappear into the club car, where the bar was located. A man of dubious charm, I thought as I entered the coach car.

The train chugged slowly through North Vancouver, paralleling the coastline. Leaving the industrial section behind, it parted residential neighborhoods; apartment buildings and houses hugged the tracks on precious real estate affording a view of the water. As the train slid into West Vancouver, along the beach, lush greenery shielded elegant homes from the curious eyes of passersby. As the skyline of downtown Vancouver across the water faded from view, the shorefront properties grew larger and the homes farther apart.

"Those are multimillion-dollar estates," a woman standing in the aisle said.

"I don't doubt it," I replied.

"West Vancouver. It's the richest city in Canada," she continued. "We haven't met yet. I'm Marilyn Whitmore." She placed a hand on the shoulder of the young woman in the aisle seat. "And this is my daughter, Samantha."

"Pleased to meet you," I said, introducing myself.

The mother was a handsome woman with strong, square features, short-cropped salt-and-pepper hair, and judiciously applied makeup. The daughter was a younger and larger version of her mother, their facial characteristics very much alike, although Samantha wasn't wearing any makeup. Two things were immediately apparent about her. She was obviously physically fit, broad-shouldered and with well-sculpted bare arms ending in large hands with thick fingers. And her expression was vacant, especially her eyes, unnaturally placid and lacking in affect, as though she might be on some sort of tranquilizing medication.

"Reggie told us you were coming on this trip," Marilyn said pleasantly.

"It was good of him to invite me. Are you both railroad buffs?"

"Oh, no," Marilyn replied. "My late husband was, though."

"And his passion for trains rubbed off on you?" I asked.

She smiled as she said, "To some extent."

"I'm just keeping her company," Samantha said. Her voice was low and husky.

"Samantha is a nurse," said her mother.

"A noble profession," I said.

"Yeah, well, they don't pay much for nobility these days," Samantha growled.

I was taken aback by the vehemence in her voice, but I said, "I'm sure that's true, considering that lives hang in the balance."

"Tell me about it," Samantha said with what passed for a laugh.

"We're about to enter the Horseshoe Bay Tunnel, more than four thousand feet long, the longest tunnel of our trip," one of the female staff announced over the PA system. Her nametag read Jenna C. She was a sprightly young woman with twinkling blue eyes and a dimple in her chin. She looked familiar, and I thought perhaps she was the young woman who'd offered Benjamin Vail a doughnut prior to our boarding. I couldn't be sure.

"And I am happy to announce that brunch is now served in the dining room," she added.

I sat with Alvin and Theodora Blevin, as planned. The fourth seat at the table was left vacant; I wondered why her son, Benjamin, wasn't sitting with us. An adjacent table was also unoccupied, and I speculated that others enjoying brunch were deliberately avoiding being close to their president.

We chatted over a fruit plate and smoked wild sockeye salmon with a bagel and crisp coleslaw. Blevin dominated the conversation. His wife said little. She appeared to be uncomfortable even being there. That she was a beautiful woman was beyond debate, but her natural beauty seemed frozen, an ice sculpture. She was as immaculately dressed as he was and sat ramrod straight in her chair, her only movement the slow lifting of the fork to her mouth. I felt sorry for her in a way. Her husband was obviously a force to be reckoned with, in a courtroom and probably at home, too.

Of course, the brief history of their marriage that I'd been given the previous night tended to heighten my curiosity. Her former husband, whose name I remembered was Elliott Vail, had disappeared and had been declared legally dead by a court. Alvin Blevin, who sat across from me this morning, had represented Theodora Vail in that proceeding. Once her husband had been deemed legally dead, Blevin had divorced his wife and married Theodora, his client—an intriguing scenario, to be sure.

But none of that entered our conversation. Blevin talked about trains mostly; his knowledge of the history of railroading in Canada was impressive, if a little too filled with minutiae for me.

After coffee, he asked me, "Will you be staying in Vancouver after the trip, or flying directly home from Prince George?"

"I'll be in Vancouver for a few days," I replied. "Reggie Weems is my host, and he's here for the whole week."

"Then you must visit the club's headquarters. It's in a downtown building I own. We have a model railroad layout I think you'd enjoy seeing. It's one of the largest in North America."

"So I've been told."

"Undoubtedly accompanied by a few snide comments," he said, glancing at other tables. He smiled. "We have three glorious days to talk trains, Jessica," he said, dabbing his mouth with a napkin and standing and holding out his wife's chair. "And you can fill us in on how a famous writer comes up with her plots."

"How do you come up with them?" Theodora asked, her first sign of interest in me.

"I'm not really sure," I replied. "I basically use the 'what if' approach. I ask myself what if something were to occur, or what if someone were to take an action, and go from there. Not very sophisticated, I admit, but it works for me."

"Works for inventors, too," Blevin said. "Well, this was pleasant and informative. Thanks for joining us. Theodora, are you ready, dear?"

When they left the table, Reggie joined me. He'd been sitting with a young couple I hadn't met yet.

"Hobnobbing with the rich and famous, I see," he said with a laugh.

"An interesting couple," I said.

"So are they," he said, indicating the couple with whom he'd just had brunch. "Newcomers to the club. First time on a trip with us."

"Husband the train buff, wife along for the ride?" I asked.

"Just the opposite," Reggie said. "She's the buff, knows a lot about early steam engines."

When I eventually returned to the coach car, Deedee Crocker was standing at a window with an open book in her palm.

"What are you looking for?" I asked.

"It's not what I'm looking for as much as what I'm looking at," she replied. "*Linaria vulgaris*. Also called common toadflax or, for those who are more romantic, butter-and-eggs."

"And they are?"

"Wildflowers. There are lots of wildflowers in British Columbia, and they're particularly plentiful growing along a railroad track."

"How nice," I said, coming to her side. "I'd noticed there were lots of flowers. Which ones are the butter-and-eggs?"

"We've passed them already, although we'll probably see them again. It's a funny name, butter-and-eggs.

They're pretty, kind of like little snapdragons, but they smell terrible."

"Why are they called butter-and-eggs?"

"The flowers are a buttery yellow and they have an orange 'nose' which is kind of an egg yolk color. If we're lucky, we might see the blue or purple toadflax. They're pretty, too."

"Do you use wildflowers in your arrangements?"

"You remembered that I'm a florist," she said, pleased. "But no, I don't use wildflowers, because I don't do arrangements anymore. I specialize in exotic plants now, rare and unusual specimens. Orchids and bromeliads and other tropical ornamentals." She launched into a description of her inventory, mistaking my interest for passion. I realized I would learn more about plants and trains on this trip than I had ever anticipated.

I noticed that a number of passengers had gone through to the club car, and when Deedee paused for breath, I excused myself and decided to join them. One of the staff, a bubbly gal named Callie, had stationed herself behind the bar.

"I make the best Bloody Marys in all of British Columbia," she announced. "Probably all of Canada, and maybe even all of the States."

"We'll put you to the test a little later," Hank Crocker said.

"Anyone game for one now?" she asked.

A few people responded and she went to work mixing her special brand of the popular drink. I settled in a club chair next to the young couple who'd been with Reggie in the dining car.

"I'm Jessica Fletcher."

"Marty and Gail Goldfinch," he said.

"Nice to meet you both. I understand you're quite knowledgeable about steam engines," I said to Gail.

Her laugh was self-effacing. "I know a little."

"More than she lets on," Martin said.

"I grew up in a house full of brothers," Gail said. "They'd never let me play with their toy trains, so I'm making up for it now."

Marilyn Whitmore entered the club car and joined us. We were in the midst of a pleasant conversation, which had nothing to do with trains, when Alvin Blevin entered the car, paused, generated a wide smile, and came to where we sat. He extended his hand to Marilyn and said, "So good to see you again, Marilyn. Sorry we didn't have a chance to chat earlier, but—"

"Hello, Al," she said, not accepting his hand. She managed a tight smile, but her tone was distinctly unwelcoming.

Martin Goldfinch rose quickly, introduced himself and his wife, and shook Blevin's hand.

"Please, sit down," Blevin said, the smile never leaving his face. "I see you've caught up with our resident author. Good for you." He laid his hand on Marilyn's shoulder and I saw her wince. "Marilyn is a veteran of many Northwind trips," Blevin said. "I'm sure she can fill you in on the pleasures ahead."

Marilyn angled her body toward me and away from Blevin.

"I hope all of you will enjoy the trip," he said, and moved away.

Gail looked meaningfully at her husband, and the Goldfinches excused themselves and went to stand at the bar.

"That was such a nice brunch, wasn't it?" I said, thinking to defuse the tension. "By the way, where's Samantha?"

"Napping. She . . ." A shadow of sadness came and went on her face.

"Did you used to accompany your husband on these trips?" I asked, casting about for a conversational topic and hoping I wasn't treading on too sensitive an area.

"Oh, yes," she said, her eyes lighting up, and I relaxed. "Some of the trips were wonderful. We rode famous trains in Europe and all over the U.S. The last one was a few years ago, the Twentieth-Century Limited from New York to Chicago. The Sunset Limited from Houston was before that. And, of course, there was the Orient Express. But you must know all about that, being a mystery writer."

"Only through Agatha Christie. I've wanted to ride the famed Orient Express for years but have never gotten around to it. Maybe this trip will inspire me."

"This is my third time on the Whistler Northwind," she said wistfully, turning to look out the window. "Living in Vancouver, we have wonderful access to it. It will always be my favorite."

When she left to check on her daughter, I picked up a magazine and browsed through it. The train's motion had an almost hypnotic effect, gently moving from side to side, a quiet ride, the only harsh sound when the train's metal wheels encountered curved sections of track.

I found my eyes getting heavy and decided to return to my seat in the coach. The brunch had had a similar effect on other passengers, some of whom had fallen asleep, wrapped in light blankets provided by the staff. I'd no sooner placed my head against a pillow I'd found waiting on my seat when a PA announcement woke me.

"We've reached the town of Squamish, population fifteen thousand. We'll be traveling right through the center of Squamish, which is an important British Columbia forestry center. And we'll soon reach Brackendale, known for its large population of bald eagles. In the winter, there are as many as three thousand of these magnificent birds. In the meantime, we hope you're enjoying the trip. I'll be pointing out places of interest as we reach them, so sit back, relax, and take it all in." Jenna, who'd made the announcement, was evidently the staff member designated to provide commentary during the trip. She placed a bookmark on the page she'd been referring to and closed the black binder. She looked at me sheepishly. "I haven't learned all the details yet," she said, tapping the cover. "Did it sound too much like I was reading?"

"You sounded just fine," I told her with a smile. "We're going to learn a lot on this trip."

She grinned back at me, tucked the binder into the corner of a seat, and left the car.

I checked my watch; we were due to arrive at the resort village of Whistler at three that afternoon and would stay overnight. Whistler was reputed to be one of North America's premier ski resorts, although there wouldn't be skiing this time of year, early July. But just the thought of settling down in a café, watching a colorful parade of people, and basking in the natural beauty of British Columbia's Coast Mountains was delicious in contemplation.

I looked around. Maeve Pinckney was still hard at work on her needlepoint. Hank and Deedee Crocker were engrossed in a game of Scrabble, the miniature board of the travel set balanced on his knee. Other passengers dozed or read or stood at windows enjoying the pristine wilderness of British Columbia. Junior, I assumed, was still at his post at the open door in the vestibule. I was about to close my eyes again when male voices caused me to sit up and turn around.

Alvin Blevin stood with his stepson, Benjamin, in the open area between the first row of seats and the vestibule leading to the dining car. Blevin attempted to control his voice, but the anger in it was palpable. I couldn't make out most of what he said, although I did hear the end of a statement: ". . . and don't you ever forget it!"

Benjamin looked as though he was poised to strike his stepfather. Maeve seemed oblivious to what was going on, but Blevin sensed my interest and broke away, flashing me one of his best smiles as he strode down the aisle.

Benjamin's shoulders seemed to fold in on themselves and he looked close to tears. Worried, I followed him into the vestibule and put my hand on his arm. "Are you all right?"

He shook his head, his misery apparent. "I hate that man," he said, his voice choked. "He may have taken in my mother, but he doesn't fool me."

"How has he fooled your mother?"

"She thinks he saved her, but she's just where he wanted her all along. My father was in the way, but he managed to get around that, didn't he? He gets around everything. Everyone falls all over themselves to do what he wants. Well, not me, not Benjamin Vail. I'm wise to him."

He looked back as Blevin, who'd stopped to talk with the Goldfinches, threw back his head in a laugh. "I'll get even with him," Benjamin muttered. "You see if I don't. He won't be laughing then." Ignoring me, he stalked to his seat and stared, unseeing, at the passing terrain.

Chapter Three

"Club meeting in the bar car."

I awakened startled. I hadn't realized that I'd drifted off.

"What was that?" I said, straightening in my seat.

"Mr. Blevin has invited everyone to the club car for a welcoming cocktail, courtesy of the Track and Rail Club," Jenna said. "I'm sorry to wake you, but he asked specifically that you come, too." The two-way radio she had clipped to her waist crackled with static. "Excuse me," she said, as she pulled it off her belt and walked in the direction of the dining car.

I stood and patted the back of my hair, which had gotten mussed when I slept. The coach was empty. All the club members had heeded the call to assembly. I stepped into the aisle and touched the tops of the seats to maintain my balance as I made my way past the lavatories to the club car.

A small but efficient bar divided the club car into two spaces, but it seemed that everyone had crowded into the front half. All the seats were occupied, and the rest of the club members were standing and chatting animatedly by the time I arrived.

I caught snippets of conversation as I slid sideways into the crowd, keeping an eye out for Reggie.

"Up to two years ago, they still had firemen."

"You're crazy. They've been running diesel since '98."

"Did you see that freight go by? A hundred and twenty cars. I counted them."

"It had a Dash Eight and a Dash Sixty-five on it."

"Can you believe it? The engine could barely make it through the tunnel."

"They obviously never went on-site to measure it. Pinckney could tell you. He's a charter member of the scale police."

"Ah, Jessica," boomed out Blevin, reaching through several people to grab my arm and draw me into his circle. "I was afraid you'd think this little do was just for club members and didn't include you. Let me get you a drink and introduce you around."

He was full of good cheer as he pressed one hand into my back and gripped a half-empty drink in the other. He pushed me toward the bar, interrupting several conversations to make the introductions.

"I believe you've met the Pinckneys and the Crockers."

"Yes."

"This is our resident Brit, Winston Rendell. He's an expert on model train layouts. Writes for *Trains* magazine."

"We've met."

"Where's Ben? Benjamin!" Blevin shouted over the tops of heads. "Get Mrs. Fletcher a drink. A Bloody Mary. And get another one for me."

"I hope you like Bloody Marys," Deedee Crocker said to me.

"On occasion," I said, my ears ringing from Blevin's thunderous drink order.

There seemed to be a tacit agreement among those who were not his fans to put their animosity toward Blevin aside and enjoy the trip. It was either that, or Callie's Bloody Marys had worked their magic to reduce the hostility enough to put a smile on all the faces. Marilyn and Samantha Whitmore were laughing at something Maeve had said, although from the direction of their gazes I had a feeling it was at Theodora Blevin's expense. Junior Pinckney was showing off the photos he'd been taking of the party with his digital camera, holding it straight out in front of him so several others could peer over his shoulder. I was impressed with the digital technology that allowed photos to be seen immediately and asked him a few basic questions about it, which he happily answered. Everyone seemed in a better mood; even Hank Crocker's morose mask had eased as he discussed his favorite topic with other railroad aficionados.

Blevin leaned down and whispered in the ear of a man sitting by the window. The man vacated the seat and Blevin swallowed the last part of his drink before climbing on the chair. He drew a silver pen from his breast pocket and tapped it against his empty glass until he'd caught everyone's attention.

"Good afternoon, ladies and gentlemen. Welcome to the annual excursion of the Track and Rail Club. We have a beautiful sunny day for sightseeing. The Northwind will be coming into Whistler in an hour or so, provided we don't have to side for any more freight trains. For those of you who've never been there, it's a great little town, plenty to do, lots of shopping for the ladies. And if you guys are not in the mood to carry packages, there are plenty of cafés to relax in while your wives spend your money."

He paused, obviously expecting a masculine chuckle, but heard only a few feminine groans and hurried on. "I hope everyone received their pins." He held up the little stainless steel pin Bruce had distributed to all members of our group at the Vancouver station.

"Mine is already proudly displayed," called out Rendell. He carried a large tan canvas shoulder bag that was covered with souvenir pins. I noticed several other men wearing baseball caps displaying theirs.

"All the guys collect pins," Deedee Crocker whispered to me. "It's like a competition to see who has the most. That's why we never miss a trip, even though Hank can't stand . . ." She nodded in Blevin's direction.

"I'd like to especially welcome some first-timers who are with us," Blevin continued. "Where are the Goldfinches? There they are." He pointed to the couple who'd raised their hands and led the club members in polite applause. "Gail's the foamer in that couple. Better watch out, Gail. These guys'll grill you on your knowledge."

"I'll try not to embarrass myself."

"And we have a celebrity aboard," Blevin went on, to my consternation. "I hope you've had an opportunity to meet the famous mystery writer, J. B. Fletcher. She's asked us all to call her Jessica. She's a guest of Reggie Weems, head of our New England chapter. Let's give a warm welcome to the charming Jessica Fletcher."

There was another round of polite applause, but Blevin was losing his audience as people again started talking among themselves.

"Let me conduct a little club business before we get back to socializing," Blevin shouted over the hum of voices. "Elections are coming up. The current slate has been nominated again. So far there's no opposition. I'm flattered, but competition is good for democracy."

"Yeah, right," Hank Crocker muttered behind me.

Blevin went on, "If you want to run, get ten names on a petition and send it in to headquarters. I promised not to use this time for any electioneering, but let me just say that you'll soon be receiving your dues bills in the mail. Once again, the administration has kept the dues at the same level. We haven't had an increase in two years, while all the other clubs have raised their dues every year. I checked. That's it, folks. Once we get to Whistler, you're on your own till tomorrow morning. The Westin has a fabulous buffet breakfast. We'll all meet up there."

Blevin climbed down from the chair. Theodora joined him. She still wasn't smiling, but she seemed to have dropped her frosty demeanor. She brushed off some imagined lint on her husband's shoulder.

"Hard to keep them focused when they're drinking," he told her.

"You were just fine."

"Didn't Ben get you that Bloody Mary yet?" he asked me.

"That's all right," I said. "I'll go to the bar myself. I might just have a glass of wine instead."

Jenna, now wearing white gloves, was serving hors d'oeuvres. She extended a tray in our direction. There were two pieces left on it. "Liver pâté on toast," she said.

"My favorite," Blevin said, flashing her a smile and a wink that caused the young woman to blush. He took the two and offered one to his wife.

"You know I hate those things," she said, turning away.

"No, thanks," I said when Blevin held one out to me.

"My gain," he said, popping them into his mouth.

There was a break in the crowd around the bar and we slipped into the space.

Callie held up an empty bottle of vodka. "Sorry, folks, I've just run dry. I would have sworn I'd stocked enough." She rummaged around the shelves below the bar and pulled out a bottle. "Wait, there's a little left in this one."

"Callie claims to make the best Bloody Marys this side of the border," said Blevin. "I make a helluva Bloody Mary myself, so I've been trying to pry her secret recipe out of her."

"You'll never get it, Mr. B," Callie said, "or I'd be out of a job." She poured her special Bloody Mary mix into a tall glass and upended over it the bottle of vodka she'd just found. "It may be a bit strong," she said. "There was more left than I thought."

"I can handle it," Blevin said.

"Coming through," said a man wearing kitchen whites and holding aloft two bottles of vodka. He was older than the other staff—probably in his thirties, to their twenties—and wore wire-rimmed spectacles. His dark hair was confined by a white kerchief tied beneath his ponytail and worn low over his brow. We moved to make room for him at the bar, and several others pressed in to take our place.

"Thanks, Karl," Callie said, taking the bottles from him.

He remained at the bar, his back to us, as Callie continued making drinks.

"Now you're going to taste something special," Blevin said, rubbing his hands together in anticipation. "Al?"

"Yes, dear?"

Theodora hesitated, as if she'd forgotten what she was going to say. "Oh, yes. Mrs. Fletcher said she wanted a white wine," his wife reminded him.

"That's all right," I said. "I don't mind."

"Callie says this is yours, Blevin," Junior said, holding out the glass. "Hey, watch it, Crocker. I almost spilled this all over you."

"Sorry," Hank said, pushing past him.

"I'll take that," Karl, the kitchen worker said. He continued to face Callie as he took a small round tray holding a Bloody Mary and a white wine off the bar and held it out for Theodora.

"Thank you," she said, lifting the Bloody Mary.

Karl turned his back to the Blevins and extended the tray to me. "You asked for white wine, didn't you?" he said, rotating the tray so the wine was closest to me.

"Yes, thank you," I said, taking it.

"Nonsense," Blevin said, lifting the Bloody Mary from his wife's fingers, and the wine from mine and switching them. "You won't know what you're missing until you've tried this."

"All right, you've convinced me," I said, resigned to drinking a Bloody Mary.

"Al, don't be so boorish," said Theodora. "Let Mrs. Fletcher have the drink she wants." She took the cocktail from my hand, placed it back on Karl's tray, and held out the glass of wine.

I'd somehow gotten myself in the midst of a tug-of-war between Theodora and her husband. "I don't really care what it is," I said. "I'm not that much of a drinker."

"Take your wine," Theodora commanded.

I reluctantly took the wine, silently resolving to stick to club soda for the rest of the trip.

"And you can have this," Theodora said, handing her husband the Bloody Mary and placing his empty glass on the tray.

"Karl, I need more celery," Callie called from the bar.

Karl, who'd moved away from us, turned, and deftly negotiated the crowd of drinkers on his way out of the car. Theodora frowned after him.

"Here, I got you the drink you asked for," Ben said, coming up behind his stepfather.

"Oh, good heavens," muttered Theodora.

"Looks like we have an embarrassment of riches," Blevin said, taking the glass from Ben in his free hand. He took a taste and called over his shoulder, "Wow, Callie, that is some spicy Bloody Mary. Really clears the sinuses. Great drink." He looked at me. "If you change your mind, Jessica, we've got plenty to go around now." He held up both drinks.

"I'm just fine, thank you, and I think I see Reggie over there. I've been meaning to ask him a question. You'll excuse me, won't you?" I stepped aside so Marilyn and Samantha could get by and walked toward Reggie, thinking that the Marx Brothers would have generated a lot of laughs with the drink routine that had just taken place.

Contrary to his promise, Blevin had begun making the rounds of the room, electioneering. He button-holed club members and bragged about how well the club was doing under his diligent management.

"C'mon, Hank," I heard him say in his best hail-fellow-well-met voice. "Can't you let bygones be? We both want what's best for the club. I've been talking with a business associate who's looking for a good accountant. I can put a good word in for you."

"You can't buy me like you've bought everyone else, Blevin. Your only interest is what's best for you, not the club."

"Three years is a long time to hold a grudge, Hank."

"Three years is a long time to get away with murder," Crocker said, pushing through the crowd to the other end of the car.

I found Reggie standing next to Rendell, who was showing off the pins that covered his tan canvas bag.

"This one was the Denali Star up in Alaska. And these are, let me see, oh, right, the Mount Hood in Oregon, the Cumbres and Toltec in New Mexico, the Eureka Springs in Arkansas. This is the Blue Train from South Africa. Real luxury, that one. Do you have this one? It's the Acadian. Runs through your state, Maine."

"I have that one, of course—Montreal to St. John— but I left mine at home. Jessica, glad you're here. Have you met Winston?" Reggie said, drawing my attention away from Blevin, who was now frowning down at Junior. "Winston writes for *Trains* magazine. Been reading him for a couple of years now. This is the first chance I've gotten to meet him. As writers, you two must have a lot in common."

"We met earlier," I said, turning to him. "And I believe you mentioned you're working on a book."

"I am indeed," he said.

"How interesting," I said. "What sort of book?"

"It'll be a history of railroads in British Columbia, including this one. Probably wouldn't interest you," he said, smiling. "It's really for people more knowledgeable. About trains, that is. A bit technical. Don't have to pander to the layman. After all, I'm not writing commercial fiction."

This was the second time Winston Rendell had referred to my writing in less-than-flattering terms. I wasn't sure if he intended to be insulting or simply didn't have any idea how rude he sounded. But I was determined not to allow his rebuff to offend me. "Even so," I said, "I'd be very interested to hear what you've learned from your research. Perhaps you can educate me."

"Don't really have time for that. Excuse me." He lifted his empty glass, nodded toward the bar, and walked away.

I raised my eyebrows at Reggie.

"Must be jealous," Reggie said. "He obviously hasn't been as successful with his writing as you have. Don't pay him any attention. I never realized he was such a snob."

"Well, I'm glad it wasn't just my imagination," I said, relieved that Reggie had seen Rendell's comments in the same light I had.

"Weems! Have you seen this?" Junior Pinckney elbowed past Rendell and shoved his camera in front of Reggie.

"Look at this, Jessica. Junior's got a shot of us boarding in Vancouver."

"How nice," I said.

"Give me your e-mail," Junior said, "and I'll send it to you when we get back to town."

"I'll be happy to do that," I said.

"Junior takes pictures of every train he rides on."

"Been doing it for more than twenty years now," Junior said.

"So Maeve was telling me. I also heard someone say you're a charter member of the 'Scale Police.' Is that another hobby?"

Reggie nearly choked on his drink at my comment, but Junior looked abashed.

"Did I say something wrong?" I asked.

"No, not at all," Junior said. "There are those of us for whom precision is more important than it is for others. I'm not ashamed to admit to being a stickler for accurate scale."

"I'm not sure I understand."

"It has to do with running model trains, Jessica," Reggie put in. "You know, the big model train layouts with elaborate landscapes."

"If you're really an expert, when you create a model

layout you try to duplicate the route of an actual railroad," Junior said. "That means not only the trains, but the environment in which they operate. For it to look realistic, the terrain is done to scale. If you're working on an HO layout, for instance, the ratio is one to eighty-seven; the trains are one eighty-seventh real size."

"Ah, so a tunnel on the model landscape has to be one eighty-seventh the size of the tunnel along the route of the railroad you're copying," I said.

"Exactly," Junior said. "Everything in the surroundings is done to scale, every building, hill, road, tree, rock; all the features should be identical to what you'd see if you took the actual trip yourself."

"That's impressive," I said.

He smiled. "Yes, it is."

"Every rock?" I asked Reggie after Junior had moved on to talk to another train buff.

"That's why they call him the scale police," Reggie said. "He goes on-site personally, with a bunch of cameras hanging around his neck, and measures everything he sees. He even had a custom software program made for his Palm Pilot to plot all the elements going into his model. Once, I heard, he hired a surveyor to confirm the height of foothills for a layout he was working on."

"I never realized model railroading was so exacting," I said.

"It isn't for everyone. Lots of people are just in it for the fun. But in any hobby, there are always people who become obsessed with the details. I'm afraid a lot of rail fans fall into that category. And they can really get hot if someone challenges the way they do things. You'd be amazed at the politics in these clubs."

"Are you thinking of Al Blevin now?" I asked.

"You don't want to be on his wrong side," Reggie said, dropping his voice. "He's not above cheating if there's someone standing in his way."

As if Reggie had had a premonition of things to come, Al Blevin's voice thundered over the buzz of the crowd: "Get out of my way!" His face was a livid red as he glared at Winston Rendell.

"What the hell's the matter with you?" Rendell returned.

"Al, you've had too much to drink," Theodora said, gripping her husband's arm. "Let's go sit down."

Blevin's shoulders twitched. He raised his fists, but crossed them in front of his chest. "You've been attacking me behind my back. Don't—think—I don't know it."

"Now, why would I do that?"

"Don't you shout at me!"

"You're the one who's shouting, old man."

The club members turned toward the altercation, conversation dying away.

"It's too noisy in here. I'm getting out." Blevin began to push toward the door. Marilyn Whitmore stood in his way. He stared at her, his eyes growing larger, his mouth in a grimace.

"What do you want, Al? Must everyone jump to your tune? Just walk around me."

The train took a curve, wheels squealing, and entered a tunnel. The light in the club car dimmed momentarily until the electric lights above the windows flickered on. Blevin reared back his head. His shoulder twitched as if he were trying to snap out a punch, but his arms stayed fixed, crossed on his chest. Another spasm shook his body and he fell backward. His head glanced off a table, knocking over a glass and spilling the remains of Callie's specialty across the lapels of his immaculately tailored tan jacket and down the front of his pristine white shirt.

The crowd gasped as their president went into a convulsion. His eyes bulged open, face by turns crimson and then blue as his body denied him oxygen, and pink again as the throes of the spasm released its hold on him.

"Come on, everyone, get out of here and make some room for him," Reggie said, herding people from the car.

They moved cautiously past the prone Blevin.

"Geez, he must have had a snootful."

"I think he's having a heart attack."

"No, it looks like a stroke."

"My cousin had epilepsy. Maybe that's it."

"Did anyone take first aid?"

"Callie, call for help."

"I did."

"I hope there's a hospital in Whistler."

"How far out are we now?"

"Don't just gawk at him. Someone help him." Theodora's face was ashen, but she backed away from her husband's prone figure. "Samantha, you're a nurse," she said. "Please do something or he'll die."

"No! I won't," Samantha shouted. She hugged herself and rocked back and forth as she stared at the stricken man.

The train emerged from the tunnel and sunlight flooded the car. Blevin's body began to tremble again. He arched back till his body was curved like a bow, only his head and feet touching the floor. His face was drained.

"Give him mouth-to-mouth resuscitation," someone said.

Samantha staggered forward and frowned down at Blevin.

"Don't do it," I said, gripping her arm. "He may have been poisoned."

"Poisoned?" Maeve gasped and slid down into a faint.

The word triggered a stampede among those who hadn't left yet. They rushed out of the car. Junior leaned over his wife, fanning her face with a railroad map.

"He's going to die. He's going to die," Samantha chanted to herself.

"You must have seen patients have convulsions before," I said, putting my hand on her shoulder.

"I won't do it," she repeated. An odd light filled her eyes. She shrugged me off and ran from the car.

Blevin's body shuddered, and he lay limp on the floor. He drew in air through his teeth and color flooded back into his face. Theodora gingerly knelt by his side. She tapped softly on her husband's shoulder and his eyes met hers. "Look what they did to you. Your nicest shirt," she said, wiping the sweat off his brow and then blotting the red stain on his shirt with a napkin. "You're going to be just fine," she said, a quaver in her voice. "You'll see. You just drank too much. Three Bloody Marys, Al. We're going to laugh about this next week." Her son, Benjamin, sat at a table near the bar, his arms and legs crossed, body hunched forward, staring silently at his mother and stepfather.

"Jessica, where did Samantha go?" Reggie whispered.

"She left." I shook my head, wondering at her strange behavior. How could a nurse turn her back on someone in need?

"What do we do now?"

"The only thing we can do till medical help arrives," I whispered back, "is keep him warm and quiet. And close the drapes near him. He may be sensitive to light."

"Sensitive to light? How do you—?"

I walked over to where Callie stood behind the counter, wringing a bar towel. "You said you called for help?" I said softly.

"I did, I did," she stammered, "but he can't have been poisoned, Mrs. Fletcher. I made his drink myself. No one's ever gotten sick before. Maybe it's just an allergic reaction. I put in a lot of horseradish this time. Do you think that did it?"

"*Shh.* It's not your fault."

Reggie shrugged out of his jacket and laid it across Blevin's chest.

Jenna, who'd been serving hors d'oeuvres only thirty minutes ago, rushed into the club car, holding a first aid kit. Bruce was close behind her. The young woman's face turned ashen when she saw Blevin lying on the floor. She sank into a chair.

"We called for an ambulance," she whispered. "There'll be one waiting in Whistler."

"How long will it be?" Theodora asked, adjusting Reggie's jacket over Blevin.

"We're almost there," Bruce said. He took the first aid kit from Jenna, propped it on a table, and snapped open the latch.

A long whistle sounded as the train rounded another curve, the shrill squeal of the wheels rending the air. Blevin's body lifted off the floor as another convulsion gripped him. Theodora scrambled away from him and climbed into a chair. The screech of metal on metal reverberated in the car, now emptied of all but a few of the club's delegation.

Jenna stared, transfixed, as Blevin's lips curled back in a grotesque grin. His eyes bulged from their sockets and his arms twitched. His skin took on an odd pallor under his tanned complexion, and a blue tinge crept into his face.

The train straightened and the wheels ceased their strident sound. But it was too late.

Junior, who'd pulled Maeve up onto a chair, looked at Blevin and pointed to Bruce's kit. "I don't think that's going to do you any good anymore," he said. He picked up his camera and took a few fast photos of the scene.

I marveled at how callously he was able to view the misfortune of his colleague.

Reggie walked to where Blevin lay and gazed into his sightless eyes. He leaned down and pulled his jacket up over Blevin's face. Theodora moaned.

Jenna gasped and began to sob.

"My God," Callie cried hoarsely from behind the bar. "He's dead!"

Chapter Four

Bruce had instructed one of the staff to escort Mrs. Blevin to another car and to send someone back to stand by the door to the club car to bar anyone from entering until we reached Whistler. Callie started to collect glasses where passengers had left them, but I asked her to leave them untouched.

"Why?" Bruce asked.

"In case they become evidence," I replied.

"Evidence? Of what?"

"I'm not a medical expert," I said, "but until the cause of death has been determined, the police will want everything to be left as it was."

"Mrs. Fletcher thinks Mr. Blevin was poisoned," Callie whispered.

"Preposterous," Winston Rendell said from the entrance. "This isn't a scene from one of your novels, Mrs. Fletcher. The man obviously died of natural causes." Rendell had barged back into the club car he'd abandoned earlier when Blevin first fell ill. I wondered if he'd come to check that Blevin had indeed died.

"You're probably right," I said to him, "but wouldn't it be better to err on the side of caution?"

Bruce agreed with me and the club car was left untouched by the staff. Of course, passengers filing out earlier could have disturbed or even moved items, but that was beyond anyone's control, certainly mine. I hoped I was wrong about the cause of Alvin Blevin's death and would gladly acknowledge that I was, should it prove to be so. But my instincts told me Al Blevin's death was no accident. I even thought I knew the poison which had taken his life. That knowledge didn't make me happy.

With everyone else gathered in the coach, I stood near Bruce in the club car as he talked on a cell phone with someone from Whistler.

"We don't know what happened to him," he said. "It appears he had a heart attack or possibly a stroke. But we"—he glanced at me—"but we decided to not touch anything in the car where it happened." He placed a finger in his opposite ear from the one to which the phone was pressed, listening to what was being said. "Why?" he said in response. "Because one of our passengers, a Mrs. Fletcher, suggested—well, she isn't sure the death was the result of natural causes." After a few additional exchanges, he concluded the conversation and slipped the phone back into his jacket pocket.

"Could I speak with you for a moment?" he asked, escorting me back into the coach. He indicated a place removed from the others. Small groups had formed throughout the car, and people were nervously chattering about what had just occurred.

"Yes?" I said when we'd taken two empty seats.

"Until it's determined how Mr. Blevin died," he said, "I'd really appreciate not having the possibility of his being poisoned spread around to other passengers."

"I understand," I said. "It's obviously supposition on my part. It's just that—"

He interrupted me. "I'm sure you have valid reasons for suspecting poison, Mrs. Fletcher, but from the standpoint of the train and BC Rail, it would be better if—"

I placed a hand on his arm and smiled. "I understand perfectly, Bruce. No more talk of poisoning until the medical folks have their say."

"Thank you."

Along with the shock and horror at having someone drop dead in the midst of a party, speculation was rampant in the car, my cautionary remark to Samantha having been overheard and then repeated by Maeve. Since Junior had taken the seat next to his wife where I had sat before, I looked around for an empty space. Reggie patted the chair next to him and I took it.

"Unbelievable," he said.

"Tragic," I said.

"I'll bet people are sorry for all the nasty things they said about Alvin."

"People express the way they feel, and no one can ever forecast someone's sudden demise. He appeared to me to be in pretty good physical shape."

"I thought so, too. Alvin was a health fanatic, aside from having a little too much to drink now and then. He was a jogger and a regular in the gym."

"Mid fifties?"

"I'm not sure how old he was, but you're probably about right." He leaned close. "Do you really think he was poisoned?"

I said in an equally low voice, "I promised Bruce I wouldn't talk about that until we get to Whistler."

"Why doesn't he want you to talk about it?"

"Because he doesn't want to set people on edge unduly. Besides, he has the railroad's reputation to protect."

"It'd be hard to taint BC Rail's reputation, Jess. It's one of the best railroads in North America."

"That may be, Reggie, but—"

I was interrupted by the sudden presence of Benjamin Vail, Alvin Blevin's stepson.

"My mother wants to speak with you."

"All right," I said. "I'm so sorry about your stepdad."

"Are you coming or not?"

"I, uh—" I looked at Reggie, who shrugged. I got up and followed Benjamin into the dining car, which was empty except for Theodora Blevin, who sat at one of the tables. She looked up at me with an expression that said, all at once, the emotions and thoughts she was experiencing at the moment.

"Thank you, Benjamin," she said, clearly dismissing her son.

"I'm staying," he said, taking up a position behind his mother with his arms crossed. He glared at me as if to dare me to upset her.

"No. That's all right, dear."

"You need me here."

"Not right now. Mrs. Fletcher and I have matters to discuss privately."

"I want to hear what she says."

"We'll talk later, Benjamin."

"But—"

"Later, Benjamin." The iron in her voice brooked no argument.

He left, and I took a chair across from her.

"I'm sorry about your husband," I said.

"It's just beginning to sink in, the reality of it," she said, her shoulders slumping as if under the weight of her suffering. "He's gone. Just like that." She snapped her fingers. "One minute he's standing on a chair welcoming everyone, the next minute he's on the floor of the club car with his face covered up. It's so—so barbaric."

I said nothing. Had I been summoned to be a listening post while she poured out her grief? I couldn't imagine why she'd choose me, unless I represented a stranger to her. Sometimes we seek strangers to confide in, content that they don't have a stake in our lives. Theodora was a woman who didn't convey emotion easily. In our short acquaintance, I'd seen very few expressions cross her beautiful face. I'd thought her arrogant, but perhaps she needed to protect herself from the unkind words of others. Or maybe she'd grown accustomed to keeping her feelings hidden when dealing with the difficulties in her life—the disappearance of her first husband, a dominating second husband, and a troubled son. In contrast to his mother, Benjamin seemed to have little control over his emotions, either pouting like a child or giving in to angry outbursts.

"Ever have anyone close to you die like this?" she asked, her eyes focused on the white linen tablecloth.

"No, not like this, Mrs. Blevin. I was with my husband when he died, but that was in a hospital setting. His death wasn't unexpected. He'd been ill for a while."

She looked up at me. "Alvin had a lot of enemies, Mrs. Fletcher. Powerful, successful men always do."

Had she come to the same tentative conclusion as I had, that her husband might have been poisoned? "Do you think someone wanted him dead?" I asked.

"He wasn't poisoned," she said firmly.

I waited.

"I know what you've been saying. You've been spreading that rumor, haven't you?"

"I don't believe in spreading rumors," I said, deciding now was not the time to tell her what I knew about the effects of various poisons, and one in particular.

"I heard you tell Samantha he was poisoned," she repeated, more vehemently this time.

There was nothing to gain by pointing out that I'd said he *might* have been poisoned. She was not in the mood to listen. Instead I said, "I don't know that for sure, but if he were poisoned, it could have been dangerous for her to give him mouth-to-mouth resuscitation. Do you know what caused your husband's death?"

"It wasn't poison," she ground out again. "You're trying to ruin his reputation."

"Perhaps he was allergic to some ingredient in the drinks," I offered, trying to give her something to hold on to until she was ready to hear the truth.

"Al wasn't allergic to anything. He was as healthy as a horse."

"I don't know what you want me to say."

"I want you to stop spreading rumors. Haven't we suffered enough? You're making it worse. Al was not poisoned." She picked up a handkerchief and dabbed her dry eyes.

I realized I was sitting with a woman who'd just lost her husband, and I didn't want to sound combative. "Everyone's understandably on edge," I said gently, and smiled. "I'm perfectly willing to sit with you for as long as you wish, but perhaps you'd prefer to be alone at a time like this."

I stood.

"Stop spreading that stupid rumor!" she growled, venom in her voice.

I said nothing, simply left the car and rejoined Reggie, who stood talking with Bruce and Callie. Other conversation in the car was muffled and somber.

"We're pulling into Whistler," Bruce said.

"I'll be glad when we're there," said Callie, who'd

been crying. Her eyes were puffy and red, and tears had streaked makeup on one cheek. "Having his body in the next car is spooky."

"Almost there," said Bruce, wrapping an arm around her shoulder. "Where's Jenna?"

"I don't know," Callie said. "Why can't we go faster? I just want to get off the train."

It did seem as though we were traveling at a snail's pace, although this wasn't a sudden phenomenon. I'd noticed since leaving North Vancouver that the Whistler Northwind was not about to set any speed records. But that was the whole point—wasn't it?—a leisurely three-day journey on a classic train with every possible comfort, much like a luxury cruise ship, taking in the beauty and majesty of British Columbia. To go any faster would be to violate the very premise of the trip. And there were other passengers in the coaches up front, passengers who were unaware of the tragedy that had taken place in the car reserved for the members of the Track and Rail Club. Speed wouldn't help Al Blevin, not anymore. Still, I knew what Callie was feeling. I'm sure we all shared her desire to reach Whistler and get away from the train, away from the dead body in the club car.

After an interminable half hour, Whistler station came into view and the train slowed to a stop. I looked out my window and saw an ambulance. Standing in front of it were a young man and woman dressed in long white lab jackets. Close to them were men wearing what I assumed were law enforcement uniforms. A heavyset man in a suit leaned against the ambulance. Beyond them were two cars parked side by side, one a patrol car with RCMP stenciled on its door. *The Royal Canadian Mounted Police,* I thought. *The "Mounties."* All I knew of that famous organization was from stories read in childhood, old movies, and photos of its officers in their distinctive brilliant red-and-black uniforms and wide-brimmed hats. I took another look at the uniformed officers. No red jackets and black pants on them. They wore drab gray shirts and blue trousers with a yellow stripe down the sides. But their hats were the familiar shape.

Bruce led Benjamin to the dining car to join his mother, and the door was shut behind them. BC Rail's onboard host returned to the coach car and used the public-address system: "Ladies and gentlemen, we've arrived in Whistler. Because of the unfortunate tragedy we've experienced, I'm going to ask you to gather up your belongings and follow me off the train as quickly and orderly as possible through this door. A bus is waiting to take you to the hotel where you'll be spending what I'm sure will be a comfortable night. Your luggage has been transported ahead of us by truck and will be in your rooms when you arrive. Please refer to your itinerary regarding any events planned for this evening and detailing how and where we'll meet in the morning for breakfast and for the bus bringing us back to the train. Thank you for your cooperation."

Once everyone was standing in the aisle, Bruce motioned for us to begin leaving. Reggie and I were the first to enter the vestibule. Bruce had already gone down the steps and stood on the platform with the uniformed officers, the man in the suit, and the two medical technicians. Reggie started down, but Bruce stopped him by raising his hand. We waited while our guest services supervisor continued to confer with the police. Finally, he looked up at us and said apologetically, "You'll have to go back inside. The police want to speak with everyone."

Reggie and I turned and informed the people behind us of the change in plans. There was much grumbling and griping, but eventually everyone was reseated and the two medical technicians entered the car. Bruce escorted them to the club car, where Blevin's body lay. Jenna entered the coach and took up her accustomed post in the front. She was very pale and clutched her black binder and the microphone to her chest.

Next to come aboard were the two uniformed RCMP officers and the large man who was obviously in charge. He seemed even bigger once inside, his tall, square frame filling the doorway. He asked Jenna for the microphone, which she handed him. After a false start as he searched for the ON button, he spoke into it. "Good afternoon, ladies and gentlemen. My name is Detective Christian Marshall, Royal Canadian Mounted Police. Sorry for any inconvenience, and I'll try and detain you for only a brief period."

His voice was resonant and deep, tinged with a Canadian accent. He was bald on the top of his head, the hair on his temples salt-and-pepper. His beard line was heavy, his eyebrows thick and solidly black. There was a look of resignation on his face, as though he'd experienced a great deal in his life as a cop and wasn't especially pleased with what he'd seen.

"Why are we being detained at all?" Hank Crocker whined from where he sat. "What does Blevin's death have to do with the police?"

A small grin crossed the detective's face, although I was sure it wasn't born of amusement. He asked, "Is there someone among you who believes the death on the train might not have been from natural causes?" He consulted a slip of paper. "A Mrs. Fletcher?"

The sound of murmuring came from the seats behind me.

"I'm Mrs. Fletcher," I said, rising.

"Please," he said, inviting me to come with him with a flip of his hand.

I followed him into the vestibule and down to the platform. Passengers from other cars who were not part of our group were in the process of leaving the train and heading for waiting buses.

"Now," he said, "what's this about poison?"

"Are you familiar with the symptoms of strychnine poisoning?" I asked.

"Go on."

I explained as briefly as possible why I thought there was the possibility that Blevin had been poisoned, and he listened patiently. I recounted the sudden onset of symptoms—the seizures, the contortions of his face, and the spastic movements of his body during the convulsions, in particular the bowing of his back when only his head and feet touched the floor. These were classic symptoms of strychnine poisoning, I told him.

"Strychnine victims are particularly sensitive to light and sound," I said. "Mr. Blevin's convulsions seemed to coincide with the screech of the wheels."

"Very interesting, Mrs. Fletcher. I'm curious as to how you know so much about strychnine."

"I've used it before."

"I beg your pardon."

"In a book, of course. I write murder mysteries, Detective Marshall."

"Ah, yes. I thought I knew the name."

"You pick up a lot of odd information in my profession."

"I'll bet you do. You know Alvin Blevin was a big

shot in Vancouver, a high-profile lawyer and business-man. You're aware of that?"

"I had an inkling from what some people said."

"He was on the train as head of this railroad club."

"That's right."

"You're a member of the club?"

"No, I'm an invited guest."

"If you're right, if he was poisoned, that would mean somebody on the train did him in, eh?"

I nodded, uncomfortable at his choice of words. Was he making fun of me?

"Since you're claiming he was murdered, maybe you can point a finger at the perpetrator. Any ideas who killed him?"

"Detective," I said, not entirely successful in keeping frustration out of my voice, "without proof, neither you nor I can state with authority that he was murdered. All I am saying is that the possibility exists. As for who might have wanted him dead, let me just add that he was not the most popular person on the train. Now, it seems to me that all this speculation can be quickly and satisfactorily put to rest by an autopsy, which I assume will be conducted, considering the circumstances of his death. The glasses from which he drank might also be of value in making a determination. I asked the train staff not to remove them."

"Very thoughtful."

"Am I excused now?" I asked.

"Of course. We'll be interviewing everyone who was with the deceased."

"On the train?"

"We'll get names and addresses, of course, and interview individuals at the hotel in Whistler. I've agreed with the management of BC Rail to allow the train to continue on up to Prince George."

"I see. What about the body?"

"It will be driven back down to Vancouver for an autopsy."

"I assume his wife and stepson will accompany it."

He nodded.

"Well, I hope I've been of help," I said. "Good day, Detective."

"Oh, you're not rid of me yet, Mrs. Fletcher. I'll be your new passenger all the way to Prince George. I'm sure we'll have lots more to talk about along the way."

Chapter Five

Detective Marshall and the two uniformed RCMP officers went row to row noting each person's name, address, phone number, and where they were planning to stay following the train trip. When that process was completed, Marshall got on the PA: "I've asked for additional detectives to be dispatched to your hotel to take statements. They'll interview you in your rooms, and I ask that you remain there until you've been contacted. I assure you it will take only a few minutes of your time. Once you've given your statements, you'll be free to enjoy everything Whistler has to offer. Thank you for your cooperation."

"Will we be continuing the trip?" Winston Rendell asked.

"Yes, sir, you will be allowed to continue." He didn't mention that he'd be accompanying us.

The check-in process at the hotel was swift and smooth, having been prearranged by BC Rail. We were staying at the Westin Resort and Spa, which had been voted by travel magazine readers the best ski-resort hotel in North America, and I wasn't surprised. A spectacular lodge built with colorful native stone and soaring timbers, it was at once sophisticated and rustic. High ceilings in the public areas were offset by warm woods, patterned slate, and wood-burning fireplaces, giving even the largest spaces a cozy feeling.

At the registration desk, I was handed an envelope containing my key and information about the resort. It included a flyer imploring us to not feed the black bears and reminding those whose suites were on lower floors to keep balcony doors closed when not in the room.

"Any suggestions for what I might do this afternoon?" I asked the clerk who'd registered me.

"Lots to do in Whistler," she said. "Ever been on a gondola?"

"As a matter of fact, I have," I said.

"The one up Whistler Mountain is terrific," she said. "Here." She handed me a discount coupon for the ride.

"Sounds good to me."

When I turned away from the desk, I found myself face-to-face with Benjamin Vail, which surprised me. I thought he was accompanying his mother and his stepfather's body back to Vancouver.

"Hello, Benjamin."

He nodded but said nothing and took my place at the check-in desk.

I rode the elevator up to the floor that had been reserved for members of the Track and Rail Club. Each of the resort's 419 rooms was a suite, and mine had a fireplace and a small terrace. The hotel's towers backed onto Whistler Mountain and faced the village, a diverse blend of low-rise buildings that I imagined would fall into an architectural category that could be called "Mountain Modern." There were lots of steep roofs with deep eaves, covered boardwalks, and sheltered balconies to protect visitors from the weather. Wood, stone, and stucco were the predominant building materials and the whole was tied together by nar-

row streets that invited exploration. The pedestrian-
only lanes curved past charming cafés and shops and
emptied into squares or dead-ended at peaceful, green
parks. My windows overlooked a cobblestone courtyard which led to the village and had a view of Black-
comb Mountain.

Minutes after I entered my room, a pleasant young
detective arrived and took my statement. He asked
what had occurred in the hour leading up to Blevin's
death. I had little more to offer than what I'd told Detective Marshall. All I'd observed was a group of people enjoying drinks in preparation for our arrival in
Whistler.

After the detective left, I freshened up and wandered into the village. Renowned as a resort for
skiers, Whistler was just as crowded with early sum-
mer visitors. Where four streets converged, tourists
laden with cameras and consulting maps filled the
many outdoor restaurants ringing the square or
spilled from the rough-hewn buildings or stand-
alone houses that accommodated clothing boutiques,
art galleries, sporting goods emporiums, and travel
agencies, not to mention every manner of souvenir
shop imaginable, hawking such must-have wares as
moose antler baseball caps and bracelets made from
dalmatian jasper. Hordes of young people and many
not-so-young people wheeling mountain bikes and
wearing hiking shoes and backpacks mingled with
the other visitors. There also seemed to be a large
number of dogs, but whether they lived with local
residents or came along with the day-trippers, I
couldn't tell. All in all, it was an energetic, eclectic
mix of people, young and old, and everyone in a
seemingly good mood.

I browsed windows and purchased a few postcards

to send to friends back home. One store window advertised Havana cigars, and I was reminded that Canada did not go along with the American ban on products from Cuba.

I gravitated to the entrance where gondolas departed to transport people up Whistler Mountain, one of two soaring peaks that attract millions of skiers, hikers, and mountain bikers each year. I'd ridden gondolas back East and always enjoyed the spectacular views they afforded. I went to the ticket window and presented the discount card.

"Senior citizen rate," the young woman said pleasantly, "and a three-dollar discount for the card."

I laughed. "Is it that evident?"

"What?"

"Recognizing that I'm a senior citizen."

She looked up, flustered. "Oh, I didn't mean to insult you."

"You didn't at all. It was just my little joke. Thank you."

"Enjoy the trip."

The fully enclosed gondolas moved through a roundhouse at the base of the mountain, stopping long enough for doors to open, allowing descending passengers to disembark and new ones to board. I stood in a short line until my turn came. I was joined by a young couple who said that friends who'd taken the ride earlier that day had seen a mother bear and her two cubs during their ascent. They seemed as excited at the contemplation of seeing the bears as they were about the ride itself. The doors closed and we began the half-hour, six-thousand-foot ascent up the rugged mountain named after the village, or maybe it was the other way around. Either way, I felt the tension of the morning lift as the gondola left the roundhouse and as the view back to the village grew smaller the higher the little car climbed.

I sat on a bench and drew deep breaths. I was glad I'd decided to take the gondola trip. A small opening above the side window let in the pristine air and transported me away from that day's events—the train, the people holding sharp views of Alvin Blevin, and especially his untimely and grotesque death. I shook my head, deliberately pushing from my mind the image of his convulsing body arched on the floor of the club car, every muscle in spasm, eyes bulging, mouth twisted into a macabre grin. Instead, the picture was replaced by the captivating scenery below and above me. Mountain bikers flew down crenellated trails that their wheels had carved into the mountainside, and hikers slowly climbed over rocks and through brush and clumps of evergreens. The village fell away faster and faster, and I joined my companions in straining to spot the bears from our Plexiglas cocoon.

At the same time, I realized how vulnerable I was, dangling from a cable high above the rugged, rocky terrain of Whistler Mountain. I wasn't concerned; such thoughts occur to everyone, I'm sure, especially when the ride gets rough as the cars bump over the connections atop the towers supporting the cable. Gondolas on their way down passed me; small children, their faces pressed against the clear walls, laughed and waved, and I returned their greetings.

"There's the bear," the young woman said.

"Where?"

I followed the direction of her eyes to a clearing in which a mother bear and two cubs could be seen foraging for food. The couple was giddy at seeing the bears, and I got caught up in their youthful enthusiasm. Yet I was equally concerned that the mountain bikers would intrude upon the bears' territory. What would the mother bear do to protect her cubs?

Our gondola finally arrived at the roundabout atop the mountain and we happily parted, agreeing that the bear sighting had been a special moment. I stepped outside the tall glass doors, went down some stairs to a gravel path, and then walked up a rise to where a large patch of snow covered the ground, even on this sunny day in July. It was cold, and the light sweater I wore wasn't sufficient to keep me warm. Even so, I basked in the clean, chilly air and drew it in, enjoying the tingling feeling it sent through my body. I wrapped my arms about myself and began a slow, deliberate, three-hundred-and-sixty-degree turn in order to take in the spectacular mountain views. Everywhere my eye fell were mountaintops still dusted with snow, some rocky and barren, others with ski trails carving delicate lines through the trees. Off to my left, partway down the mountain, a cobalt blue pond reflected the clear sky.

Halfway through my slow pirouette, I saw the dark-stained wooden lodge which housed the gondola station. Rock music blared from outside speakers, and young people streamed in and out of the tourist shop and nature exhibit next door. The loud commercialism made me sharply aware of the contrast between the beauty of nature and humankind's dubious additions to it.

Through the glass walls of the station, I could see the moving cars circle inside, discharging and taking on passengers. An open deck greeted those arriving. I realized that in winter, skiers would have to descend the broad wooden steps before they could don their skis. I was about to continue my personal, circular tour of my surroundings when the sight of someone walking out onto the deck stopped me. It was Benjamin Vail. He came directly to where I stood.

"This is a surprise," I said pleasantly. "I thought you and your mother were going back to Vancouver." When he'd been in line behind me at the hotel, I'd assumed that was still the plan, delayed perhaps by some logistical problem. But his appearance on the top of Whistler Mountain, at precisely the time when I was there, couldn't have been a chance occurrence.

"She went," he said. "I'm staying."

"I see," I said, not really seeing at all why he wasn't accompanying his grieving mother. "So, here we are. I have the feeling it's not a coincidence that we've both ended up here."

He stared at me for what seemed a long time, although it was only seconds. As I looked into his eyes, I saw something I hadn't noticed before. Yes, there was the somber, brooding look that he seemed always to display. But there was also a profound sadness, a vulnerability that came through. It wouldn't have surprised me if he'd burst into tears at any minute. Instead, he straightened up and took a deep breath.

"Why are you butting in?" he asked.

"Butting in? I'm afraid I don't understand."

"Blevin."

"What about him?" His use of his stepfather's last name, delivered with such detachment, was disquieting.

"He's dead. Let him be."

I shook my head and made a few false starts at responding. "I don't have any point of view in your stepfather's death, Benjamin, aside from feeling sorry for you and your mother."

"It was a heart attack. He had a weak heart. He wasn't poisoned. You're trying to make it look like something sinister."

Blevin had been painted as a man proud of his physical fitness. No one had mentioned a weak heart, and I doubted it was true. But here was the stepson delivering a message similar to the one I'd received from his mother earlier that day.

"I'm not trying to make it look like anything," I said. "I merely raised a question. Did your mother tell you to follow me up this mountain in order to talk to me?"

"I do my own thing. I don't need my mother telling me what to do."

"Well," I said, "you've managed to find me here alone, and you've delivered your message. Is there anything else you want to talk to me about? If so, I'd appreciate hearing it, Benjamin, because frankly, I'm ready to go back down. I'm cold."

As I waited for a response, I tried to process why he was there and what he'd said. Had he decided on his own not to accompany his mother to Vancouver with his stepfather's body, or had that been her decision? Had his mother dispatched him to issue a threat to me? If so, why? What did they hope to accomplish? Did it mean they'd believed that Blevin might have been poisoned and had some reason to quash the information and keep it from being made public? If that was the case—if he had, indeed, been poisoned—was the mother or the son a murderer?

"Did you decide to stay in Whistler overnight just to tell me to 'butt out'?" I asked, shivering as a cold wind whipped across the bare mountaintop.

"No," he said. "I have my own reasons."

Despite the discomfort I was feeling, both because of the cold and because of his unexpected appearance, I took advantage of the moment to ask him, "Were you close to your stepfather?"

The question seemed to take him by surprise. He snorted, "No way on this earth."

"It must have been difficult for you when your mother married Alvin Blevin. Had you been close to your own father?"

"My father is none of your business."

"Perhaps," I said, "but then neither are my suspicions about how someone died your business, even if it involves your stepfather."

I was about to ask about the circumstances under which his father had disappeared, but he drew a deep breath, rammed his hands into the pockets of his black jeans, and said, "Just leave us alone, okay? You're pushing in your nose where it doesn't belong. Blevin dropped dead of a heart attack. That's it, Mrs. Fletcher. That's it." He turned and walked back toward the roundabout.

I lingered in the gift shop before getting in a gondola for the descent to the village. The scene with Benjamin was like a dream that never happened. It was a silly exercise on his part—and that of his mother if she'd been involved. Rather than encourage me to drop the topic, their admonitions raised red flags. Why were they so eager to pass off Blevin's death as being from natural causes?

I looked for the bears all the way down, hoping that no mountain biker careening down a path would come face-to-face with a protective momma bear. The return trip seemed much longer than the ascent had been, and I was happy to get off and be on solid ground.

Whistler was still bustling when I returned from my ride up the mountain. The square I'd visited earlier was even more congested, thanks to the attraction of a performance by street musicians. I was hungry and perused menus outside the many restaurants and cafés on the square's perimeter. I chose a place called Araxi, and as I was about to enter, I spotted a familiar face. It was my Whistler Northwind fellow passenger Marilyn Whitmore. Her daughter was not with her.

"May I join you?" I asked, indicating the empty chair at the outdoor table she occupied.

"Yes, of course," she said. "Are you enjoying your afternoon?"

"I took the gondola up Whistler Mountain."

"I could never do that," she said. "I have an appalling fear of heights. That's why I like trains. I avoid planes whenever possible."

"I actually enjoy flying," I said as a waiter delivered a menu and took my drink order, a glass of red wine. "I have my private license."

"Oh?"

"It's ironic, really. I have a license to fly, but I don't drive."

"That's funny."

"Where's Samantha? Is she shopping?"

"I left her back in the room sleeping. The shock was too much for her, I'm afraid."

A nurse shocked over someone dying? I thought. But I didn't express my surprise. Instead I asked, "Did the police interview you?"

"If that's what you can call it," she replied with a wry smile. "Just a few questions. You?"

"The same. They don't seem especially concerned at this juncture about Mr. Blevin's death."

Her eyebrows arched. "But they will be if you have your way?"

"I don't consider it 'my way,' " I said. "Whatever the truth is will be good enough for me."

My wine was delivered. Marilyn held up her glass, which contained something undoubtedly more potent than my cabernet. "To a pleasant rest of the trip despite what happened this afternoon."

I raised my glass in a halfhearted response and we drank.

She looked out over the square, and a thoughtful expression appeared on her face. "Sad, isn't it," she said, "that some people die and few people care."

"An old friend of mine says that when you're dead, all bets are off, even for the most reviled of people."

"Like Alvin Blevin."

Since she'd decided to enter this area of discussion, I said, "I gathered from comments made by some members of the club that he wasn't especially popular."

She sighed as she said, "That's a gentle way to put it."

"Some of the complaints seem to be about how he ran the club, that he was too dictatorial. Do you feel that way, too?"

"It may sound callous, but if someone killed Al Blevin, I can't say that I'm sorry. He wasn't a nice man."

A shadow crossed the table and I looked up. The waiter apologized for interrupting our conversation. "May I tell you about our specials?"

We placed our orders, and talk shifted to more mundane topics: her favorite restaurants in Vancouver, the wonderful service on the train, the bears who lived on the mountain. Throughout our meal, I tried to keep my mind from racing back to murder. I wanted to talk more about Blevin with Marilyn, to find out why she didn't like him, who else didn't like him, but the opportunity had passed. Of course, if the autopsy proved Blevin had indeed been poisoned, I could raise the topic again.

While outwardly I advocated awaiting the results of the postmortem before commenting on the cause of Blevin's death, inwardly I had no doubt about its nature. I had studied too many books on methods of murder and had sat in too many lectures on forensic investigation to question what had been obvious to me. A murder had taken place. But how long would it take the Mounties to come to that conclusion? A week? Reggie and I could be on our way back to the States by then. If the autopsy and chemical analysis of the glasses proved me right—and I was sure they would—the information might come too late for me to be involved in the questioning. Was I willing to leave the inquiries solely in the hands of the Canadian authorities? They were fully competent, of course, but then I was already on the scene, and I knew all the potential suspects. I could be very helpful to the Mounties, couldn't I?

While I was musing about the investigation, a school choral group assembled in the square in front of the restaurant, and Marilyn and I listened to the a capella singing, charmed by their sweet voices. When the group had finished their miniconcert and dispersed, Marilyn said, "I'd better get back and see how Samantha is doing."

"I hope she's feeling better," I offered.

"Samantha is—well, she's fragile, has been ever since her father died. She wasn't able to save his life, and she took it particularly hard."

"How did he die?"

"Heart attack. Samantha blames herself for not being there. She was late coming home. Thinks if she'd been able to do CPR, he would have lived. It's nonsense, of course. He had a weak heart. She couldn't do anything about that. But she doesn't see it that way.

The therapist suggested we get away for a while. I was hoping this trip would help her to relax and give her a new outlook, but . . ." She shrugged.

"I'm so sorry," I said. "It must be difficult for you as well."

"She'll be right soon enough. I think Al's death just brought it all back."

She was about to leave the table when Detective Marshall came to the railing separating the dining area from the square. He'd changed into casual clothing and carried packages.

"Good evening, ladies," he said. "Enjoy your meal?"

"Very much," I said. "It looks like you've done a little shopping."

He grinned. "Picked up a few things for the grandchildren. Always do when I'm away. Well, have a good evening." He gave us a small, awkward bow and walked in the direction of the hotel.

"He evidently believes you," Marilyn said.

"About what?"

"About Blevin being poisoned."

"Perhaps," I said, "but I've decided that until there's something tangible to support my theory, I'm considering Mr. Blevin's death to be nothing more than an unfortunate accident. I enjoyed having dinner with you and our conversation, Marilyn."

"We'll have lots more time to continue it," she said. "See you in the morning."

I stayed behind at the table for a few minutes before heading back to the hotel. I knew I'd only half meant what I'd said. My intentions were good. *I should consider Alvin Blevin's death to be of natural causes unless proved otherwise. I shouldn't race to conclusions before proof is placed before me*, I told myself. Yet, back at the hotel, I found two uniformed Royal

Canadian Mounted Police officers stationed at each
end of the hallway. Their presence reinforced the
impression that my observations were being taken
seriously.

Chapter Six

As I approached the hostess's desk outside the hotel's Aubergine Grille the following morning, a pile of newspapers caught my eye. Smiling out from the front page of the *Vancouver Sun* was Alvin Blevin. The photo had been taken on a golf course; he wore casual sports clothes and held a club. The headline above the picture read PROMINENT VANCOUVER ATTORNEY DIES. I picked up a copy and read the brief story, bylined by someone named Eugene Driscoll. He'd obviously had little information upon which to base his piece. He reported that Blevin had died of a presumed heart attack on the Whistler Northwind shortly before its arrival in Whistler and went on to say: "Famed mystery writer Jessica Fletcher is aboard the Northwind. Efforts to reach her and other passengers traveling with Mr. Blevin were unsuccessful." An autopsy was pending, Driscoll wrote. A capsule history of Blevin's professional life followed.

"One for breakfast?" the receptionist asked, after returning from seating another party.

"Yes, please."

We were on our way across the large dining room toward a small table near a window when Maeve

Pinckney extended her hand from where she sat with her husband, Junior. "Sit with us," she said.

Junior was wearing his ubiquitous backwards baseball hat and a maroon sweatshirt with GEORGIA TECH in white across the chest. A copy of the newspaper was unopened on the table.

"I assume you saw this," Maeve said, pointing to the Blevin story.

"I just picked it up."

"Big-shot Blevin gets his picture on the front page," Junior said, finishing what had been a tall stack of pancakes, sausage and bacon, and hash brown potatoes.

"I think we should be a little respectful of him, Junior, now that he's dead," his wife chided gently. She seemed to choose her words carefully when addressing her husband, as though saying the wrong thing, however innocuous, would provoke him.

"I didn't like the man, Maeve. You know that. He always had his eye out for you, and don't think I didn't notice you fixin' your hair or makeup whenever he was around."

"You're just imaginin' things, Junior, although it's nice to think of you as bein' jealous after all our years together. It's very flatterin'. Isn't that right, Jessica? Alvin was just trying to be charming to all the ladies. He never paid me any extra attention."

Junior's answer was to pick up the paper and turn to the sports section.

"How are you feeling?" I asked her.

"I'm just fine. Why do you ask?"

"I was concerned when you fainted," I said.

"Silly ol' me," she drawled.

Junior grimaced as he said, "Maeve's the only person on the train who thinks Blevin was a good guy. He charmed the pants off her." He shook his head and resumed reading.

Maeve frowned. "Now, Junior, I think we've had enough conversation about Alvin Blevin, may he rest in peace. We're on vacation, and you get to take pictures of all the trains with your new digital camera. Junior is a wonderful photographer, Jessica. You should have him show you some of the photos he's taken."

Junior peered at me over the newspaper. "I've got two sixty-four-megabyte cards. Lets me take almost three hundred pictures. Camera's got a built-in zoom. Thing's a monster. Can't buy a better one. I can take pictures clear as a bell from three inches away to fifty feet. I'll show it to you when we're back on board."

"Thank you," I said, smiling to myself that Maeve had managed to distract her husband and smooth the waters.

She delicately dabbed her lips with her napkin. "You should eat, Jessica. It's a wonderful buffet, part of our package."

"I will in a moment," I said, sipping my coffee.

I looked to the room's entrance and saw Detective Marshall being led to an empty table next to the window. He wore the same suit he'd had on the day before and carried a briefcase. Maeve followed my gaze and said, "He's still here."

"Yes, he is," I agreed.

Junior looked over the top of the newspaper again. "Don't know why they'd have the police involved," he muttered. "Blevin dropped dead, that's all. Happens all the time."

I looked at Maeve, whose expression was hard to read. She was a pretty woman, subtly made up to accent her beauty, although she needed no artificial enhancements. It was also apparent that she had a voluptuous figure, a classic hourglass shape that was only partially contained beneath the full clothing she wore. *Had her obvious charms attracted Alvin Blevin?*

I excused myself and went to the buffet. Reggie had just entered the restaurant and joined me.

"Sleep well?" he asked.

"So-so," I said, placing a variety of fresh fruit on my plate. "You?"

"Was awake most of the night. Couldn't get Blevin out of my mind."

"I understand," I said, adding a yogurt and a blueberry scone to my breakfast.

We were at the end of the long buffet table when he said, "I thought Benjamin Vail was supposed to go back to Vancouver with his mother and the body."

"No, he said that—"

"You talked to him?"

"Yes. Yesterday."

"You did? How did that happen?"

"It's a long story, Reggie. Where did you see him?"

"Out in the courtyard this morning."

"We'd better get to the table and eat this before the bus leaves for the station," I said. "I'm sitting with the Pinckneys. Would you like to join us?"

"I've already taken a place with the Goldfinches," he said.

"Then I'll catch you later."

My meal was interrupted several times when a few other members of our group stopped by the table to say good morning and to ask whether there was anything new about Blevin's death. I occasionally glanced over at Detective Marshall. He seemed engrossed in whatever he was reading, which appeared to be papers taken from his briefcase.

I finished my breakfast and was about to leave when

Maeve stopped me with "His son doesn't seem too upset with his death."

"What son?" I asked.

"Blevin's stepson," Junior said. "Benjamin."

"Why do you say that?"

"The way he acts," Maeve said. "Tell her, Junior."

"I saw him this morning, outside. I snuck out for a smoke and—"

"Junior still smokes now and then," Maeve said, wrinkling her nose at an imagined odor of tobacco.

"I've cut way down," he said in defense. "Anyway, I went outside to have a cigarette and I saw the kid with Jenna."

"Jenna from the train?"

"Yeah. The cute one."

Maeve leaned close to me. "Junior says they looked lovey-dovey."

"You'd think he'd show a little more class," Junior said, standing and motioning for Maeve to join him.

"Comin'?" Maeve asked me.

"I'll be right along."

I was almost sorry to get on the bus and leave Whistler. It would have been nice to spend a few leisurely days there, exploring the quaint village and enjoying the hotel's amenities. All the seats were taken in the front of the bus, and everyone was strangely quiet. I walked down the aisle toward the back, where I could see a few empty rows. But when I reached the first one, I realized it was already occupied. Benjamin Vail, in a green-and-white-striped shirt and well-worn jeans, sat slouched down, his head turned toward the window, his pea jacket and carry-on bag thrown in the seat beside him. I moved to the next row and sat down.

The Whistler Northwind's staff was lined up next to

the train when we arrived. Callie, the most overtly bubbly of the staff, forced a smile as we filed by and began boarding. It must have been especially difficult for her since she'd mixed and served the drinks that Blevin had imbibed, possibly providing the poison that had been the cause of his demise.

My attention turned to Jenna. She was a very pretty young lady, petite and perky, with light blue oval eyes, her brunette hair in a stylish bob; she usually wore a mischievous smile on her lips. Junior's claim to have seen her being "lovey-dovey" with Benjamin that morning was difficult to believe. Jenna's and Benjamin's personalities were polar opposites, she lively and vivacious, he the quintessential brooding, angry young man. Then again, I'd learned long ago not to judge what attracts one person to another.

I also reminded myself that Junior Pinckney might not be the most credible of witnesses when it came to evaluating people and their relationships. My conversations with him, as brief as they were, revealed what I considered to be a hardheaded man, opinionated and without much tolerance for disagreement. Not that he was unpleasant. He was just not someone I would seek out to sit next to on a long flight.

People gravitated to the seats in the coach car they'd occupied the previous day, except for Benjamin, who disappeared. I didn't see where he went. Junior immediately stationed himself in the vestibule, and Maeve took the window seat next to me and pulled out her needlepoint. Detective Marshall sat alone at the rear of the car. *What is he going to do for the rest of the trip?* I wondered. My question was answered shortly after we pulled out of Whistler station. The big detective left his seat and engaged the club's newcomers, Martin and Gail Goldfinch, in conversation.

I drew out a map provided by BC Rail and identified our route and the scenic treasures we'd pass on the way to the town called 100 Mile House. It was deep in the heart of British Columbia's Cariboo territory, where a gold rush in the mid and late 1850s had opened up the rugged region to development. I looked up at the sound of Jenna's voice over the public-address system.

"I'll be pointing out many sights along the way," she said, "including the mighty Fraser River, the longest river in British Columbia. We'll be passing high above it; the sight is truly spectacular. The river is the site of a large salmon run each year where the salmon fight the currents and rapids to spawn upstream. We usually read a little poem about salmon."

"A poem?" someone grumbled.

Jenna picked up her black book from the seat in front of her and turned to a page she'd marked. I noticed that her pretty face was not as brightly lit with a smile as it had been previously. Was Blevin's death distressing her? Was there truth to what Junior had said, that she had a personal relationship with Benjamin Vail?

She began reading, her tone of voice serious:

I hesitate to be unkind, but the salmon has a one-
    track mind,
Once every season full of fire, he swims upstream
    higher and higher,
Up canyons steep, up rivers deep, through rocks
    and rills, up streams and hills
Up glassy glades, up high cascades;
Until at least on one bright dawn, he gets there
    just in time to spawn,

Now having wooed his salmon cutie, and having
   done his salmon duty,
In quiet waters he will drown,
Pondering with his dying bubble,
Just why is sex so darn much trouble?

People laughed at the punch line. Jenna's mouth
fought against a smile, finally letting a grin break
through. "If anyone has any poems or jokes of their
own," she said, "I'm sure everyone would love to hear
them." There were no takers. "Perhaps later," she said.
"I'm giving you time to think up your best stories. You
won't get off the hook so easily next time." She replaced the book on the seat and disappeared into the
vestibule.

"She's lovely, isn't she," Maeve said. "Nice to be that
young and have your whole life ahead of you."

"Yes," I said, "but there are advantages to getting
older, too."

"You're right. Ah always say ah'm getting better,
aging like a fine wine." She winked at me and went
back to her needlework.

I picked up my map but again was distracted when
Bruce came from the dining car and summoned Detective Marshall to accompany him. When they'd disappeared into the vestibule leading to the dining car,
Reggie poked his head into the coach and motioned
with his finger for me to join him.

"I think you were right," he said, pulling me to the
side.

"About what?"

We stood at the door opposite the one where Junior
Pinckney was leaning out, taking pictures. It was
noisy out there with the rumble of the train on the
tracks, the squeal of the wheels on every curve, and

the wind whipping through the open window, hitting
us in the face. Reggie brought his mouth within inches
of my ear.

"About Blevin being poisoned."

I turned my back to Junior and looked out the open
upper half of the doorway Reggie and I shared.

"How do you know?" I asked, glancing to be sure
that Junior wasn't trying to listen in on our conversation.

Reggie, too, checked our immediate area before saying into my ear, "I overheard Bruce talking with somebody on his cell phone. He said he'd get the detective
right away."

"And?"

"It had to be bad news, Jess."

"Why do you say that?"

"Bruce sounded like it was urgent."

"Well, I suppose we'll find out soon enough."

"Enjoying the view?" Winston Rendell asked. He'd
stepped in behind us and stood with a pipe in his
mouth. "Bloody silly rules they have about smoking,"
he said, extending the unlighted pipe. "No smoking
anywhere on the train."

"We'll be at 100 Mile House soon enough," I said,
wondering if he'd been eavesdropping, "and you'll be
able to enjoy that pipe." We chatted a few minutes before I excused myself.

I returned to the coach and stood in the aisle stretching my legs and watching the landscape passing by
outside the large windows. A few rows back, Deedee
Crocker was standing as well. She was flipping
through a book on the wildflowers of British Columbia, although on this section of the journey, the only
plants I could see were acres and acres of sagebrush. I
was restless and kept turning over in my mind con-

versations I'd overheard or had with my fellow passengers. Was there a clue I'd missed, a comment that had deeper meaning than I'd recognized at the time? I had questions for Reggie, but they would wait until we could speak in private. There were too many people eager to listen in on any talk concerning Theodora and Alvin Blevin.

A few minutes later, Reggie also left the vestibule and came into the coach car. This time I indicated to him that I wished to talk. The club car was no longer off-limits; the police had had the rest of yesterday afternoon and all night to collect potential evidence. Reggie and I went there and paused just inside. We were alone, but the vision and sounds of yesterday's party, and Blevin's gruesome death, were very much with us. We took chairs along one wall.

"Reggie, tell me how Elliott Vail disappeared," I said.

"What makes you ask about that?"

"Just curious, I guess. I was going to ask Benjamin about it yesterday, but I don't think he would have told me anyway."

"Well, you can understand that, Jess." He glanced out the window. "We'll be coming soon to the spot where he disappeared."

"Oh, my. Do you mean he disappeared on one of these train trips?"

"Yes. Three years ago, on this very route."

"You never mentioned that, Reggie. How could you keep something so dramatic a secret?"

"Because I wanted this to be a pleasant ride for you. It was an opportunity for you to revisit Vancouver, and I didn't want to spoil it for you with rumors and nasty stories from the club's history."

"No wonder the Crockers and the Pinckneys were

surprised to see Theodora on this trip. I'm amazed, too. It must have been painful for her to revisit this scene. Why would Blevin subject her to it?"

"Who knows what really goes on in a marriage?"

"What happened to Elliott Vail?"

"I don't really know a great deal. The story is bizarre. Elliott was on the Whistler Northwind three years ago. Theodora was with him. And the guy disappeared."

"Were you on that trip?"

"No. It's the only trip I've missed in recent years, which is why I wanted to come on this one. But I heard all about it from a dozen people who were with Elliott and Theodora."

I thought for a moment before asking, "How do you disappear from a train like this? Where do you go?" I gazed out the window. The train was traveling along a ridge overlooking a canyon. We'd passed dry rolling hills that had reminded me of Texas and Wyoming. Now the hills were cleft by the Fraser River, a narrow stream of brown water far below. What vegetation there was was low and scorched by the sun. We hadn't seen any signs of habitation for miles.

"When we get to the overpass that crosses Fraser River, you'll understand a little better, Jess. It's a spectacular view, way up high over the river and canyon. Some people can't even bring themselves to look down. You know, fear of heights."

"Are you saying that Elliott Vail fell into that river?"

"No, jumped, Jess. At least that's the speculation."

"Speculation?" I couldn't restrain my incredulity.

"Yeah, as far as I know. I mean, I was never privy to all the details. I heard there was a suicide note and—"

"Vail left a suicide note?"

"So I understand."

"What did it say?"

"Never saw it, of course. But the story is that he'd been despondent for a long time. Theodora told people she was concerned about his mental state and thought another trip on this train would pick up his spirits. Others on that trip claimed he was acting strangely, agitated and nervous. At any rate, he was last seen alive on the train just before it crossed the Fraser. After that, Theodora said she couldn't find him. She never did. The consensus was that he jumped into the river from the overpass. Of course, if you ask Maeve Pinckney, she'll say Theodora pushed him off."

I sat back and digested what he'd said. "How could it be possible that his body was never discovered?"

"It's pretty wild country, Jess," Reggie explained.

"Still."

"I know, I know. You'd think they'd at least find his remains after a while. But they didn't. There are a lot of wild animals in these hills, cougars and bears. Maybe that's why."

Here was another mystery to match the death of Alvin Blevin. Theodora Vail Blevin had not been very fortunate in her choice of husbands. Or had she? "Was there insurance money involved?"

Reggie shrugged. "There must have been. Some people said Theodora collected a bundle, but you can't prove it by me. I always wondered why an insurance company would pay off for a suicide, but—"

"They generally will after two years have passed," I said. "What—" I started to ask another question, but Hank and Deedee Crocker entered the car and took chairs next to us. Deedee was holding her book on Canadian wildflowers.

"Hello, folks. Beautiful day, isn't it?" Hank's usual gloom was nowhere in sight.

"Have you heard anything new about how Al died?" Deedee asked.

I shook my head.

"Well," said Hank, "I thought that poem Jenna read about the salmon making love was great. If they ask for jokes from us again, I've got a few."

"That's . . . wonderful," I said, glancing at Reggie.

"Ah, here comes Callie. I could use a drink," Hank said. "I'll have one of your signature Bloody Marys, Callie. I hope they haven't closed the bar for the rest of the trip just because Blevin died."

I saw Callie shiver. "No, sir," she said, her smile tight. "But it's a bit early. I'll be opening the bar after lunch."

"I think I'll take a little walk," Reggie said, standing.

"I'll join you." As I rose to follow Reggie, I saw movement in the back of the club car. We had thought we were alone but never checked the portion of the car that extended beyond the bar. Someone had been standing there, just behind the wall of glasses and bottles, listening to our conversation. He was still there. I could see the edge of his green and white sleeve. It was Benjamin.

In the Summit Coach, Bruce was conferring with the kitchen worker, Karl, who'd delivered the extra bottles of vodka during yesterday's fateful party. The cook left, and Bruce asked me how I was doing.

"Good," I said. "You?"

"As well as can be expected. We'll be having lunch soon. Just got the menu from the horse's mouth, halibut or terrific chicken potpie, the Northwind's own special comfort food."

"Sounds wonderful," I said.

Detective Marshall, who'd been seated next to Gail Goldfinch as I passed on my way from the club car, got up and came to where I stood with Bruce and Reggie.

"Can you spare me a moment, Mrs. Fletcher?"

"Of course."

He turned and headed up the aisle toward the club car from which I'd just come, passing Benjamin coming the other way. Reggie and I looked at each other, and I knew what my friend from Cabot Cove was thinking. I was about to be told the results of the autopsy.

Chapter Seven

I followed Detective Marshall down the length of the
Summit Coach, trying not to feel too self-conscious as
more than a dozen pairs of eyes watched our
progress and mouths whispered comments along the
way. We walked through the front lounge of the club
car, past Deedee and Hank, who were playing Scrabble, past the bar, where Callie was setting up for the
afternoon, and stepped into the quiet salon at the
back of the train, where Benjamin had been hiding
not five minutes ago. To the left of where we entered,
a built-in entertainment unit held cupboards below,
bookshelves above, and a large-screen television
perched on the counter between. The unit was dark
wood, and its back formed the rear wall of the bar
we'd just passed. As in the front lounge, chairs in this
one were lined up along the windows but faced into
the room. At the far end, two tables flanked the glass-
paneled door that looked out on the tracks and the re-
ceding landscape.

"Have you received the results of the autopsy yet?"
I asked.

"Not yet," he answered, starting to pace. "I'm talking to everyone who witnessed Mr. Blevin's death. So
please don't feel I'm singling you out."

"I understand."

"I just want to go over what it was you saw and heard to make you suspect a poisoning. And I'd also like you to give me an idea of the relationships you've observed, those you think might have had a grudge against the deceased."

I noticed that he avoided using the word "victim."

"I can only tell you what people have said to me, but I don't want to throw suspicion on anyone. After all, you're not even sure a murder has taken place, are you?"

"That remains to be seen."

"My argument, exactly. I'm uncomfortable pointing fingers."

I watched as he walked back and forth like a lion trapped in a too small cage. He was a man who found it difficult to hold still. Perhaps the act of moving paralleled the pace of his thinking. He stopped briefly and looked at me, his broad shoulders hunched forward, fists shoved in his jacket pockets.

"Let's just stick to what you saw and what you heard before Mr. Blevin became ill."

"All right. I walked into the party late, after it had already started." I described for him how Alvin Blevin had introduced me to members of the Track and Rail Club, how he'd made his announcements to the crowd, and how he'd insisted I try Callie's Bloody Mary. I stopped and felt myself grow pale.

"What's the matter? Don't you feel well?"

"I just realized that one of the drinks Alvin Blevin consumed might have been originally meant for me."

"I beg your pardon?"

"I mean, he was intent upon my sampling the drink Callie is famous for. I had said I'd just as soon have a glass of wine, but he was insistent. When the waiter brought the drinks on the tray, there were two glasses, one with wine and the other a Bloody Mary. Mr. Blevin pushed the Bloody Mary into my hands, but Mrs. Blevin was adamant that I have the wine." I shivered. "I drank the wine, and he drank the Bloody Mary."

"Do you think that was what caused him to get sick?" he asked.

I barely heard the question. How close had I come to swallowing the drink intended for Alvin Blevin? To being poisoned myself? My heart beat rapidly and I felt a cold sweat coming on.

"How well do you know the people on this train, Mrs. Fletcher?"

"Except for Reggie Weems, I never met any of them before a few days ago." I pulled a handkerchief out of my jacket pocket and patted my brow. "I can't imagine that *I* was the intended victim. It makes no sense."

"I agree," he said.

"I think I'd like to sit down."

"Please. I didn't mean to be rude. I just think better on my feet. Why don't you sit here?" He led me to an upholstered barrel chair, and I sat slowly, retracing in my mind the sequence of events of the afternoon in question.

"You know," I said, "Benjamin also brought him a drink."

"How many drinks did Mr. Blevin consume?"

"I'm not sure. He had a half-empty glass when I arrived, and he took the Bloody Mary from the waiter's tray, and Benjamin—that's his stepson— gave him another. I only saw him sip one, however. Later, when he was lying on the floor, I overheard his wife say to him that three drinks were too much. So perhaps he drank them all, but I can't say for sure."

"What was his demeanor before he became ill? Was he in a good mood, a bad mood?"

"He seemed very cheerful to me." I concentrated on the scene and began to let go of the tension that had gripped me at the prospect of having escaped death by poison. "The others around him seemed to be cheerful as well, although when Mr. Blevin tried to make up with Hank Crocker, Mr. Crocker rebuffed him."

Marshall took a step back so he could see into the front half of the car, where the Crockers had been seated. "They're gone," he said. "Tell me about that."

"Mr. Blevin said three years was a long time to hold a grudge. Mr. Crocker responded that Blevin was getting away with murder and then walked off."

"What was he was referring to?"

"I haven't the faintest notion," I said. "I have no firsthand knowledge of their history. Reggie Weems told me only that Hank Crocker objected to the way Alvin Blevin ran the club and together with others had instituted a lawsuit against him. You'll have to ask Reggie—or Hank—for more details."

He pulled a spiral pad from his breast pocket and made a note in it. "What about the other passengers at the party? I heard he got into a fight with someone."

"If he did, I didn't witness it, unless they were referring to his altercation with Winston Rendell."

"What happened there?"

"It was strange. People were socializing. Then, without any provocation I was aware of, Blevin began yelling at Rendell to get out of his way. That was the first symptom, really. But it wasn't until he complained about the noise that I began to suspect something was really wrong."

"How's that?"

"Well," I said, thinking back to what I'd learned

about strychnine poisoning, "it takes about ten to twenty minutes before the effects of the poison show up. Restlessness, irritability, and anxiety are early symptoms."

"Really, Mrs. Fletcher, there are many reasons why a person could be irritable that have nothing to do with poison," he said.

"You're right, of course. At first I didn't think anything of his confrontation with Winston Rendell, except perhaps that Blevin was a very rude individual. But later, when he talked about it being too noisy, I began to suspect foul play. Sensitivity to light and sounds are hallmarks of strychnine poisoning. And his convulsions were practically by the book."

"You told me before that you used strychnine in one of your mysteries. What made you choose that particular poison?"

"It's not a difficult substance to obtain, really. It's a common rodenticide."

He raised an eyebrow at me.

"Gardeners use it," I said, "for killing mice or rats or moles."

"Wouldn't someone taste that in his drink?"

"Not if the drink had a really strong flavor of its own. Callie's Bloody Marys certainly qualify there. Blevin himself commented on how spicy they were."

He thought for a moment before asking, "What do you know about that couple from the South, Mr. and Mrs. Pinkeye?"

"I think you're being funny, Detective. Their name is Pinckney," I said. "Maeve and Junior."

He ducked his head, but I caught a hint of a grin. "Yes, the Pinckneys. I asked the husband for his real name, and it was something like Beauregard Jubal Pickett Pinckney, Jr. 'Junior' is easier."

"No doubt," I said. "He certainly is a rabid fan of railroads. I don't think he's left his post at the open door in the vestibule except to eat."

"So I've noticed. He told me Mr. Blevin was quite the ladies' man."

"Really?"

"He said something along the lines of no woman being safe in the deceased's company."

"I hadn't heard that," I said. "Blevin was certainly a handsome man, very sure of himself. Rich and powerful, too. I wouldn't be surprised that some women would be attracted to him."

Marshall grunted, and I took that to mean he agreed.

He stood at the rear window, his back to me, and looked out at the tracks growing narrow behind us. My mind wandered. He reminded me in some ways of my dear friend from London, George Sutherland, a Scotland Yard inspector I'd met many years earlier when in England as a guest of the then reigning queen of mystery writers, Dame Marjorie Ainsworth. I'd been Marjorie's weekend houseguest when she was brutally stabbed to death in her bed, and Inspector Sutherland was dispatched to the scene. We'd gotten to know each other during that investigation and had remained fond friends ever since, interested perhaps in more, although neither of us had taken steps to advance that possibility.

I'm always curious about people's lives outside their work. Detective Marshall had bought gifts for his grandchildren. I wondered what this RCMP detective's life was like when he wasn't investigating murders in British Columbia. Did he have a wife? Did they discuss his cases over dinner or on Sunday drives?

He turned and for the first time gave me a soft smile. "You will, of course, keep me informed of anything you might overhear that would have bearing upon this unfortunate incident."

"Of course I will. And I trust you'll let me know once you've received word on the autopsy."

His smile widened. "This is a new experience for me," he said, "having a murder mystery writer as an unofficial partner."

"I'll try to be as helpful as I can," I said.

He left the club car and I followed, but as I passed the lavatories, the door to one of them opened and Maeve Pinckney appeared, her eyes red rimmed.

"Are you all right?" I asked.

"Oh, yes," she said, but there was a quaver in her voice. Before I could offer anything, she walked quickly down the aisle toward our seats.

What's that all about? I wondered. Behind me, the other lavatory door opened and Junior Pinckney emerged.

"Is your wife all right?" I asked him. "I saw that she's been crying and—"

"Maeve? She's fine. She's a real waterworks, cries over Hallmark commercials, for God's sake. Don't pay any attention to her."

What an insensitive comment, I thought as I walked down the aisle, intending to speak with Maeve to see whether there was anything I could do for her. But Detective Marshall had beaten me to it. She'd taken my seat against the window; he filled the seat she usually occupied. I stopped halfway down the car and stood at one of the windows. I was taking in the passing scenery when Jenna came on the PA.

"Lunch is about to be served," she said. "We'll be reaching the Fraser Canyon soon, one of the most spectacular sights on the trip. And we'll be passing the ginseng fields, the most profitable legal cash crop per acre grown in British Columbia."

"I wonder what the illegal crop is," Reggie said, coming up behind me.

"I'd rather not know."

"Share a table, Jess?"

"Love to."

As we waited in the aisle for others to leave their seats and file into the dining car, I asked Reggie, "Was Blevin a womanizer?"

My Cabot Cove friend guffawed. "Al Blevin was notorious for getting whatever he wanted," he said. "But that's another story. Come on, I'm famished. I hear the chicken potpies are to die for."

As it turned out, Reggie's rave review of the chicken potpie wasn't misplaced. It rivaled the best from my friends' kitchens back home.

But food wasn't my preoccupation of the moment. My natural instinct to know about people had kicked in and was running in high gear. It didn't matter whether Blevin was poisoned or not, at least not for the moment. I was now determined to find out as much as I could about his obviously controversial life. This need to know is a common curse among writers, at least the ones with whom I'm friendly. While the characters in my novels are creatures of my imagination, they're often based on real people I've known or heard of, properly disguised, of course. My fascination with asking "what if" was now operating full-time.

I intended to ask Reggie more questions about Blevin's love life over lunch, but the Goldfinches joined us and had questions of their own, not about Blevin but about Elliott Vail's disappearance three years ago. I only half listened while Reggie related what he'd told me earlier, but my interest picked up when Martin asked, "Had Mrs. Vail been having some sort of a relationship with Blevin *before* her husband disappeared?"

"That was the rumor," Reggie answered, "but you can't prove it by me."

Gail Goldfinch chimed in with, "There must have been a lot of insurance money involved."

"Why do you assume that?" Martin asked.

"Oh, I don't know," she said. "Just the way she looks and carries herself."

"Al was loaded," Reggie said. "She didn't need to bring money into the relationship."

"Still, two and a half million dollars wouldn't hurt, would it?"

I'd been silent during the exchange. Now I joined the conversation. "I wonder what was said in the suicide note."

"Oh, was there a suicide note?" Gail asked. But there was something in the tone of her question that didn't sound genuine to me.

"Was it ever made public?" Martin put in.

"Not that I know of," Reggie said. "I asked Al about it once. He told me the court proceedings and decisions were sealed by the judge."

The subject was dropped for the rest of the meal, and topics shifted to talk of old trains and the passing scenery. The Goldfinches excused themselves after a dessert of double chocolate truffle cake, leaving Reggie and me alone at the table.

"Nice couple," he said. "Always good to have new blood in the club."

"There's something odd about them, but I can't put my finger on it."

"They look pretty normal to me."

"Reggie," I said, changing the topic, "I asked you before lunch about Al Blevin's reputation as a womanizer."

"Doesn't matter, does it," he said, "now that he's dead?"

"Do me a favor and satisfy this naturally curious mystery writer."

He laughed. "Going to base a book on this?"

"His death is intriguing, is it not?"

"Especially if he was poisoned."

"Even if he wasn't."

He nodded toward a table at the opposite end of the dining car, closest to the coach car. Maeve and Junior Pinckney were in the process of vacating it. Reggie leaned close. "It's not the sort of thing that I ever noticed," he said, "but Junior there has hinted that he caught his wife in a compromising position with Blevin."

"Oh? When was that?"

"A few years back."

"Before Elliott Vail disappeared."

"Yeah. Sure. It would have been five or six years ago."

"Was Blevin married at that time?"

"Might have been. Or between marriages."

"How many times was he married?"

"Three that I know of, not including Theodora."

"Any children?"

"I never saw him with a kid, but if he does have any, I imagine they'd live with the mother. Maybe Junior knows. Ask him."

"I will."

Maeve saw us looking at them and gave us a wave, which I returned.

I shook my head. "I certainly don't know Maeve very well, but I simply cannot imagine her taking up with Alvin Blevin."

Reggie grinned. "Remember what Henry Kissinger answered when he was asked why so many women were attracted to him?" He adopted what passed for an imitation of Kissinger's accent: "Vimmen love power!"

"Not this voman," I said, laughing and standing. "We should be getting close to 100 Mile House soon, shouldn't we?"

"Right. But first we have to cross over the infamous Fraser Canyon. It's a sight not to be missed."

A few minutes later, Jenna's voice came over the PA to herald the train's approach to Fraser Canyon. Her announcement woke many of those whose heads had started to droop following a satisfying lunch, and there was hustle and bustle as people stood in the aisle or kneeled on their seats to get a better view. We'd been paralleling the Fraser River for a while. Now we were about to begin the breathtaking crossing of the canyon. We were on a long curved section of track that afforded a view ahead of what looked like an elongated, spindly trestle held up by matchstick legs.

"It doesn't look as though it can support us," I commented to Bruce, who'd entered the car carrying his ubiquitous clipboard and cell phone.

He laughed. "Oh, it can support us, Mrs. Fletcher. Always has."

Spaces next to the windows on the scenic side were all taken, so I wandered into the vestibule, where, no surprise, Junior was hanging out the upper half of the door, baseball hat on backwards, digital camera trained on the unfolding vista. He wasn't the only one there. Hank Crocker, a video camera in his hand, was trying to push Junior aside. But Junior wasn't budging.

"Move, damn it!" Crocker barked.

"I was here first," Junior said, not turning.

"You're always here. Come on, stop hogging the door."

"Go to the other side. The view is just as good."

"If it's just as good, you go."

It was getting nasty. I decided to move into the dining car, where I could sit and enjoy the view from one of its windows.

In the small foyer that led into the dining car, a figure was pressed against the window, his back to me. These windows didn't open. There was no breeze to ruffle Benjamin's hair, no fresh air tainted with the slight smell of oil that the train gave off. It occurred to me that this portion of the trip could be exactly why Benjamin Vail had continued on the Northwind while his mother returned home to mourn her second husband. Had he never seen where his father had disappeared? Had he wondered all these years what had happened to send Elliott over the edge? Did he worry, as so many children of suicides did, that he had contributed to his father's demise by some word or deed? His was not a pleasant personality, but my heart went out to Benjamin as he strained against the glass, struggling to see where his father had died.

I passed through the foyer without lingering, careful not to disturb the young man's privacy at such a difficult moment, and paused next to the service cabinet. At the far end, Karl was setting the tables with fresh linen. I stepped into the car and heard a voice with a distinct British accent. Winston Rendell came into view. He was speaking into a cell phone and pacing along the wall.

". . . of course I'm sure," he said. "The bastard is bloody well dead, and good riddance."

Before I could back away, he turned and saw me. His expression went from surprise to anger. "I'll call you later," he said into the phone, slipping it into his pocket and forcing a smile at me.

"Enjoying the view, Mrs. Fletcher?" he said.

"I haven't seen very much of it but—excuse me."

I returned to the vestibule, where Hank Crocker and Junior Pinckney continued to jockey for position at the half-open and prized place by the door. Hank spotted me and said to Junior, "Let Mrs. Fletcher have some time here."

Junior snorted as he considered Crocker's suggestion.

"No, that's all right," I said.

Hank gave Junior a little shove away from the door and followed him to the opposite side, leaving the space at the door unoccupied. Although I wasn't especially keen on standing in the rush of air coming through the open upper portion of the door, I appreciated the gesture and went to where they'd been standing. At first, I stood back a few inches from the door, uncomfortable doing what they'd been doing, leaning on the closed lower portion and extending their heads through the opening.

"Afraid to look down, Mrs. Fletcher?" Rendell said from behind me. He'd come from the dining car and was now a foot from my back. "Fear of heights?"

"No," I said, closing the gap in front of the door and placing my hands on the ledge. I leaned forward, poked my head out into the wind, and peered down into the canyon and at the river that appeared to be miles below. The view was spectacular; the train had slowed and was barely moving, giving passengers more time to appreciate the dramatic scene.

Suddenly, the closed bottom portion of the door gave way and swung out, taking me with it. I was doubled over on it, my stomach the fulcrum point, my head and torso jutting from the train, the tips of my shoes barely maintaining contact with the edge of the vestibule floor. Below was Fraser Canyon, so distant and menacing, its muddy river and harsh terrain beckoning as it allegedly had done to Elliott Vail three years ago. The train jerked forward and the door swung wider; my feet left the metal edge of the floor. In another moment the door would bang backwards into the side of the train and I would be knocked off, tumbling hundreds of feet down into the jagged rocks and churning water.

I screamed; the rush of air carried away the sound.

"Help!"

I felt a tugging on my skirt, then hands on the waistband, pulling me and the door back toward the vestibule. Those same hands then grasped my shoulders and completed the task of bringing me to safety.

"Oh—thank heavens, you—were here," I said to Samantha Whitmore as I slumped against the wall of the vestibule, shaking, taking in gulps of air.

"That was close," she said, pulling me farther away from the door, which was still unlatched. "Are you injured? Are you feeling pain anywhere?" she asked as she ran her hands up and down my arms and examined my eyes. Even through my shock and confusion, I realized that this was a Samantha I hadn't seen before, solicitous and capable.

Bruce, the Northwind's guest services supervisor, hurried in from the coach and came to my side. Keeping one hand on my shoulder, he slammed the bottom half of the door shut and jiggled the handle. "I saw you through the window," he said, shuddering. "This has never happened before, I promise you. These doors are always locked. I check them myself." He returned his full attention to me. "Are you all right?"

"I'm—yes, I think I'm all right—shaken but otherwise—okay." The words came out in short bursts as I struggled to catch my breath. "I thought—"

"Yes?"

"I thought Mr. Rendell—he was right behind—me—when it happened."

"Did he—? Are you saying—?"

"No. Don't misunderstand." I tried to draw in a deep breath. "It's just that he was here when it happened." I looked at Samantha. "I assumed *he* was the one who grabbed me."

"There was no one behind you when I came along," Samantha said.

"Did you do anything to the door to make it open like that?" Bruce slammed his hand on the door to test the lock.

"I don't think so. Mr. Crocker and Mr. Pinckney were at the door before they made room for me."

I looked across the vestibule, but the two men who'd been battling each other for the best view had abandoned their posts and disappeared.

"I'll talk to them," Bruce said.

"Yes, do that. I'm feeling a little better," I said. "I think I'll return to my seat."

"Of course. Can I get you anything? Coffee or tea or a brandy?"

"No, nothing. Wait, yes. Maybe a cup of tea."

"Right on it." He rushed away.

"You almost died," Samantha said, her concern now turned to pique, "and he offers you tea."

"Samantha, I can't thank you enough."

She raised her hands as if to ward me off, took a step back, and shook her head. The disturbed expression was back in her eyes. "Don't have to," she muttered, turning to leave. "Didn't want another death on my hands."

Alone in the vestibule, my back to the wall, I took a shaky breath. I'd said I wanted to return to my seat, but I wasn't actually certain my legs would support me yet. I turned my head and looked intently at the latch. *Who loosened that door? Was it Rendell? He was right behind you,* I told myself as I replayed the scene in my mind. *He taunted you, and you foolishly leaned closer to the door to move away from him. Had he released the latch and walked away so he could claim that he wasn't there when I fell to my death? If so, why? He was introduced to me as a colleague, a fellow author, yet he's consistently made disparaging remarks about my writing. Surely his resentment of me couldn't justify murder. There must be something else I'm missing.* I ran a trembling hand through my hair. I'd obviously interrupted an important phone call, and he hadn't been happy. But was what I'd heard enough to tempt him to murder me?

I took a deep breath and blew it out. My hammering heart had slowed a little, and I thought my legs might hold me now. I entered the coach and slowly made my way down the aisle. I had almost reached my seat, where Maeve Pinckney was working on her needle-point, when Hank Crocker stopped me. "Enjoy the view?"

"I, ah—"

"This is where he went off," Crocker whispered.

"Pardon?"

"Vail. He must have been really desperate to take a plunge like this."

"All suicides are acts of desperation," I offered, feeling a little light-headed; I grabbed a seat-back for support.

"I never bought it," he said, his voice low. "Didn't make any sense. He wasn't the kind of guy to kill himself that way. Elliott was not a very physical guy, you know? I'd figure him to take some pills or stick his head in an oven. Jump from way up here? Nah. And how come nobody saw him go, you know, from a window or something? Everybody's looking out the window at this point in the trip."

But Bruce had been the only one to see me dangling over the gorge. Or was he the only one?

"Excuse me," I said, and slid past Maeve into the security of my comfortable chair.

Jenna brought me a cup of tea.

"Bruce said to tell you it's ginseng. From British Columbia. Our ginseng is considered the best quality in the world, the most beneficial." As she spoke, she flipped the catch holding the little table flush with the seat-back in front of me—*Just like an airplane*, I thought absently—and put down the teacup and saucer.

Being seated, and drinking the hot tea, helped calm me, although I needed two hands to lift the cup to my lips. Maeve, ignorant of my ordeal, chatted on about how halfway into a train trip, she always began to get bored, and how nice it was to have me to talk to, to while away the hours. Of course, her needlework was a compensation. She had many beautiful pillows to show for her train time, and whenever I was in Atlanta, I must stop by and visit with her and Junior, and she would take me on a tour of her completed projects.

I listened with half an ear, but her conversation required no response except the occasional "Hmmm." When I finished my tea, I let my head fall back and closed my eyes. Maeve continued talking a little longer and then stopped. I could feel the movement of her hands as she worked rapidly on the stitches for her next pillow.

With my eyes closed, the image of being suspended over the yawning chasm roared back into my mind.

One awkward movement and I would have hurtled to my death. My body would be lying dashed against the rocks instead of sitting safely in a plush seat as the train rattled along toward its next stop. Odd scraps of thought floated through my brain. I was grateful I'd kept up with my exercise program. I'd needed all my stomach muscles to keep from sliding off the swinging door. I felt my toes curl tightly from the tension and made a conscious effort to relax them, thankful that I hadn't lost my shoes—or my life.

Horrifying as it was, I forced myself to relive the experience, to concentrate on the details. Mentally, I retraced my steps from the time I'd entered the vestibule until Samantha pulled me back from the brink of death. Even if a motive wasn't clear, Winston Rendell hadn't been the only person with the opportunity to tamper with that lock. Junior and Hank had been competing for the best view. Had one of them released it accidentally? Purposely? No, it didn't make sense. They had no reason to want to harm me. Who *would* have a reason? Benjamin had been there, too, only steps away. I had thought him completely involved in seeing where his father had died, but could there have been a more sinister explanation for his presence? And there was my savior, Samantha, a disturbed young woman with an unpredictable personality. She'd said she didn't want another death on her hands. She could have been referring to her father. Or she could have been referring to Blevin. Had she truly happened by? Or had she created the situation from which she'd rescued me?

I wrestled with more questions. Should I tell Detective Marshall about what happened? Would he think I was trying to make my case more dramatic? Was this simply a potentially tragic accident that fortunately had ended happily? Was it a warning to "butt out" as Benjamin had instructed me on the top of Whistler Mountain? Or did someone want me out of the way—permanently? I was raising the specter of murder. Was the murderer trying to kill the messenger?

"You must have been having a bad dream," Maeve said to me when I opened my eyes and sighed. "You were frowning and your face was all screwed up. Would you like me to ask Jenna to get you another cup of tea? Of course, ginseng is supposed to be very stimulating, so perhaps you'd like something else."

I thanked her for her concern but declined her offer. Instead, I got up to stretch and looked around the coach car. Detective Marshall stood talking with Martin Goldfinch, whose wife sat reading a book. Samantha was sleeping again, her head on her mother's shoulder. Winston Rendell sat alone peering out the window, his face set in a scowl.

Jenna came on the PA and read from her book.

"Ladies and gentlemen, I'm sure you enjoyed the spectacular views of the canyon and river. Fishing rights on this portion of the river are reserved exclusively for members of the First Nations. We'll be coming up on the ginseng fields in a few minutes; you'll know it when you see miles and miles of fields covered in black plastic. A little later, we'll be reaching Taylor Lake, almost four thousand feet high, the summit of our journey. In the meantime, Callie informs me that the bar is open."

Jenna made an attempt at a smile, but since Blevin's death, she had yet to recover her earlier bubbly personality. I wondered if there was something more on her mind as she quickly disappeared into the dining car. People got up and headed for the club car, including Maeve, leaving her seat open. Detective Marshall waited for the others to leave before coming down the aisle and taking the unoccupied space next to me.

"Have you heard anything?" I asked, settling back into my seat.

He nodded solemnly.

"And?"

"I'll have to start reading your books, Mrs. Fletcher," he said softly.

"Poisoned?" I murmured.

"Uh-huh. And it was strychnine."

Chapter Eight

"I'd like to keep this between us, Mrs. Fletcher, if you don't mind," Detective Marshall said, his voice muffled behind the hand he'd drawn across his mouth.

"Of course," I said, looking around at the small group that had gathered for afternoon cocktails. "No one will hear it from me. But I'm sure you know that a secret like this won't remain a secret very long."

"Yes, I realize that."

"Why don't we move to the back of the car where we can speak more freely?" I suggested.

He escorted me to the rear of the club car, where someone had pushed two of the little round tables together and set up a game of checkers, the red and black disks lined up in the rows of squares, awaiting players.

"I have our Vancouver office running background checks on all the passengers, and another detective will join me when we arrive at 100 Mile House," he said, studying the checkerboard as though he might start playing at any moment. "For now, I intend to concentrate on the folks who were in the room when the deceased was drinking."

"You will reinterview everyone on this train, I assume."

"Focusing on those in this car, of course."

"The staff as well. Have you spoken with them?"

"Of course, although I don't expect anyone to offer much that's different from their original interviews back in Whistler."

"With all due respect to your other officers, Detective Marshall, those initial interviews were cursory, at best."

"Necessarily so," he said. "I don't suppose you'd have much interest in internal police affairs, but there is a jurisdictional dispute brewing over Mr. Blevin's death."

"Oh?"

"Because he was such a prominent member of Vancouver society—and now that it appears he was murdered—the Vancouver police will wish to take over the investigation. They've already started, in fact."

"Did they inform Mrs. Blevin of the poisoning?"

"I'm sure they must have by now, but they haven't notified me yet."

Jurisdictional disputes, more aptly termed "turf wars" between law enforcement agencies, always seem to arise in high-profile cases. Tension between such agencies as the FBI and local police departments are common, and I wondered how serious such disputes could become in Canada. I asked.

My question brought forth a smile from the big, dour detective. "Actually, Mrs. Fletcher, we tend to get along quite nicely, at least here in British Columbia. Oh, we have our moments of disagreement, but nothing serious. Because everyone on this train will conclude their trips back in Vancouver, the municipal force is arguing that it makes logistic sense for the city boys to take over. However, I'm pressing to stay on the case. We'll see how it pans out."

"You've established that everyone will return to Vancouver?"

"That's what they all say. Once we arrive at 100 Mile House, my colleague and I will verify everyone's travel plans through their ticketing."

I reached into my handbag and retrieved my airline ticket, which indicated that my return flight from Vancouver would be three days after we returned to the city from the Whistler Northwind's final stop in Prince George. I handed it to him.

"Yes, precisely," he said, handing it back. "I'm sure everyone will be happy to cooperate."

"I would hope so," I said.

"Perhaps even the murderer."

He sat next to the tables on which the checkerboard sat, crossed his long legs, and looked out the window at the passing countryside, his craggy face set in deep thought. I didn't intrude on whatever he was thinking, although my mind was racing as I recalled the circumstances surrounding Alvin Blevin's murder, my own brush with death temporarily set aside. It came back into focus quickly, however, when Winston Rendell poked his head into the salon where we were sitting. He seemed surprised to see me there with Detective Marshall.

"Beg pardon. Didn't know this area was occupied," he said, leaving quickly. His expression had been distinctly uncomfortable and he'd avoided my gaze. Was a guilty conscience plaguing him? Was he worried that I would influence the police, point them in his direction, accuse him of murder or attempted murder?

I shivered. Until I knew who was responsible for unlocking the vestibule door, I would look upon certain members of our entourage with suspicion. And he was one of them.

"What do you know about that chap?" Marshall asked me.

"Very little," I said. "He writes for *Trains* magazine, and he mentioned once that he's working on a history of BC Rail. You've spoken with him?"

"Yes. That's not quite the story he gave me. Told me he was in the railroad business."

"Well, perhaps he meant his writing was a business."

"Didn't sound that way."

"Oh?"

"And it's not going very well, I take it."

"He said that?"

"Not in so many words. He said something along the lines of Mr. Blevin's death coming at an inopportune moment, although he added that it probably didn't make much difference because the deal had already gone astray."

"They were in business together?"

"Talking about it anyway. But it's over now, obviously."

"Did he seem angry about that?'

"Not especially. Wouldn't have put him in an especially good light to admit he was angry at Mr. Blevin about a failed business deal, eh?"

"Would have made him a suspect," I injected.

"Exactly."

"I interrupted him on the telephone today," I said, and recounted what I'd overheard.

"May not mean much. Looks like most of the people in this club weren't fans of the deceased."

But I wondered if it did mean something. If Rendell had murdered Blevin over a business deal gone sour, it also would have given him a motive to eliminate one meddlesome female who was insisting that a crime had taken place.

The detective fell silent again. He focused on the checkerboard, brow furrowed, tongue running over his upper lip.

"Shame," he said without looking up.

"What's a shame?"

"There's a checker missing."

I looked at the board. He was right. One red checker wasn't there.

"I would have enjoyed a game," he said. "Do you play?"

"I have. Where could it be?"

"The checker?"

"Yes."

We both looked at the carpet under the tables, but the missing piece wasn't there. "Maybe in the cupboard," he said, pointing to the cabinet beneath the TV and VCR.

"Let me take a look."

I knelt by the cabinet and opened one of the doors. Inside were assorted board games, some in boxes and some not, and a few books scattered among them. It looked as though previous players hadn't been especially careful about putting away the pieces in the games, something that always irks me. I pushed aside some of the boxes as I searched for the missing red checker and spotted it in a corner of the shelf, wedged between the side of the cabinet and a brown cardboard box. I reached in to slide the checker toward me, toppling a pile of game boards, which slid off each other, revealing the label of the box.

"I think you'd better come look at this," I said.

"You found it?" he said.

"Yes," I said, holding up the checker. "But I found something else, too."

Marshall squatted down beside me. "What is it?"

"Take a look at that box."

He reached into his breast pocket, drew out a small flashlight in the shape of a pen, twisted the top, and aimed the narrow beam at the label. "Paget's Garden Guard," he read. "Powdered bait for the control of pocket gophers, ground squirrels, and other rodents. Highly poisonous. Wear gloves when using this product."

"Look at the small type on the bottom," I said. "It says 'strychnidin.' "

"Do you think—?" he said

"I don't know," I replied, "but I'll bet it's the source of the strychnine that killed Mr. Blevin. Easy enough to test."

Marshall instinctively removed a handkerchief from his pocket, lifted the box from the shelf, and placed it on the counter next to the television. He glanced at me and winced. "You didn't touch this, did you?"

"No." I immediately knew what was bothering him. He wasn't worried that I'd come in contact with a poison. The container might yield vitally important fingerprints.

"Good," he said, frowning. "I don't understand why my men didn't see this when they went through the place."

"Perhaps it wasn't there then. Or maybe they concentrated on the other part of the lounge where Blevin fell ill."

"Maybe. They'll have to answer that question. Have a seat. I'll be right back." He went around the corner to the bar and returned a moment later with a large green garbage bag, in which he wrapped the box. He pulled a rubber band over the plastic to hold it in place, and took his seat across the tables from me, placing the package on the chair beside him.

"I must say, Mrs. Fletcher, staying close to you during an investigation tends to—well, how shall we say it?—tends to reap rewards, eh?"

"Only because of a missing checker," I said.

"Be that as it may, you might well have discovered how the strychnine found its way into the bar car. Nothing I can do with it until we reach 100 Mile House." He checked his watch. "Which won't be long from now. In the meantime, are you up for a game?"

I was soundly trounced in the two games of checkers I played with the RCMP detective, although I felt I had an excuse for my losses. While my mind was distracted during the moves, he seemed totally focused on the board and his options, as though no one had been murdered the day before in the other end of the very car in which we sat.

We parted as the train approached the town of 100 Mile House, with these words from him: "Keep your eyes and ears open, Mrs. Fletcher. I have the feeling that I'm in league with a woman whose senses are especially keen."

Being human, I was gratified to be on the receiving end of such a compliment. I suppose acceptance by a detective like Marshall was especially pleasing because that hadn't always been true. In other murder cases in which I'd found myself inadvertently involved over the years, the investigating authorities had not always been especially receptive to my ideas or hunches, even my presence in general. But while Detective Marshall didn't seem to fall into that category, I was well aware that I could quickly wear out my welcome unless I continued to produce useful evidence. And if I was successful, would the killer be coming after me—again?

Chapter Nine

The buses were waiting for us when we got off the train at 100 Mile House, and I joined other members of the Track and Rail Club on the line waiting to board one of them.

"Oh, aren't they cute?" Deedee Crocker squealed, pointing at the grassy hill that butted up against the train platform.

"They're not cute when you're trying to putt on the golf course," Callie said, coming up beside her.

I gazed at the grassy verge and at first didn't see what they were looking at. But a quick movement and a chirping drew my attention to a small head poking out of a hole. Then a whole body emerged and a little animal sat up, front paws hanging in front of its chest, black eyes paying sharp attention to our slowly moving group.

"What are they?" Hank asked.

"Pocket gophers," Callie replied. "And those bigger guys over there are marmots, or ground squirrels."

A dozen pairs of human eyes turned toward the little animals. Several dozen pairs of rodent eyes stared back.

"Ooh, they give me the creeps." Maeve shuddered.

"It's just a squirrel," Junior said. "You've seen those at home."

"They're not the same."

"Close enough. When did you become so squeamish? You're the one always putting down bait and trapping the mice in our basement."

"That's only one at a time. And at home I don't have so many of them staring at me."

"If they're looking at you, it's just because they're scared you're going to come after them."

"They're a real problem up here, especially on the golf course," Callie put in. "There are so many of them, we had a green that all but collapsed because of the large number of tunnels underground."

"What's the golf club doing about it?" Hank asked.

"There's not a lot that can be done," Callie replied. "You can poison them, but there's hundreds more where the first wave came from. We just grin and bear it."

"Poison them?" Deedee said.

"Bad choice of words," Callie said. "Sorry."

On the bus, I was disappointed to learn from Bruce's onboard announcement that we would not all be staying overnight in the same hotel. I'd looked forward to the opportunity to get to know certain others in the party a little better, perhaps over dinner. Half of the group, including Detective Marshall, was dropped off at a hotel not far from the train station, and my contingent was driven to the Hills Health Ranch and Spa, a bucolic, sprawling facility surrounded by horse paddocks, open fields, and forests. The young men who transported our luggage from point to point in a truck had arrived an hour earlier, testimony to the Whistler Northwind's leisurely pace and BC Rail's efficiency, and our luggage was already in our rooms. My accommodations were on the second floor, a sparkling clean, albeit spartan room, typical of other health spas

I'd visited, with windows and a small balcony overlooking a volleyball court, located next to a trailhead entering the woods.

Dinner, a barbecue for members of the Track and Rail Club, was scheduled to begin in two hours. I showered, dressed in a fresh outfit, and ventured out for a walk. It was a lovely late afternoon, the sky a deep blue with only an occasional passing high white cirrus cloud. I'd read the ranch's brochure before leaving my room and was impressed with the variety of programs on offer: nature walks, aerobics, supervised workouts with weights, horseback riding, yoga, stretch classes—even belly dancing. And of course, the requisite body and facial treatments expected of a full-service spa. Sampling them all wasn't an option, although a session with one of the ranch hands to demonstrate horse whispering really appealed to me.

I wandered to a corral where horses were being rounded up for feeding. Jenna, whom Junior Pinckney claimed he'd seen with Benjamin Vail at the hotel in Whistler, leaned on the fence watching the ranch hands perform their task. I came to her side.

"Beautiful here, isn't it?" I said to break the ice.

She jumped at my voice and turned to look at me quizzically.

"I didn't mean to startle you."

"Oh, you didn't," she said, issuing a smile.

"I love watching horses," I said. "They're so majestic."

"Yes, they are."

"Are you staying at the ranch?" I hadn't seen any of the staff at our previous hotel.

"No," she said. "We have our own quarters on the train."

"I didn't know that."

"The car right behind the engine," she said. "We sleep there and have our own bathrooms and kitchen."

"Sounds nice."

"Actually, I grabbed a ride here to get away."

I laughed. "Too much of the close quarters?"

She nodded. "We all get along great, but sometimes you have to—well, get away. Callie plays golf. Bruce always manages to find a movie theater. I just like to be by myself."

"I know what you mean," I said.

She fell silent, watching the slow swish of the horses' tails as they lined up around the trough. "People think he was murdered, don't they?"

I didn't respond.

"Everybody is saying it. You said it."

"Who else is saying it?" I asked.

"Everyone. You spoke with the detective. What does *he* say?"

"He doesn't share much with me," I said. It was only a partial lie. He'd shared some things, specifically that Blevin had been poisoned, but I assumed there were other things he'd held back.

"We've never had anything like this on the train before," she said. "I suppose we'll all be suspects."

"That's usually the way it works," I said. "Everyone is a suspect until ruled out. Didn't the police do the same thing when Elliott Vail disappeared?"

"I don't really know. Anyway, why would one of us want to kill Mr. Blevin?" she asked.

"Us?"

"The staff. Detective Marshall said he's sending someone to our car later to ask more questions."

"That's his job." It didn't escape my notice that she knew about Elliott Vail. How? Had Benjamin told her? I let it go for the moment, instead saying, "You and the rest of the staff must have known Mr. Blevin from previous trips."

"A couple of us did, at least the ones who've been working for a few years. I mean, I think I only met him once before. I didn't know him."

"But you'd met him before this trip. Callie, too. Who else?"

Her expression turned hard. "Why are you asking that?

"No reason. Just curious."

"You sound like the detective."

"He would never have me asking questions on his behalf. I can assure you of that. No, no. He's a professional. I'm just . . . a naturally curious person. I'll bet you are, too."

"What do you mean?" she asked suspiciously.

"Well, you must meet all sorts of people on the train. People who are pleasant and easy to be around, and people who give you a hard time. A service business is like that, right? I bet you're probably good at sizing up the passengers pretty quickly."

She relaxed. "That's true, you know. Some of the passengers can be a real pain. And you can spot them a mile away."

"The manner in which someone treats people who provide service often says a lot about them. Take Mr. Blevin, for instance. Those of you who knew him from previous trips might be in a position to offer some insight into his life." I kept my voice rhetorical. "Was he kind to the staff or arrogant? Was he well liked by his colleagues? Or were there people from the club who had a grudge against him?"

"You mean, would someone be so angry with him that they killed him?" she asked angrily, tears welling up in her eyes.

"That's assuming, of course, that he was indeed murdered. What did *you* think of him?"

She seemed to soften a bit. "I thought deep down he must be a really nice man. He always smiled at me. I never saw him fight with anyone, except Be—well, no, forget I said that. He got along with everyone."

"Were you going to say Ben? Stepfather and stepson—that's a tricky relationship. There are bound to be irritations."

The stiffness returned. "I don't know anything about their relationship."

I had to probe in another direction, and I knew which one would help me most. "How long have you worked on the Northwind?"

"Why do you want to know?"

"Oh, just a hunch. Were you on the trip when Mr. Vail disappeared?"

"What does that have to do with anything?"

I wasn't sure how far to take the subject but decided since I had her one-on-one, I might as well plunge forward.

"I wondered if you were working on the Whistler Northwind when Ben's father fell overboard," I said. "It's such a remarkable story. As I understand it, Mr. Blevin represented Mr. Vail's wife, Theodora, in court. And he succeeded in having Mr. Vail declared legally dead. It must have been covered on television. It was quite a legal breakthrough. Then Mr. Blevin married Mrs. Vail. That's a provocative scenario, I'm sure you'll agree. Certainly, the staff would have remarked on it."

"I wouldn't know," she said icily, returning her attention to the horses. "I don't watch television, and I don't gossip about the passengers."

I decided to switch tacks and see if I could jar a response from her. "I'm thinking of watching the horse whisperer tomorrow morning," I said. "Have you ever seen one?"

"No."

"Can you sneak away for an hour?"

"No. We have to report for duty at eight."

"Of course. By the way, I spoke with Benjamin yesterday. It must be so difficult for that young man to have lost his father under mysterious circumstances and then see his stepfather die before his eyes."

She didn't hesitate. "I have to get back to the train," she said. "I'll see you tomorrow. Have a nice evening."

I watched her walk briskly up the hill, appearing ready to break into a run at any second. No question about it, this pretty young woman who'd been so upbeat and pleasant at the start of the trip now had something very weighty on her mind. My mention of Benjamin and his father had obviously upset her. The question was, why? If there was a relationship between Jenna and Benjamin, perhaps even a romantic one, she might know a great deal about the people involved in this affair. If so, I wondered what Benjamin's mother, or his stepfather, had thought about these two young people being together.

The dining room at the Hills ranch combined a western theme with hotel comfort. Spindle-backed wooden chairs cozied up to well-spaced tables set with white linens and fresh flowers. The rich brown log walls were lightened by large picture windows overlooking the woods. Hanging plants also seemed to bring the outside in. Here and there, colorful rugs brightened the plank floors. A gentleman played old-time melodies on an upright piano located next to the buffet and salad bar.

A section of the large room had been reserved for members of the Track and Rail's party, and I sat at a

table with the Pittsburgh Crockers, the Atlanta Pinckneys, Marilyn Whitmore and her nurse-daughter,
Samantha, of Vancouver, and to my distinct discomfort, Winston Rendell.

The waitress invited us to help ourselves from the
buffet, and I went to the line at the salad bar and
picked up a plate. Junior Pinckney was behind me.

"Careful what you tell that Brit," Junior said under
his breath.

"Pardon?"

"That writer, Rendell. He says he's writing about the
trip, but he keeps asking questions about the club's
dues and funds, and about Blevin's way of running the
club and using the funds."

"Maybe that's good," Hank Crocker said, reaching
in front of me to take a plate. "Put Blevin's shenani-
gans in print."

"What good would that do?" Junior asked. "Blevin's
dead now. That was the best way to straighten out the
mess he made."

Reggie joined the line and nodded toward Rendell.
"Speaking of steam engines," he said.

"Were we?"

"Rendell. I just heard he's cornered the market on
old steam engines."

"How did he do that?"

"Bought 'em up, two hundred of them. He must be
rich as Croesus. I had no idea, did you?"

"No! You said he was a writer."

"Well, he is, but apparently he's got his fingers in a
lot of business pies, too."

"What's he going to do with the steam engines?"

"He intended to sell them off as scrap metal, but
when he became aware of the resurgence of interest in
old steamers, he changed his plans and has been re-

furbishing them. More money in that, I guess. Word has it he's even considering building new ones to meet the demand. He spent a lot of time with Blevin. I wonder . . ."

"What are you wondering, Reggie?"

"If maybe they had some sort of business deal going on between them."

Detective Marshall had drawn that same conclusion, but I didn't mention it.

Once we'd gotten our salads, we went outside where a young man in a chef's white uniform stood over a huge charcoal grill. "Steak, chicken, or ribs?" he announced loudly. The odors wafting from the grill stimulated my appetite, and I ordered chicken. Samantha Whitmore, who was ahead of me in line, waited for me to be served. As we walked back to the restaurant together, she said, "I want to talk to you."

"All right. Care to give me a hint as to what it's about?"

Maeve Pinckney, carrying a plate overflowing with ribs, came to where we stood.

"Later. It's personal," Samantha told me, and went through the door held open by a waitress.

The rest of dinner passed without conversation about the death of Alvin Blevin. But Junior became animated over dessert when Hank Crocker mentioned a club member's model railroad setup. "I've seen it," Junior said, "and it's all wrong. His proportions are out of whack."

"The scale police at work," Hank Crocker grumbled.

"That's the trouble with you people," Junior said. "You all claim to care about accuracy, but you don't pay any attention to it in your own model setups. You ought to be ashamed of yourselves. That big, fancy layout at Blevin's office isn't right, either."

"He always said it was," Crocker said. "Hell, he spent a damn fortune in club money on it, all for his personal pleasure. The man was a disgrace. Excuse me. I need some air."

His departure prompted others to get up and go, leaving only me and the Whitmores. Samantha, who'd said little during dinner, waited for her mother to excuse herself.

"Coming, dear?"

"In a little while, Mother." She waited till Marilyn left the room.

"Want to have that talk now?" I asked.

Samantha glanced at the other members of the group who lingered. She shook her head. "Do you swim?"

"Yes," I answered.

"Join me in the pool? Say twenty minutes?"

"I'll be there."

Although I seldom have an opportunity to swim when I travel—there just never seems to be a good time—I always pack my bathing suit. I'd peeked into the room housing the indoor pool while taking my walk prior to dinner and was impressed with its size and cleanliness. The people who ran the ranch and spa were obviously sticklers for hygiene and order. There wasn't a piece of furniture or a towel out of place.

I changed in my room, slipped into a terry cloth robe and slippers provided by the ranch, and headed for the pool house, where Samantha was already in the water doing laps. She wore a one-piece black suit that hugged her tight body. I admired her stroke. Her arm muscles bulged as she plowed her way through the water. Her smooth motions in the water suggested she spent considerable time in swimming pools. I wondered if she used the activity to exorcise her demons.

I poked my foot in the water and was somewhat disappointed at how tepid it was. Like all indoor pools, the humidity level was high. Living in Maine gets you accustomed to cold water, particularly in the ocean, where the water is bracing—frigid to newcomers—even on the hottest days of midsummer. I prefer cold water.

I submerged myself and did a backstroke toward Samantha, resting at the opposite end of the pool. She pulled herself up from the water and sat on the edge of the pool, cocking her head and hitting the opposite side with the heel of her hand to dislodge water from her ear.

A family with two small children had been in the pool when I arrived, but they soon departed, leaving us alone.

"You said you wanted to talk to me about something personal," I said.

She nodded and spent a few seconds collecting her thoughts and deciding how to say what was on her mind. She seemed to study her fingers, pressing each one, as if counting off arguments in her mind.

"You owe me," she said at last, glancing in my direction and then looking back down at her hands.

"If you're referring to saving my life when the vestibule door came unlatched, you're right," I said. Despite the warm water surrounding me, I shivered at the image of being dangled over the Fraser Canyon with only a swinging door to keep me from plunging to the ravine below. "I owe you my thanks, and I'm very grateful that you were there and that you had the good sense to grab my skirt to pull me back in."

"You owe me more than thanks."

What was she trying to tell me? Did she want some compensation for her actions? A reward? It hadn't occurred to me to offer her money as thanks. Was she looking for public recognition, a story in the newspaper? I hadn't praised her in public. Perhaps I'd been remiss, and she wanted people to know how brave she'd been—and she had—to reach out, putting her own life in jeopardy to save mine. "Samantha, I apologize for not talking about how wonderful you were. I should have given you credit, told everyone how you saved me. I guess I wasn't thinking—"

"That's not it." She was becoming agitated.

"What? What is it you'd like me to do?"

Her mouth worked, but she couldn't get the words out. At last she blurted, "Keep the police away from my mother."

"I don't understand."

"My mother didn't do it," she said loudly.

"Didn't do what?"

"Kill Blevin."

I said nothing.

"You believed he was murdered from the beginning, didn't you? 'Poisoned,' you said. 'He may have been poisoned.' You told me not to touch him. I heard you. You said it."

I'd told her not to give him mouth-to-mouth resuscitation, but now was not the time to correct the record. "It was only speculation," I said.

"Yeah. But now it's been confirmed."

When I didn't respond, she shouted at me, "Hasn't it?"

"Yes," I said. "How did you find out?"

"Rumors are flying on the train. You think I don't hear them, but I do. I won't let you hurt her."

"Why do you think that I or the police would suspect your mother?"

"Because Blevin killed my father." Her voice was low now, almost whining.

I frowned up at her. I tried for a reasonable tone, trying to calm her rising hysteria. "That's quite an accusation," I said. "But that's not what your mother told me. She said your father died of a heart attack."

"He never would have had that attack if Alvin Blevin hadn't swindled him." She angrily dashed tears from her eyes. "He did it. I know he did it. He did it on purpose." She began rocking back and forth, hugging herself, her feet pressed against the side of the pool. A long moan escaped her.

I put a hand on her knee. "How did Alvin Blevin swindle your father?" I asked softly.

Her body stiffened and she glared at me, her face twisted by the loathing she couldn't contain. "Al Blevin was a self-centered, conniving, dishonest, vile human being."

I took a step back. The virulence of her hatred startled me. "What did he do? What happened?"

It was Marilyn who answered. "I'll tell you what happened."

I hadn't seen her come into the pool room; I'd been so intent on her daughter. She was standing on the side of the pool, watching Samantha closely.

"Ma, Ma. She won't tell him. She promised."

"What happened, Marilyn? Why does Samantha say Alvin Blevin killed your husband."

Marilyn sighed. "Just as good as." She walked behind her child, knelt down, and began massaging Samantha's shoulders. "Robert was Al's partner in a land deal in West Vancouver. It was worth millions. Robert threw himself into the project, devoted two years of his life to it. The last two years of his life."

I waited for her to continue.

"He died before the deal could be consummated. Blevin had cheated him, tying up construction with red tape until Robert ran out of money. Blevin scooped up the project and finished it without him. We never saw a penny from it."

Samantha swallowed a sob.

"C'mon, honey," Marilyn said. "Let's go back to our room."

"I hated him," she said to her mother. "I hated him."

"I know. Let's go."

Samantha stood and looked back to me. "She didn't kill him. And I don't want you to think she did."

"I don't think she did," I said, "but it really doesn't matter what I think. Blevin's death is now strictly a police matter."

"And you have an in with the police. Don't think it hasn't been noticed how close you and Marshall are." She was shouting again. "Did you tell the detective that you suspect her?"

"No. Of course not."

"Don't tell him. You owe me that. I saved your life. The police don't have to know about my father's dealings with him."

I understood her concerns and was even sympathetic. But asking me to withhold information from law enforcement caused my back to stiffen. Someone had been murdered in a cruel fashion. Whoever did it would have to pay for that crime, no matter who it was.

"If I'm asked by Detective Marshall, I won't lie," I told them.

Marilyn's expression said she was offended at the notion. "I would never ask anyone to do that, Jessica," she said. "But not offering more than one is asked doesn't constitute perjury. What I just told you, I told you in confidence. Blevin contributed to my husband's heart attack; I have no doubt about that. But that doesn't mean I would ever think of killing him. I just want you to know that."

"I understand," I said.

"Let's go, sweetheart," Marilyn said to her daughter.

Samantha backed up a few steps and ran at the pool, diving over me, her body a graceful arc above my head. I moved to the side but was not swift enough to avoid the splash that engulfed me when she torpedoed into the water. I lost my footing and went under with a gasp. Water hit my lungs and I rocketed to the surface, choking and coughing, struggling for air.

"Samantha! I'm ashamed of you," Marilyn chided. "I'm sorry, Jessica. Are you all right?"

I nodded, but the water still in my lungs kept me from speaking.

Samantha pulled herself out of the other end of the pool, got to her feet, and went to the chair where she'd put her robe and slippers. Mother and daughter left me alone in the water.

I rested by the side of the pool until my breathing was regular again, and I coughed only occasionally. I couldn't put the incident out of my mind as I went to my room to change out of my bathing suit into street clothes. Samantha was ill, I now knew. It was becoming harder for her to maintain the illusion of normality. True, she was protecting her mother. But was she also protecting herself? She was a nurse, which meant she would have learned something about poisons. She had access to strychnine—anyone who bought rat poison did—and she would be aware of the lethal dose. She had motive, too. Not only had her mother lost her husband, allegedly due to Blevin's business dealings, but Samantha had lost a father. Had her father's ruin and subsequent death enraged the daughter? Enraged her enough to kill?

I needed a distraction. I went downstairs to browse in a gift shop on the property and bought a few souvenirs to take back home. The clerk told me that the rose hip oil was a specialty of the house. They grew the roses and made the oil themselves at the ranch. Celebrities swore by it for their complexion. She gave me a sample to try.

After paying for my purchases, I stepped out onto a broad deck at the front of the shop. It was still bright out. The farther north we went, the longer the days were, the sky remaining light well into the time it would have been dark at home. I walked to the end of the building, where there was a bench. The deck wrapped around to the side and I heard muffled voices coming from that direction. I was tempted to peek around the corner to see who was meeting away from the eyes of other visitors, but I didn't have to. A male voice was followed by the sound of female whimpering, and Maeve Pinckney appeared, a handkerchief to her face. I started to say hello, but she glanced at me with nervous eyes and ran down the steps in the direction of the hotel.

I expected to see her husband follow, but the man who emerged from the side of the building was not Junior Pinckney. It was Winston Rendell.

Chapter Ten

"Enjoy your evening at the ranch?" Detective Marshall asked as I boarded the Whistler Northwind for the final portion of our three-day journey, the longest leg that would culminate at Prince George.

"Yes," I said, "especially the horse-whispering demonstration this morning."

"And what is that?" he asked.

"Did you see the film *The Horse Whisperer*?"

"Afraid I didn't."

I explained how a young female ranch hand at Hills Ranch had demonstrated that morning how she controlled her horse through body language and the movements of a small whip she carried, never touching the horse with it but cueing the animal by the various positions in which she held it, aided by subtle verbal sounds.

"Would it work on people?" he asked, a glint in his eye.

"I doubt it."

I watched him go up the aisle and disappear into the bar car. Junior Pinckney, his baseball hat on backwards, had already taken his position at the half-open door in the vestibule when I wandered through on my way into the dining car. I wanted some time to think undisturbed and the dining car was usually empty, likely the reason Winston Rendell conducted his telephone calls in there.

Rendell wasn't there, but Benjamin was just leaving. He glared at me. "I hope you're satisfied."

"I beg your pardon?"

"Blevin. The cops say he was poisoned. Now they're harassing my mother."

"I'm sorry about your mother, Benjamin, but I'm not to blame for the truth of your stepfather's death."

"Yeah, right." He stomped past me, nearly knocking me over.

In the dining car, Jenna and Karl were setting the tables, distributing the fresh flowers that graced every meal. I sat at a table and moved my seat back so as not to disturb the tableware they had so carefully arranged. "Am I all right over here?" I asked.

"You're just fine," Jenna called out as she carried an empty tray from the car.

"Good morning, Mrs. Fletcher," Karl said, placing a small vase of baby carnations on the table. He was dressed in his kitchen whites, his black hair pulled into a ponytail, white kerchief tied in back, riding low on his brow. Another kerchief, this one red, was tied around his neck.

I stared at him, and he smiled. "I'm sorry," I said. "Good morning, Karl. Please excuse my rudeness. For a moment there, you looked familiar to me, but I can't place where I may have seen you before."

"No apologies necessary," he said, pushing up his wire-rimmed spectacles where they had slid down the bridge of his narrow nose. "I must have that kind of face. People have told me that before."

I noticed he wasn't quite as young as I'd first supposed. His tanned face was unlined, but his neck and hands were those of an older man. *Kitchen work takes quite a toll*, I thought wryly. Aloud, I said: "Can you spare a moment to talk with me?"

"Certainly. How may I be of assistance? Would you like some coffee, a snack?"

"No, thank you. I was hoping to ask you about Alvin Blevin."

A dark look passed over his face and then his features relaxed back into the bland expression he always wore. "Terrible tragedy," he said. "That detective was talking to us last night. All the staff are really upset."

"It must be very difficult, especially for Callie."

"Yeah. Jenna, too. I think she might've had a crush on him."

"Surely Mr. Blevin wouldn't have encouraged that."

"Why not? She's cute."

I'd noticed that Jenna seemed very subdued following Blevin's death, but I'd suspected that she was worrying about Benjamin. It hadn't occurred to me that she might have been mourning Blevin. Now I wondered if his alleged womanizing had extended to a woman young enough to be his daughter.

"Karl, you brought in two fresh bottles of vodka when you came to the club car that day."

"I see where you're going with this, Mrs. Fletcher. The Mountie asked about that, too. But they were sealed. Callie opened them at the bar."

"Did you see anyone drop anything into Mr. Blevin's drink?"

He shook his head.

"Who might have had an opportunity to handle his glass?" I asked.

"Gee, Mrs. Fletcher," he said in a tone that struck me as ironic. "You were there. It was a pretty crowded party. His drink got passed around to several hands before it landed on my tray. In fact, it was originally supposed to be for you, wasn't it?"

That was true. And I remembered Junior passing the glass, and Hank nearly spilling it as he pushed through the crowd. Also, after Benjamin had brought him another Bloody Mary, Blevin had left one of the drinks on a table where anyone could have dropped in the poison. This line of questioning was not going to produce anything helpful. I tried another.

"How long have you worked on the Northwind?"

"Why would you want to know that?"

"Were you working for the Northwind when Elliott Vail disappeared?"

He startled. "No, ma'am, but I certainly have heard about it. Do you think the two deaths are connected?"

"I'm not sure," I said.

"That's a scary thought," he said, laughing softly. "*I'm* not sure I'll want to keep working on this train with that kind of stuff going on. Speaking of work . . ."

"Of course. I've kept you. My apologies."

"No problem. But I don't want them to come searching for me. We have a pretty tight schedule to keep. If I can help you again, let me know."

He placed two more vases on the remaining tables and left the car.

I stared out the window watching the passing scene. We were paralleling a broad stream, a tributary of the Fraser River. Along the banks, reeds and other boggy grasses swayed in the steady breeze, which painted ripples on the pale green surface of the water. Small brown ducks took flight when the engineer blew the train whistle, flapping away from the noisy animal snaking through the countryside. Overhead in the clear sky, an eagle wheeled. Intruding into my thoughts, as we glided by this pastoral landscape, were two disquieting questions: *Who killed Alvin Blevin? And why?*

An image of Theodora Blevin came to mind. Was I foolish in discounting the widow herself? Many an errant husband had been killed by a jealous wife. Too, Blevin was a very wealthy man. Money was another potential motive. There had been suggestions, notably by Maeve, that Theodora might have killed her first husband. Did she fit the description of a serial killer? Benjamin had hinted that Blevin was responsible for his father's death, but that could have been wild speculation. He didn't like his stepfather. What had been his relationship with his father? Elliott's demise had been labeled a suicide, but could it have been a murder? I had been truthful when I'd said I didn't know if these two deaths were related. But if they were, was the same person responsible for both?

Maeve was working on her needlepoint when I returned to my seat and slid in next to her. I was puzzled by her rendezvous with Winston Rendell the night before. Perhaps Junior was justified in his jealousy. Perhaps she had indeed had an affair with Alvin Blevin. Was Winston Rendell her new paramour? If so, she hadn't been very happy with him from what I'd witnessed. But somehow, I didn't think their encounter was what it seemed to be superficially. Maeve was a pretty woman and aware of it. She dressed carefully and in a way to show off her figure, but she didn't wear anything that could be called provocative. She impressed me as an open and direct person, rarely watching what she said. Instead, what was on her mind came tumbling out before she could think better of it. Too, she struck me as being content in her marriage, if not completely delighted with her husband. Was I not seeing her clearly? I'd been fooled by people before, and I probably would be taken in again. Of course, as Reggie had pointed out: Who really knows what goes on between a husband and wife?

"How did you enjoy the Hills ranch last evening?" I began.

"What? Oh, fine. Just fine," Maeve said. "Ah took a nature walk this morning with Deedee Crocker. She was showin' me all the wildflowers. Very pretty."

"Beautiful countryside," I said.

I hesitated to delve into her personal business but took the plunge anyway. "Maeve, I saw you with Winston Rendell last night. You looked upset." I stopped, hoping she'd fill in the blanks I'd left for her. She didn't disappoint me.

She frowned and her lips formed a hard line. "It's Junior's fault."

"What's Junior's fault?"

"He's so jealous, it makes other men think there's something going on there."

"What do you mean?"

"He talks about his suspicions. You heard him. Hints I had an affair with Alvin Blevin. Preposterous. Now, Alvin did pay me attention, mind you. He was very complimentary, but always the gentleman. And ah'm a lady, and a faithful one. I've told Junior that over and over, but he persists in his accusations."

"So Rendell overheard Junior talking and decided to flirt with you?"

"That's the way it appeared to me. Junior went to take pictures of the horses after dinner, and Winston asked if I'd like to take a walk. At first I thought he was just being pleasant. Ah like to flirt a little—what Southern woman doesn't?—and I like it when men are attracted to me, but I don't draw them on, if you know what I mean."

I thought perhaps Maeve did "draw men on," but I wouldn't say that.

"Anyway, he starts talking about Alvin and asking how close were we? I got real hot—angry, I mean. Ah told him I never had an affair with Alvin Blevin, don't know about his personal life, and to stop asking me about him. Then he starts asking about you."

"Me?"

"Yes. What did we talk about while we were sitting together? Did you ask me questions about Alvin Blevin? I said: 'That's enough. I told you ah'm not interested in Alvin Blevin. Our little walk is ending.' And then he grabbed me."

"Grabbed you?"

"He pulls me in and tries to kiss me, says I should be sweet to him and he'll be sweet to me. He can buy me nice things. That's when I ran." Her eyes filled with tears, and she sniffed delicately. "If Junior didn't make those comments, none of that would've happened."

My guess was that it would be a while before Maeve accepted an invitation from another man to take a walk. And perhaps that was just as well. I patted her hand and she gave me a watery smile.

Jenna entered the car and took the microphone as the train chugged away from the station.

"Good morning, ladies and gentlemen," she said, forcing a modicum of gaiety into her voice. "Did everyone have a pleasant stay at 100 Mile House?"

There were murmured expressions of assent.

"We'll be serving lunch in an hour or so," she said. "In the meantime, sit back and enjoy the scenery and the ride. This area of the country is known for its wildlife. You might spot deer or a bear. We've seen them before along this route. And eagles, lots of bald eagles." She quickly replaced the mike in its holder on the wall and disappeared into the dining car.

The narrow channel I'd been gazing at when I was in the dining car had been replaced by a beautiful lake. It was too bad I was preoccupied by the murder. This could have been a lovely, relaxing journey. The British Columbian countryside was rough and beautiful at the same time. I marveled at the men and women of an earlier century who had matched their grit against the rugged landscape, seeking their fortune in the gold mines buried in the Cariboo territory. I would have enjoyed concentrating on the natural history and the human one, appreciating the gentle glide of the train as it followed the storied gold rush trails. But this trip had a different focus. And it was too late now to turn my mind to the original center of attention.

Most of the passengers were standing in the aisle admiring the view. Junior had come in to announce that he'd caught a shot of a bald eagle lifting a fish from the water with its sharp talons. He offered to show the picture to anyone interested, but they'd have to meet him in the vestibule; he was going back to scan for more eagles.

It occurred to me that I hadn't seen Reggie Weems this morning. I rose from my seat and glanced around the coach car. No sign of him. I excused myself to Maeve and strolled back to the bar car where I was surprised to see Reggie deep in conversation with Detective Marshall. I was about to leave when Reggie motioned for me to join them.

" 'Morning, Jess," he said.

"Please, have a seat," Marshall said, indicating a chair next to him. "Mr. Weems and I have been discussing some logistic matters."

"Like how to make sure we don't lose anybody once we get to Prince George," Reggie clarified.

"Do you think that's a possibility?" I asked.

"It's always a possibility that a murderer might wish to separate himself from the crowd," Marshall said.

"Or herself," I offered.

"Yes, of course," said Marshall.

"I understand you and a colleague checked everyone's travel itineraries," I said.

Marshall nodded. He looked as though he hadn't slept much; large, dark circles surrounded his eyes. "That was accomplished last night," he said. "All seems in order. But that is not to say that someone—anyone—might not decide to alter their plans in order to avoid further scrutiny."

I wondered why the detective had taken Reggie into his confidence, in a sense had made him part of his team. Marshall evidently sensed what I was thinking because he said, "Mr. Weems appeared to be in charge of this junket. I've asked him to lend some insight into the unfortunate death of Mr. Blevin."

"I'm really not in charge," Reggie said. "I just—"

"No matter," Marshall said. "I would be less than honest if I didn't admit I need some help in this investigation. Mrs. Fletcher has already weighed in—to good effect, I might add—and I have expressed my appreciation." He shifted in his chair and recrossed long legs. "Look," he said, "unless it's Mrs. Blevin, someone among you poisoned Mr. Blevin. We'll soon be arriving at our final destination, at which point everyone—at least according to their official travel plans—will fly back to Vancouver, which, technically, is out of my jurisdiction. My counterparts with the Vancouver police have asked me to provide as complete a picture of the suspects as possible. I'm arguing that my knowledge

and experience will be helpful to the continuing inquiries. If I can show them how far our investigation
has already proceeded, I think my superiors will see
the wisdom of keeping me on the case. Although
everyone has been interviewed since the murder, the
information gathered has necessarily been sketchy, at
best. You, Mr. Weems, know these people quite well
through your long involvement with the Track and
Rail Club."

"I know most of them," Reggie said, "but not
everyone. I'll do anything I can to help." He looked at
me. "And I know Jessica will, too. What do you want
us to do?"

Marshall chewed his cheek and looked to the ceiling
before answering. "Prepare for me a synopsis of each
person on this train with respect to Mr. Blevin's
death."

"What should we include in it?" I asked.

"Anything bearing upon the relationship between
the men and women on the trip and the deceased."

"I'm afraid I can't contribute much to that," I said.
"I've just met them."

"Yes," Marshall said, "but you seem to have an in-
satiable curiosity, Mrs. Fletcher, and your powers of
observation are keen. I have no doubt that you've
managed to get some of them to open up to you or,
failing that, have heard your share of conversations."

I smiled and said, "I'm not sure I take that as a compliment, eavesdropping on the conversations of others."

"I mean it as a compliment," Marshall said. "A good
investigator always keeps his ears open, whether he's
on a case or not. You never know when something you
overhear will become an important piece of evidence. I
have a feeling you'd make a crackerjack investigator."

"I'll take *that* as a compliment," I said. "Thank you."

Marshall stood and stretched. "Bad lower back," said the detective, twisting his torso.

"C'mon, Jess. Let's put our heads together," Reggie said, rising from his seat, too.

The train entered a curve and the squeal of the wheels straining against the metal tracks made conversation difficult. I touched Marshall on the arm and raised my voice. "Have you tested the box yet?" I asked, referring to the rodenticide we'd found in the games cabinet.

"What?" He cupped a hand behind his ear.

"The box," I said loudly.

Just then the train righted itself on a straightaway and the squealing stopped.

"What box?" Reggie asked.

"I'll explain a little later," I said. To Marshall: "I assume there's no reason not to tell Reggie."

"No reason at all."

The three of us left the bar car together, causing eyebrows to rise as we passed their seats. A few people had poked their heads into the bar car while we huddled there but quickly turned and left. Marshall took a seat across the aisle from the Goldfinches, while Reggie and I slipped into a pair of seats away from the rest of the passengers.

"Might as well get started," he whispered.

"Might as well," I said.

With the exception of breaking for lunch, Reggie and I spent the afternoon comparing thoughts about possible suspects on the train. We initially tried sitting together in adjacent seats in the coach car, but after only a few minutes we realized that wasn't going to work. Other passengers kept walking by and leaning in our direction, trying to overhear what we were saying. We

finally decided it was foolish to attempt to act noncha-
lant and went to the dining car, where we sat at a table
at the far end. Everyone seemed to realize we were
doing some sort of work together and left us alone, including at lunch; no one suggested joining us. The
only person who did intrude was Jenna. She asked
twice whether she could get us anything, and her at-
tempts to see what I was writing on the yellow legal
pad I always carry with me made it plain that service
wasn't uppermost in her mind.

We finished talking shortly before it was announced
that dinner would be served in a half hour. I'd filled
three pages in my yellow pad, torn them loose, folded
them into a small wad, and placed them in my purse.

"I can't think of anything else," Reggie said as we
left the table to return to the coach car.

"Nor can I," I said.

Everyone displayed intense interest in us as we
went to our individual seats. I saw that Detective Marshall was now sitting with Deedee Crocker, whose
husband was in the vestibule looking out the second
half-open door.

"Where have *you* been?" Maeve Pinckney asked
when I'd settled down beside her.

"Oh, I had some work to do," I said lightly. "I have
a mad habit of bringing my work with me wherever
I go."

"Writin' a book with Reggie?" she asked.

"Writing with—? No, but he's helping me with—
helping me with a scene I'm having trouble with."

She nodded and gave me a knowing smile. I wasn't
kidding her or anyone else.

I sat at dinner with the newcomers, Martin and Gail
Goldfinch. To my surprise, Winston Rendell joined us.

"You were a busy bee today," Rendell said as an appetizer of Dungeness crab cakes and a frisée salad was served. He had put on a cheerful demeanor, having decided, I suppose, that sugar was preferable to vinegar in dealing with me.

I repeated my weak story about having brought work with me on the trip. I didn't expect follow-up questions, but Martin Goldfinch said, "I saw you huddled this morning with Detective Marshall. What's new about Mr. Blevin's murder?"

"Nothing, as far as I know."

"Oh, come, Jessica," he said, raising his brows and looking at me over half-glasses he'd donned to read the menu. "Don't be coy. We're all in this together, aren't we, like survivors of a plane crash. We know Blevin was poisoned, and we're all suspects. What does the detective say?"

"I might ask you the same question," I said. "I see that you've had a few conversations with him."

"Questions is what he has to say. Just questions." He leaned closer to me. "Is it true that Blevin had an affair with her?" He nodded in the direction of Marilyn Whitmore, who sat with her daughter and Reggie.

Another rumored affair, I thought, *this time with Marilyn Whitmore.* "I wouldn't know," I said. "You aren't suggesting that Detective Marshall told you that, are you?"

"No," Goldfinch said, sitting back and laughing. "Just one of a couple of hundred rumors making the rounds."

"You Americans are bloody fond of rumors, aren't you?" said Rendell.

Gail Goldfinch smiled and said, "That's a case of the pot calling the kettle black, if ever there was one. You Brits are the kings of tabloid journalism. When I was on vacation in London last year, it seemed as though the whole city thrived on rumors, particularly about the royal family."

Rendell seemed annoyed at Gail's comment and looked around the dining room as though seeking escape. I said to him, "I understand that you and Mr. Blevin were involved in a business deal that wasn't going very well."

My question took him aback. "Who told you that?"

Detective Marshall had been the source of that news, but I needed to keep him out of it. "I'd prefer not to say."

Visibly rattled, Rendell cleared his throat a few times before saying, "Not true at all. For many years Al Blevin and I had discussed setting up a company together, but we never developed the idea very far."

"What sort of business?" Gail asked.

"Developing a new generation of steam engine," Rendell replied slowly, speeding up as he continued. "There's a resurgence in interest in the old smoke belchers, and we thought we might try to tap into that attraction." He straightened in his seat, evidently deciding how the story would end. "Unfortunately, Al died before we could take it to the next step."

"It was going well; it was on track?" I asked.

"Yes, quite," Rendell said, "if it's any of your concern."

That seemed to be the end of it, for the moment. But as we prepared to vacate the table, Gail asked Rendell, "Was Elliott Vail involved in your business venture with Blevin?"

"Vail?" Rendell said, laughing. "What a silly question. Of course not. How could he be? The man is dead."

"Why do you ask?" I said.

Gail shrugged and stood. "No reason," she said. "Dinner was delicious. The maple salmon was yummy."

"You've asked questions about Elliott Vail before. How do you know about him?" I asked. "You two are new to the club."

"How do you know about him, Jessica?" Gail responded sharply. "You've never been on this train before, either. His suicide was hardly a secret. Lots of people on board have mentioned it to us."

"That's right," her husband put in. He pulled her away from the table, and I realized that it was the first time I'd seen him touch his wife.

Reggie had left the dining car ahead of us and was sitting alone in a window seat. I joined him.

"Pick up anything new at dinner?" he whispered in my ear.

"Just that Mr. Rendell admits he was involved in a business venture with Alvin Blevin, something about manufacturing steam engines."

"That's not new," Reggie said. "I told you that the other night."

"True, but Rendell now claims the business deal wasn't going sour. He told Detective Marshall that it was. What about you? Learn anything to add to our notes?"

"Just that the Whitmores wear their hatred of Blevin on their sleeves, but Mrs. Whitmore keeps saying how ridiculous it is to suspect them. I can't blame her. She's really a nice lady. But now that I know she thinks Blevin's actions contributed to her husband's heart attack, I'm more tuned in." During our meeting that afternoon I'd told him of my conversation with Marilyn Whitmore at the pool at the Hills ranch. "Her daughter's a strange one; a very angry lady is my read," he said. "Smart, though. She worked in a toxicology lab in Vancouver."

"Worked? Past tense?"

"Yeah, according to her mother. She said something about Samantha being on a medical leave."

"Toxicology?"

"Yeah. Oh, sure, I see what you're thinking. Toxicology. She'd know about poisons and things like that."

"Yes, she would."

Detective Marshall stopped at our row, and people in nearby seats turned in our direction.

"Lovely dinner, wasn't it?" he said, loud enough for them to hear.

"Very nice," we agreed.

He quietly dropped a slip of paper on Reggie's lap and said, "Well, I think I'll get back to my book. We'll be in Prince George before we know it."

We waited a moment before seeing what the note said: *Meet me at eight at RCMP's Prince George headquarters.* He'd signed it "CM" and included the address.

Reggie put the paper in his shirt pocket. We nodded at each other, smiled at those who were overtly directing their attention at us, and sat back to enjoy what was left of the trip. Like all trips I'd taken that were coming to an end, I felt a certain sadness at reaching our final destination. The murder aside, the ride on the Whistler Northwind had been a pleasant, unhurried experience. Taking the murder into consideration, it was an experience I'd not soon forget.

Jenna came on the PA and announced that our luggage would be in our rooms at the hotel, as it had been at previous stops. She then thanked us for traveling on the Whistler Northwind, said it was a pleasure serving us, and wished us a safe trip home.

"Where do you guys go now?" Hank Crocker called out.

"The staff?" Jenna asked.

"Yes. You and Callie and Bruce and the rest of them."

"Some of us fly home and others turn right around and go back to Vancouver," she said.

"Better tell them to watch out for the Bloody Marys." Crocker laughed at his own joke, but he was the only one.

Jenna placed the microphone back in its wall holder with more force than necessary and left the coach car.

I asked Reggie if he'd noticed a change in Jenna's demeanor since the beginning of the trip.

"Yeah," he said. "She used to smile more. She doesn't seem as happy as she was when we got started."

"I forgot to put that on our list for Detective Marshall," I suggested.

"Probably means nothing," Reggie said. "Maybe she has woman troubles, you know what I mean? My niece is always complaining about that PS something-or-other."

"Still . . ."

I hadn't mentioned to Reggie that there might be a personal relationship between Jenna and Benjamin Vail. Junior Pinckney claimed to have witnessed them in the courtyard of the Westin Hotel in Whistler. And I remembered seeing them together outside the railroad station in Vancouver, but I hadn't heard their conversation. She might simply have been welcoming him to the Northwind. I dug in my purse for the wad of notes that Reggie and I had put together and added "Jenna-Benjamin?" to the long list of observations.

Less than an hour later, the train chugged into Prince George, the lumber capital of British Columbia. Before reaching the station, we passed through what must have been miles of wood products awaiting export: myriad piles of felled trees for the sawmill; stacks upon stacks of cut lumber; and hundreds of flat cars, on which the finished products, sealed in plastic, stood ready to join the long line of freight cars on the journey southward.

Clouds had moved in and the sky was gray; raindrops spattered the clear dome of the coach. I got up, intending to take a last look around before we were instructed to leave the train. In the front section of the club car, the bar was closed, the wooden counter wiped clean. No bottle or glass was in evidence to remind visitors of the fatal party that had taken place there. But the careful observer would have seen the faint red stain on the carpet from the Bloody Mary that spilled when the poison in his system knocked Alvin Blevin down. I pictured the meeting of the Track and Rail Club, people happy, animated, anticipating three days of old-fashioned train travel, an opportunity to commune with fellow foamers, to discuss the focus of their passion, brag about their model railroads, and trade train lore. And into this joyful gathering had stepped a murderer.

"Revisiting the scene of the crime, Mrs. Fletcher?" Benjamin stood in the entrance to the rear salon.

"Why did you stay on the train, Benjamin? Don't you think your mother needs you at a time like this?"

"My mother doesn't need anyone," he muttered, and then thought better of it. "My mother has lots of friends to console her."

"Why did you stay on the train?" I persisted.

"I think you've already figured that out, Mrs. Fletcher. My father died on this train. I needed to see where. I needed to know why."

"And did you find the answers you wanted?"

"No. But the trip wasn't wasted."

"Wasn't wasted? Are you referring to the death of your stepfather?"

"My mother's husband, you mean. He had no relation to me. I was just in the way, something to push aside to get to my mother."

"Aren't you a little old to play the rejected child, Benjamin?"

He smirked. "No fooling you, huh?"

"I know there was tension between you."

"That's an understatement. I hated him, plain and simple."

Jenna's voice came over the public-address system, announcing our arrival in Prince George.

Benjamin walked toward me and stopped. "You think I killed him, don't you?"

"Did you?"

He brushed past me, leaving the club car. "I'd like to see you prove it," he called over his shoulder.

Chapter Eleven

The inclement weather was not flattering to Prince
George. The city was saved from obscurity by the rich
lumber-filled mountains on its outskirts and its citizens' passion for the beauty of the outdoors, but the
grim downtown, a collection of faceless industrial
buildings, was not inviting. The bus passed a series of
rundown motels, and I sighed with relief when the
driver pulled up to the Ramada, a modern, if architec-
turally uninspired, hotel.

Reggie and I had agreed that being seen going off together after having huddled on the train all afternoon
would only fuel speculation on the part of other passengers. We arranged to leave the hotel separately and
to hook up at a restaurant he'd chosen from a guide-
book, Ric's Grill. I begged off a couple of other dinner
invitations, saying only that I had other plans without
specifying. I'm always uncomfortable lying about anything, as justified as it might be on occasion, and
learned long ago to keep it simple, lest I have to remember later what has been said.

The rain had stopped and Reggie was waiting for
me when I arrived. The restaurant had low lighting,
black-patterned upholstery, and high wooden di-
viders, making it easy to hide from prying ears and
eyes—the perfect setting for an assignation. I felt as if

we were acting in a film noir and that Sam Spade
would show up at any moment. We asked for a booth
as far removed from the others as possible, ordered our
dinners, and took a final stab at the list we'd compiled
before heading for our meeting with Detective Marshall at RCMP's Prince George headquarters. I added a
few notes to what we'd already written, and by the
time dessert had been served, we felt satisfied that
we'd covered everything Detective Marshall was expecting of us.

"I have to admit," Reggie said, as he pulled out a
credit card to pay the bill, "that I'm pretty excited
about this."

"Excited?" I said, not sure I would have used that
word.

"Yes," he said. "I mean, I've never been asked by a
homicide detective before to come up with who killed
somebody. I feel like some amateur detective in one of
your novels, Jess, coming to the rescue of the police
and cracking a difficult case."

I laughed and patted my friend on the shoulder.
"Well," I said, "don't get too excited, Reggie. Detective
Marshall has asked us only to report what we've observed, not to point the finger at any individual. That
would be unwise."

"I know, I know," he said as we stepped out onto
George Street, Prince George's major downtown avenue. "Still, if what we've come up with makes the difference in bringing a murderer to justice, I'll be pretty
proud."

"As well you should be. Come along. According to
my city map, police headquarters is only a few blocks
this way."

Detective Marshall was summoned from the back of
headquarters upon our arrival and led us to an inter-

rogation room that was, at least for this person who'd spent some time in such rooms, surprisingly pleasant. It was softly lighted, as opposed to having the usual harsh overhead fluorescent lights intended to unnerve people being interrogated, and its furniture—chairs with arms padded with red vinyl, and a table absent scars and cigarette burns—was anything but threatening. I'd been in police rooms in which the two front legs of simple wooden chairs had been cut off a half inch to cause the individual being questioned to constantly lean forward, an uncomfortable and ultimately fatiguing posture. Not the case here. The chair frames were metal—and level.

"Please," Marshall said, "have a seat. Coffee? Tea? A soft drink?"

Reggie opted for coffee; I asked for tea. They were served by a uniformed officer along with a small plate of sugar cookies baked in the shape of a moose. He left the room, and Marshall, who'd removed his suit jacket and hung it on a coat tree in a corner, took a chair at the head of the table. Reggie and I sat across from each other.

"Now then," Marshall said, "you are very kind to allow me to interfere with your free evening."

"It's our pleasure," Reggie said.

"I'm not sure how pleasurable it will be, but thank you nonetheless. Might as well get started. What have you come up with?"

I took our notes from my purse and spread the pages on the table. Marshall glanced at them and said, "You've put a lot of work into this. I appreciate that."

"We've covered everyone and everything we could," I said. "Like me to begin?"

"Please," Marshall said, pulling closer a pad of white lined paper that had been on the table and uncapping a pen.

I looked to Reggie to see whether he preferred to present our notes, but he nodded at me and sat back, a satisfied smile on his face.

"Let's start with the deceased's immediate family," I said. "There's his wife, Theodora, who appeared to have been a loving, caring wife, at least from what I was able to observe."

"But a cold woman," Marshall said.

I smiled. "You noticed."

"Hard not to," he said. "Go on."

"We—Reggie and I—have nothing specific to point at to implicate her in her husband's murder. But, of course, there are the intriguing events surrounding her marriage to him."

"The disappearance of her former husband, Mr. Vail," said Marshall.

"Exactly," Reggie said.

"I don't know if there is any connection between Vail's disappearance from the Whistler Northwind three years ago," I said, "but we thought it was worth noting."

"And I agree," Marshall said. "I mentioned it to the Vancouver police, and they said as far as they were concerned, it was still an open folder."

"What can they do at this juncture?" Reggie asked. "They never found the body."

"True," Marshall replied, "but there's evidently been speculation since the hearing that Mr. Blevin might have—how should I say it?—that Mr. Blevin might have used undue influence to persuade the judge to declare Vail dead."

"Undue influence?" I repeated. "A bribe?"

"That would be undue influence, eh?" the large detective said. "Let's see what the city boys come up with on that score. Next? The son?"

"Yes," I said. "Benjamin Vail, Blevin's stepson."

"Not an especially pleasant young man," said Marshall. "Did either of you observe the tenor of the young man's relationship with his stepfather?"

Reggie and I paused before he said, "Jess saw them arguing on the train."

"Oh?"

I recounted the brief, angry exchange I'd witnessed between Blevin and Benjamin and then told Marshall of my trip up Whistler Mountain when Benjamin joined me unexpectedly—"he told me to 'butt out' "—ending with Benjamin's taunting "prove it" just before we got off the train.

"You didn't mention that Theodora told you to stay out of it, right after Blevin died," Reggie said.

"That's true," I said, and recalled being summoned to the dining car by Benjamin to receive Theodora's stern warning to stop saying that her husband had been poisoned.

Marshall grunted. "It seems mother and stepson would prefer that murder not be mentioned in the same breath with his death."

"Which makes them pretty suspicious," Reggie said.

Marshall ignored Reggie's editorial comment and said, "Go on, Mrs. Fletcher."

I consulted my notes. "I assume the train's staff has been questioned," I said.

"Of course."

"I ask because it's possible that Benjamin Vail might be involved in some sort of relationship with the hostess, Jenna."

"What do you base that on?" the detective asked.

"Observation and hearsay. I saw them together before we left Vancouver. And Junior Pinckney claims to have seen them acting 'lovey-dovey' back at Whistler."

"'Lovey-dovey'?" Marshall said, smiling.

"His description," I said. "Also, Jenna's demeanor changed dramatically following Blevin's death."

"Perhaps she was simply shocked," Marshall offered. "She's a young woman. Witnessing a death, and now knowing it was murder, could be very upsetting."

"Undoubtedly," I said. "But I thought it was worth mentioning."

"And I agree," he said. "Everything is worth mentioning in a murder investigation."

"Did the kitchen staff have anything to offer?" I asked.

"No."

"There was that one fellow who delivered bottles of vodka to Callie at the bar shortly before Mr. Blevin died. His name is Karl. I talked with him. He suggested that Jenna had a crush on Blevin."

"I spoke with him at length, as well as Callie," Marshall said. "In fact, I even got her secret recipe for Bloody Marys." He reached into his pocket, pulled out a piece of paper, and unfolded it. "Tomato juice, Dijon mustard, celery salt, pepper, lemon and lime juice, horseradish, dill weed, Worcestershire sauce, and Tabasco to taste." He looked up, his face deadpan. "I'll have to try it when I get home."

"Did she have anything else to say?" Reggie asked.

"No. And neither did the other staff," Marshall said, replacing the recipe in his pocket. "They claim to know nothing about what happened."

"I assume you're going to contact the human resources people at BC Rail," I said.

"Why would he want to do that?" Reggie asked.

"To check the background reports on all their Northwind employees," Marshall put in, smiling at me. "We're already on it." He looked at his notes. "Who's next?" he asked.

"The couple from Pittsburgh, Hank and Deedee Crocker."

I'd written: *He's an accountant; she's a florist. His dislike of the deceased is palpable. Sued Blevin over alleged misuse of club dues to build model railroad layout. Her work as a florist might bring her in contact with poisons used to control insects and rodents. He acts glad Blevin is dead, has made crude comments about it.*

Marshall listened as I read my notes to him, shifted in his chair, recrossed his legs, and finally said, "If Mrs. Crocker had access to poisons, her husband would have access to them, too."

I moved on to Maeve and Junior Pinckney.

"No love lost between Blevin and Mr. Pinckney," I read from my notes. "Junior suspects his wife engaged in some sort of relationship with Blevin. She denies it, but her husband makes snide comments about it all the same."

Marshall cleared his throat and tried to repress a smile. "Somehow, someone called 'Junior' shouldn't be a murdering sort."

"Excuse me," Reggie said, "but I thought you couldn't ever decide who was the murdering type."

"And you are correct," said Marshall, sobering. "I've known murderers who were the least likely individuals to commit a violent act, pillars of their communities, while secretly pulling wings off butterflies. Jealousy would certainly be a motive for Mr. Pinckney to have murdered a rival for his wife's attention. Of course, had her alleged relationship with Mr. Blevin gone sour, she, too, might have had a motive to want him dead." He looked at me and grinned. "I'm playing your 'what if' game, Jessica."

"So I see," I said.

I slid the notes across the table to Reggie. "Why don't you go over a few names?" I suggested.

"Oh, sure, Jess." He perused the pages. "Let's see. The new couple, Mr. and Mrs. Goldfinch. Had a long talk with them over lunch the first day. Said they've been married four years, live in Hartford, Connecticut, no children. She's a housewife; he works in computers, he said. The wife is the rail fan, but I have to say she's not as knowledgeable as I thought at first."

"I have a hunch they're not married," I said, causing Marshall to sit up straighter and look at us.

"They don't act like a married couple to me," I explained. "At least not based upon my observations over the years of how married couples behave together."

"What do you mean?"

"They never touch each other, for one thing. They don't look at each other when they're speaking, even if they're speaking about the same topic. And Gail talked about when *she* was in London on vacation last year."

"What's suspicious about that?" Reggie asked.

"If you went on vacation with your husband, wouldn't you say 'we'? She said 'I,' not 'we.' "

Reggie winked at me. "Well, *I* wouldn't be on vacation with a husband."

"Should be easy enough to check out their story," Marshall said. "Now that you mention it, I had the feeling they were not being straightforward with me."

"If they're not married, why would they say they are?" I wondered aloud.

"Maybe they're awkward about traveling and sleeping together," Marshall offered.

"In this day and age?" Reggie said.

"I'm sure there are still some who share the sort of

decorum Detective Marshall is talking about," I said in his defense.

We fell silent for a few seconds. I broke it. "I found it interesting," I said, "that Gail—Mrs. Goldfinch, if she is that—tossed out a precise figure when we were discussing how much insurance Theodora might have collected after the disappearance of her husband."

"She did?" Reggie said.

"Yes," I said. "Don't you remember? We were talking in generalities, but she said something along the lines that two and a half million would be a tidy sum for Theodora to bring into her marriage to Al Blevin."

"Oh, yes. I do remember. But how would she know?" Reggie asked. "I never heard that figure before and I've been in the club a lot longer than they have. If a rumor had surfaced about how much Theodora stood to gain from Elliott's death, I would have heard it before the Goldfinches. Anyway, the court record was sealed." He looked to me. "Wasn't it?"

"Yes, it was, as I understand it," I said. "And your question is the right one. How *would* she know?"

"Assuming her information was correct and it was two and a half million," Marshall said.

"Yes, assuming that," I said.

"She might have tossed out that figure just to indicate large sums in general," Reggie said.

"Two and a half million is not a round number," I replied.

Reggie looked down at our list. Next were the mother and daughter team on the trip, Marilyn and Samantha Whitmore. But although he raised them, I had the most to say about them.

I told Detective Marshall about my confrontation with Samantha at the pool, shocking both men when I explained why she claimed to have saved my life.

"I can't believe you never said anything," Reggie said.

"Now, don't be offended, Reggie. You can see I'm fine. I didn't want to make a fuss. What's more important is that Samantha and her mother both believe that Blevin cheated Mr. Whitmore out of a business partnership and was directly responsible for his fatal heart attack."

Marshall said, "I don't doubt Blevin was capable of ruthless business dealings, at least from what I've been able to ascertain. But claiming he'd brought on another's coronary is a bit of a stretch, wouldn't you agree?"

"Perhaps," I said. "But Marilyn perceives it that way. She certainly is aware that her comments place her in a bad light. She asked me not to mention it to you."

Marshall sighed. "Someone else anxious to avoid suspicion. What about the daughter?"

"Samantha worked in a toxicology lab," Reggie quickly said.

"I can see why Marilyn worries about her," I said. "She's not well, that young woman."

Marshall slowly shook his head, stood, and stretched against an unseen pain in his body. "It never fails to amaze me," he said absently, to no one in particular.

"What's that, sir?" Reggie asked.

"How a man can go through life alienating others to the extent that they would like to see him dead."

"I know of a few women who've done that, too," I said.

"Oh, yes," Marshall agreed. "Cruelty is an equal-opportunity trait. I've always believed that if you're going to bother getting up in the morning, you might as well be pleasant and treat people decently. Otherwise . . ."

"Otherwise you end up like Al Blevin," Reggie said.

Marshall resumed his seat. "You have more, I'm sure."

"Not much," I replied. "There's the British businessman, Winston Rendell."

"Yes. We've talked about him before," Marshall said. "Always harder to check up on someone from another country. Diplomacy and all that. Even so, this meeting has been most productive. Keep it up, eh? Let me know if you find out anything more."

"Will you still be involved in the investigation once we're back in Vancouver?" I asked.

He laughed and said, "Oh, I'll keep my hand in. I like to think the chaps in the big city can't possibly do it without me. You'll be seeing me, I assure you."

He gave us each a card with his cellular phone number on it, and we bade him good night.

Reggie and I walked back to the hotel.

"So, who do you think did it?" he asked.

"I'm not sure," I said. "Benjamin hated his stepfather."

"But the Whitmores—Marilyn and Samantha—were none too fond of Al either."

"True. There are many with a motive. But there's one we need to find out more about. And I think I know someone who can help us look into the background of Winston Rendell."

It was still light out at ten o'clock when I returned to my room at the Ramada, and I wondered if we were far enough north to see the northern lights. It had been a long day, and I struggled to stay awake, even setting my alarm for midnight in case I fell asleep.

The number was in my address book. I remembered the strange sound of the rings on the other end. The connection was made and a masculine voice said, "Good morning. Scotland Yard."

Chapter Twelve

After I brought my luggage down to the lobby the next morning, I found Reggie having breakfast in the hotel café. We were shortly joined by Winston Rendell, who startled us by pulling out a chair and sitting down without asking if we wanted company.

For a man who'd been consistently rude to me and might even have made an attempt on my life—I still didn't know who had unlatched the vestibule door— he was in an expansive mood, smiling and chatty. He had won three hundred dollars in the hotel casino, he told us.

Reggie's spirits were also high, although he lamented that the train portion of the trip was over. "I always hate getting on a noisy jet aircraft after riding a great train like the Whistler Northwind," he said. "Jets are so . . . they're so modern."

Rendell laughed. "Better get used to it," he said. "The way things are going, there won't be any passenger trains left except for commuter ones. I wouldn't be surprised if BC Rail stopped running the Northwind. They're losing money on every trip."

"I hope you're wrong," I said. I found his apparent glee at the misfortune of others to be offensive. "Train travel is lovely. And if the Northwind stops running, it would be a shame for all the people who made our time aboard so enjoyable."

"Despite a certain murder having taken place?" Rendell said.

"Fortunately, most of these trips don't involve murder."

"Speaking of murder," he said, "what's new with the investigation?"

Reggie and I glanced at each other before I said, "I don't think anything is new, except that the Vancouver police will be joining the RCMP."

"I assume Detective Marshall questioned you as he did everyone else," Reggie said.

"Sure. I had nothing to tell him. Blevin was rude to me as usual, and I left the car once he went into his death dance. Anyway, when the local cops take over, the charming Detective Marshall will be gone from the scene." He said it with a smirk.

"You don't like him?" I asked as my breakfast was served.

"He's not exactly Inspector Morse or Adam Dalgleish, now, is he?" he said, referring to famous fictitious investigators in the mysteries respectively of Colin Dexter and P. D. James. "He's a buffoon."

"I certainly disagree with that," I said, feeling myself getting heated at his disrespectful comments, even though I knew he was baiting me. "Behind that easygoing facade is a very smart man, a sharp investigator."

"You should know, Mrs. Fletcher. You spent enough time with him. What did he have to say last night?"

"Last night?"

"Yes. At police headquarters."

"How did you—?" Reggie started to say.

I wasn't going to pursue the conversation, but Rendell cleared up how he knew our whereabouts the previous evening by saying, "Enjoy your dinner at Ric's? They make great drinks."

"You were there?" Reggie said.

"At the bar. You walked right past me, but I saw you. When you left, I figured I'd see where you were going. You know, maybe you knew Prince George's hot spots."

"You followed us?" I was astonished.

"Don't look so shocked, madam. It's not a crime to follow someone down the street. When I saw you walk into police headquarters, I figured you were meeting with the good detective."

He wanted Reggie and me to know that he was keeping tabs on us. That was clear. I had a feeling he was not quite so blithe as he was straining to convince us he was. Rendell was worried about Marshall. Why? What did he think Marshall had found out about him that the Vancouver police might not know? Was his ticket to safety getting Marshall off the case? He was bound to be very disappointed. Detective Christian Marshall was planning to stick around, and so was I, at least for the next few days.

"You seem to show a great deal of interest in our activities," I said. "Maeve Pinckney said you were even asking about conversations she and I had when we sat together. I wonder why that would be of interest to you."

Rendell quickly wiped his mouth with his napkin and stood. "She's just another foolish woman," he said, his good mood flown. "Her blather is certainly nothing to heed." He forced a smile, but his nostrils were flaring when he added, "Well, see you on the bus. You'd better watch out, Jessica Fletcher. I might switch from railroad history to murder mysteries. I'll write one about Alvin Blevin's murder. Guaranteed best-seller."

Reggie was incensed on my behalf. "Some nerve," he muttered after Rendell was gone. "Tells you to watch out because he's going to write a bestseller."

I smiled at him. "Maybe he will," I said. "Write a bestseller. I just hope he doesn't start telling everyone about our meeting with the detective."

"It would be just like him to do that," Reggie said.

"You're right," I said, "and there's nothing we can do about it. Might as well go. We don't want to miss the bus."

We were taken to Prince George airport, where we boarded a WestJet flight to Vancouver. A front had passed through the area overnight. The showers were gone, but there was a brisk breeze in their wake. The plane shuddered on takeoff, buffeted by the winds, but we soon reached our cruising altitude with only blue skies ahead.

My seat was next to Reggie's; Marilyn and Samantha Whitmore sat across the aisle. Marilyn had been truthful when she'd said she feared flying. Throughout the short flight she looked absolutely petrified. Her face was pale, and her hands gripped the armrests with the resulting white knuckles. Samantha seemed unconcerned about her mother's distress; she stared out the window, her attention focused on the landscape below.

Another bus awaited us at Vancouver Airport, but I suggested to Reggie that we take a taxi to the Sutton Place Hotel. I'd picked up conversations while waiting for our plane in Prince George that Winston Rendell had indeed been talking about our meeting with Detective Marshall, and I wasn't in the mood to answer questions about it.

We arrived well ahead of the others, and were greeted with an unreserved welcome from the doorman. A bellman was on the spot in seconds to handle our luggage, but first he directed me to the concierge's desk, where I was handed an envelope. From it I pulled two folded pages torn from the local newspaper and a handwritten note:

> *Dear Mrs. Fletcher. My name is Gene Driscoll. I write for the Vancouver Sun and am covering Alvin Blevin's murder. (See enclosed tear sheets.) I would like very much to interview you regarding this case. Please call me at your earliest convenience.*

Attached to the newspaper clips was his business card.

I recognized his name from the article by him I'd read at breakfast back in Whistler.

I put his material in my purse and headed to the elevator.

Back in the same suite I'd enjoyed before leaving on the Whistler Northwind three days earlier, I relaxed. It was almost as though I'd just gotten off a ship and was again enjoying my land legs. The suite, so spacious and tastefully decorated, gave a sense of harmony, of being at home base after a long journey. After the rustic and unadorned rooms we'd stayed in on the trip, it was nice to feel a bit pampered in the elegant Sutton Place.

In the marble bathroom, I unpacked my toiletries—I'm obsessive about completely unpacking as soon as I arrive in a hotel room, even if my stay is to be for only a few days—and sat at the window looking out over Vancouver. Now that I was back where I'd started the trip, I realized I didn't have any concrete plans for the rest of the day and evening. The Track and Rail Club's itinerary didn't have anything scheduled until the following day: an early-morning presentation by a railroad historian in one of the hotel's public meeting rooms; a tour to area sights, including the famed Capilano Suspension Bridge; and a farewell meal on the Pacific Starlight Dinner Train. But before that, the club's board of directors was scheduled to meet at club headquarters, the office building owned by Alvin Blevin. It was a schedule that didn't leave much time for investigation, much less leisure. How was I going to pursue my suspicions about Blevin's killer if I was running from one social obligation to another?

Reggie and I had parted in the lobby. He was off that evening to meet friends at Cin Cin, one of the best restaurants in town. "It's beautiful. The food is sensational. You'll love it," he'd said. I had begged off. He was concerned about deserting me, but I assured him I welcomed an afternoon and evening on my own. However, my plans got back on track when the phone rang.

"Mrs. Fletcher?"

"Yes?"

"This is Theodora Blevin."

Hearing from her was a shock, and my momentary silence testified to it.

"Hello," I said.

"I wasn't sure whether you were back in Vancouver yet but thought I'd try. How was the rest of the trip?"

Other than that, Mrs. Lincoln, how did you enjoy the play?

"It was—it was fine."

"I was wondering if you were free this evening."

She certainly had a talent for catching one off guard.

"This evening? I—yes, I am, as a matter of fact."

"I'm having a few close friends for dinner and would be pleased if you'd join us."

"Are you sure—?" I started to say, but decided it

wasn't my business or place to question why she'd be having a dinner party so soon after her husband's murder. I was also tempted to ask why I would be invited to dinner with "close friends" but discarded that question, too. Others had characterized Theodora Blevin as an aloof woman, and this call did nothing to alter that characterization. I could barely remember the days that followed when I'd become a widow. Frank's death had been expected; yet I was consumed with grief. I certainly didn't hold dinner parties. Then again, I reminded myself, judging how another person reacts to loss based upon one's own response isn't fair.

"Yes, I'm available for dinner this evening," I said.

"Good. I'll have my driver pick you up at the hotel at seven. Is that all right?"

"Seven would be fine."

"I look forward to seeing you," she said, just before she disengaged and the click reached my ear.

I wondered if Benjamin would be there. Were they planning to team up to persuade me to "butt out," as they'd tried before? I shook my head, trying to sort out what Theodora might be thinking, but it was a fruitless exercise. I would go to dinner and see what played out. In the meantime, the lovely weather outside my window beckoned. A nice walk seemed in order. After three days spent mostly sitting on a train, the exercise would be refreshing, and there were still many shops I hadn't had an opportunity to visit.

I'd changed into walking shoes and was almost out the door when the phone rang again.

"Mrs. Jessica Fletcher?" a male voice asked.

"Yes? This is she."

"My name is Joel Jillian, Mrs. Fletcher. I'm a detective with the homicide division of the major crimes section, Vancouver PD. I hope I'm not disturbing you."

"Oh, not at all. I was on my way out for a walk. I just got back from a three-day train trip."

"Yes, ma'am, I know."

Of course he knew, I thought. *The Mounties had obviously given him my name.*

"What can I do for you?" I asked.

"Christian Marshall of the RCMP suggested I contact you once you got back to Vancouver."

"About the death on the Whistler Northwind," I said.

"Exactly. Detective Marshall indicates you've been extremely helpful to him during the investigation."

"Well, that's very flattering, Detective Jillian, but I'm afraid I didn't have a great deal to offer Detective Marshall. What little I know, however, you're welcome to hear."

His laugh was youthful and gentle. "I think you might be a bit too modest, Mrs. Fletcher. At any rate, we're getting pressure from all angles to solve this thing pronto. Naturally, we're working closely with E Division, but—"

"E Division?"

"RCMP's headquarters for Vancouver. It's been their investigation ever since the death occurred, but now that the body and the suspects are back here in Vancouver, we've caught the case."

I sighed. From the moment I'd witnessed the gruesome death of Alvin Blevin, I'd found myself consumed with its aftermath. As a passenger continuing on the trip, it was hard to disassociate from the murder and its subsequent investigation on the Whistler Northwind, even if I'd wanted to. But as I talked to Detective Jillian a different set of feelings invaded me. It was as though the murder investigation had broken into two distinct phases—the train and its stops to the

north, and now its continuation in the city, with different players and undoubtedly different ground rules.

"All we're asking, Mrs. Fletcher, is that you give us
the same cooperation you gave Detective Marshall."

"Did you have something specific in mind?"

"We understand you're having dinner with Mrs.
Blevin."

They must be tapping her phone—or mine, I thought,
but didn't say it out loud. "Yes. I just received the invitation."

"Don't put yourself in any danger, but do let us
know if she says anything incriminating."

"I hardly think Theodora Blevin issued a dinner invitation so I could be her confessor, Detective."

"Agreed. We just want to keep you safe, Mrs.
Fletcher, and we appreciate your continued cooperation."

"Thank you for that, and if, in my contact with fellow passengers, something strikes me as relevant, I'll
be happy to let you know."

We spent another few minutes discussing the level
of crime in Vancouver and the Vancouver police department's working relationship with the Royal Canadian Mounted Police. "Detective Marshall sends his
best," Jillian said. "He's had quite a career with the
Mounties."

"He's a fine man," I said, standing and trying to
stretch with my head and shoulder holding the phone
to my ear. "I really must go. I need to get a little exercise after three days on a train."

Yet after we hung up, I hesitated. I was only hours
away from having dinner with Alvin Blevin's widow,
who was certainly a suspect in the murder.

Dinner?

Why was she hosting a dinner party so soon after

her husband's death at the hand of someone she undoubtedly knew?

What if she had played a role in her husband's death?

Why had I been invited?

And what about the disappearance of her previous husband, Elliott Vail? I'd forgotten to ask the detectives about that. I was eager to get to the bottom of the case, but frustrated as well. There was so much to know and so little time left before Reggie and I were scheduled to fly home.

Chapter Thirteen

I pushed the button and waited for an elevator to arrive at the lobby level, eager to shower and change after my brisk walk.

"Mrs. Fletcher?"

I turned to see a tall young man with an unruly shock of red hair. He was wearing a brown corduroy jacket, a blue denim shirt, a red tie, jeans, and construction boots.

"Yes?" I said.

"I'm Gene Driscoll, the *Vancouver Sun*, Mrs. Fletcher. I've left you a couple of messages and—"

"Of course. I'm sorry I haven't gotten back to you yet."

"Do you have time for an interview?"

"I can't imagine why you'd want to interview me," I said. "You're covering Mr. Blevin's murder."

"Right."

"I really don't know anything about it aside from having been on the train when he died."

"But you were the first one to say he'd been poisoned."

"That was just a lucky guess on my part, Mr. Driscoll. Oh, here's my elevator."

"Please," he said, touching my elbow to keep me from getting on, "I won't take much of your time."

The elevator doors closed.

"I don't think it's appropriate for me to comment on an ongoing investigation," I said after pushing the button again.

"What did you hear on the train about Elliott Vail?" he asked.

"Elliott Vail? Why are you interested in him?"

"I suppose you haven't heard, Mrs. Fletcher. There's an investigation into Alvin Blevin's representation of Vail's wife, Theodora. There are rumors that he may have convinced the judge to rule in his favor by means other than legal argument."

Were he still alive, I thought, *the authorities would be closing in on Alvin Blevin.*

"The insurance company, Merit Life, hasn't dropped the case either," Driscoll added.

Another elevator arrived.

"I thought they'd already paid his widow," I said, holding a hand against the open door to keep it from closing.

"They did," he said. "But their U.S. headquarters is still investigating. If it can be proved that the judge was illegally influenced to declare him dead prematurely, that'll open the case again. Insurance companies don't cough up two and a half million bucks that easily."

"That was the amount they actually paid?"

"Yeah."

A buzzer sounded, indicating someone was interfering with the elevator doors, keeping them from closing. I was that someone.

"The Vail question could have a bearing on the Blevin murder, Mrs. Fletcher," he said, his voice urgent. "Think about it. Vail's widow gets two and a half million dollars and marries Blevin, who handles her case in court. There's Vail's kid, Benjamin, who ended up being arrested for attacking Blevin after he married his mother. And—"

"Come on up," I said. "I only have a little time before I'm scheduled to leave for dinner, but I'd like to hear more of what you have to say."

"I came to hear what *you* have to say," he said with a chuckle, following me into the empty elevator. The door closed and the buzzer stopped.

"Then we'll have a two-way conversation," I said. "The best kind."

"I just have this feeling, Mrs. Fletcher, that the two events have to be linked," he told me, when we'd settled on the sofa in my suite.

"I agree," I said, putting on my glasses and pulling out the newspaper clips he'd sent me that I'd stashed in the desk drawer, "but only because I share your feeling. What's important is that there be evidence to connect them. Have you come up with any?"

He removed a pen from his pocket, opened a slender reporter's pad, riffled through the pages, and shook his head. "The widow collects the money and marries her attorney, Al Blevin, and now she's a widow again. That's a heck of a coincidence. I wouldn't want to marry that lady, figuratively speaking, that is. Literally, too, for that matter, although she's pretty good-looking for an old broad."

I raised my eyebrows and peered at him over my glasses.

"Sorry. That wasn't politically correct, was it?"

"It wasn't polite, either," I said. "Are you saying you think Theodora Blevin murdered both her husbands?"

"Wouldn't be the first time something like that has happened. Of course, we can't prove Vail was murdered because his body was never found. Makes me wonder if she had an accomplice in the canyon to help her get rid of the evidence."

"You're making a very big assumption there," I said.

Driscoll shook his head and laughed. He'd settled his lanky frame on the couch and was sunk back into the cushions, his long legs crossed. He said, "What I'm wondering is if Blevin's life was insured by the same company. Then they'd be taking a double hit."

"There is another possibility, you know," I said.

"What's that?"

"Elliott Vail could still be alive."

It was the first time I'd voiced an idea that had been rolling around in my mind for a while. But what would Vail stand to gain by staging his own disappearance? Unless . . . His wife had collected his life insurance money and now was a widow again. Could she have been responsible for Blevin's death? Was she planning to reunite with her first husband? Had that been their plan all along? But if it was, did Benjamin know about it? Would they make him suffer the loss of his father only to have Elliott resurface years later? If so, how could they do that to their son?

"I bet Merit Life would like to prove that," Driscoll said. "It would save them a bundle."

"I beg your pardon? I was distracted. What was it you said?"

"Merit Life. If they can prove Vail is alive, they get their two and half million back."

"That's exactly what I'm thinking," I said. "Do you know where Merit Life is headquartered?"

"Sure. Hartford, Connecticut. That's where lots of insurance companies have their headquarters. Their Canadian affiliate is in Vancouver."

"What else have you found out while you've been chasing down this story?"

"The rumor is that Theodora Vail was getting it on with Al Blevin before her husband disappeared."

"Do you know that for a fact?"

"No, ma'am. Scuttlebutt."

"Is there any way to prove it?"

"Not unless you can find a witness to testify to it. But it wouldn't make much difference. Infidelity is hardly news these days."

"Of course, if Elliott Vail *was* murdered," I said, "then it would provide a motive."

"True."

"You mentioned downstairs that Benjamin Vail was arrested for having attacked his stepfather. When did that happen?"

He chewed his cheek and briefly closed his eyes before answering. "I think it was right after Blevin married Theodora Vail. The police got a domestic disturbance call and went to Blevin's house. They took the kid off in handcuffs, but Blevin refused to press charges, and the matter was dropped. The story is in one of those clips I gave you."

I offered him a soft drink from the suite's minibar, which he declined.

"Mrs. Fletcher," he said, closing his notebook.

"Yes?"

"I've been doing all the talking, but I came here hoping to get a quote from you."

"I'd like to be as helpful as you've been, Mr. Driscoll, but I'm afraid you know a great deal more than I do."

"That's not what Detective Marshall of the RCMP thinks."

"He told you that?"

"Not directly. I got it from one of the other passengers on your trip." He flipped through the pages of his spiral-bound pad. "This person said that Marshall enlisted you and a friend of yours—a Mr. Reginald Weems—to help with the investigation. True?"

"Who said that?"

"Can't tell you. Confidential sources and all that. So, is it true? Did the Mounties ask you to help with the investigation? Not exactly standard police procedure."

I wasn't sure how to answer. Obviously, this young reporter had it right and had gotten it from a credible source. It would be another thing to acknowledge it for public consumption.

"Detective Marshall asked me and Mr. Weems to tell him what we'd witnessed the day Mr. Blevin died, which we did. I'm sure others on the train were asked the same question and cooperated, too." I looked at my watch. "Now, Mr. Driscoll," I said, going to the door and placing my hand on the knob, "I'm afraid I have another appointment. I appreciate the job you have to do, and I respect it. I also assure you that I really don't have anything to offer you—at this juncture."

He cocked his head. " 'At this juncture,' " he repeated. "Does that mean you might have something to tell me at another time?"

"That's always a possibility," I said, opening the door.

"Promise I'll be the first reporter you call?"

"Yes," I said. "You'll be the first."

"I guess I can't ask for more than that," he said.

"Thanks for your time."

"And good luck with your investigation."

After he was gone, I dialed Reggie's room. I was expecting his voicemail but he answered in person.

"Reggie, it's Jessica."

"Change your mind about joining me at Cin Cin

tonight? I was just on my way out the door, but I can wait another few minutes."

"No, thanks. I have a dinner appointment soon."

"I thought you wanted to be on your own."

"Now, don't get offended. I'll fill you in tomorrow. But listen; this is important. Do you do any business with Merit Life?"

"Merit? Sure. I've placed a lot of policies with them. Why?"

"Merit's Canadian affiliate is the insurance company that issued the policy on Elliott Vail's life."

"It is? I never even thought about who the insurer was. How did you find out?"

I told him briefly about the reporter's visit and what I'd learned from him. "Know anyone really well at Merit?" I asked.

"As a matter of fact, I do."

"Think you can find out the name of the investigator working the Vail case?"

"What are you up to, Jessica?"

"Just following a hunch."

Chapter Fourteen

Theodora Blevin's driver was parked in front of the hotel when I came down from my room a few minutes before seven. He was a short, chubby man dressed in the requisite chauffeur's black suit, white shirt, and black tie. He opened a rear door, pressed it closed behind me, got behind the wheel, and pulled away.

"Lovely evening," he said over his shoulder as he joined traffic on Burrard Street.

I agreed. "How long have you been driving for Mrs. Blevin?"

"Quite a few years, ma'am. Actually, I was Mr. Blevin's driver until . . ."

There was no need for him to finish the sentence.

"You have my sympathies."

"Thank you, ma'am."

As he turned left on Georgia, I recognized the route. It was the same one our bus had taken on its way to join the Whistler Northwind at the beginning of our ill-fated train trip into northern British Columbia. We drove into Stanley Park, Canada's largest urban park, designed by the same landscape architect, Frederick Law Olmsted, who'd designed New York's Central Park, and headed for the Lions Gate Bridge, which would take us into West Vancouver, home to the city's most exclusive waterfront community. I recalled Marilyn Whitmore's comment as the train passed through the area that West Vancouver was the richest city in Canada.

"Know the history of Lions Gate Bridge?" the driver asked as we approached it.

"A little," I said.

"The Guinness family, the beer people, built it in 1938," he said. "It cost them six million U.S. dollars. King George and Queen Elizabeth were here to open it officially in 1939. The city bought it back from Guinness in 1963 for six million."

"A bargain for the city," I suggested.

"I suppose it was," he said.

Traffic was heavy once we were on the bridge, testimony to how quickly bridges and highways become obsolete as traffic handlers. On the other side, we turned left and followed Marine Drive until reaching a property surrounded by a high hedge. Two police cars flanked the entrance. The driver got out and punched in a code on a keypad, which activated the gates. We drove through and pulled up in a circular driveway in front of a Tudor-style home where a half dozen other vehicles were parked. He assisted me from the car and escorted me up a short set of steps to heavy wooden double doors and pressed the doorbell. A few moments later the doors swung open and Theodora appeared. She wore a black floor-length sheath with a neckline that hugged her throat, a suitable scrim for the expensive gold jewelry she sported. She flashed a weary smile and said, "Welcome. I'm so glad you could make it. Please, come in."

I followed her from the expansive black-and-white marble foyer decorated with sleek, modern black designer tables and chairs through a wide archway to the living room, which was decidedly less contemporary in feel. The furniture was heavy wood and more traditional. The walls were covered with a red fabric, accented with gold, and the expensive Oriental carpets picked up those colors. A fireplace spanned an entire wall, its mantel covered with small photos in gold leaf frames.

There were five people in the room when Theodora led me in, three women and two men, their dress indicating this gathering had not been billed as an informal one. They had drinks in their hands and were congregated near French doors that led to a patio and garden. They turned at our entrance.

"My friends, may I introduce the famed crime novelist, Jessica Fletcher."

I wished she hadn't given me billing, but I ignored it and went through the ritual of introductions. A member of the household staff approached and asked if I wanted a drink. "A white wine would be nice," I told her.

As I engaged in the requisite sort of conversation between people at a party who'd just been introduced, my eyes went to the wall above the fireplace. A large oil painting of Alvin Blevin dominated the space, and I was reminded of my initial reaction when his widow had invited me to a dinner party. Only a few days had passed since his murder, hardly time enough to grieve but sufficient to plan and execute a social gathering. Of course, with the sort of money his widow enjoyed and the household help it could buy, hosting parties wasn't especially difficult or time-consuming.

The others at the gathering represented themselves as being close friends of long standing with both Al Blevin and Theodora. I silently wondered whether they were thinking what I was thinking, that a formal dinner party was premature. Theodora seemed to anticipate such thoughts when she said, "I want you to know that asking you here this evening was not a decision I took lightly. And I admit to a certain self-serving motivation. You were among our closest friends, and I felt a need to have you here, around me, at this dark moment."

It was a lovely sentiment. But if true, *why was I there?*

Again, Theodora did a bit of mind reading. "I invited you, Jessica, because of everyone who was on that train with Al and me, you obviously have the most reasoned view of what occurred." She added to her friends, "It was Jessica who first speculated that Al was poisoned. I didn't believe it—I didn't *want* to believe it—but she proved to be correct."

"I don't doubt it," one of the men said, "considering your career solving murders in your books."

I didn't have a chance to respond because one of the three women, who'd introduced herself as Nancy Flowers and didn't seem to be connected with either of the two men, said, "Teddy says the police don't have a clue as to who killed Al."

It took me a second to realize she was referring to Theodora. "I'm sure they're doing everything possible to solve the case," I said.

"And you should know, Jessica," Theodora said. To the others: "Jessica has maintained a close relationship with the police."

"What do they have to say?" one of the men, the Blevins' accountant, asked.

"Yes, what *do* they have to say, Mrs. Fletcher?" Benjamin Vail lounged against the arched opening to the living room, his arms folded over his cable knit sweater and his wide-wale corduroy-clad legs crossed at the ankle. I wondered how long he'd been there.

"Benjamin, dear. You're late," his mother said, "and you haven't changed for dinner."

Benjamin pushed off the molding and sauntered into the room. He flung himself into an armchair and looked around at the other guests. "Ah, yes. We must dress for dinner, jacket and tie, or jacket and ascot, like my friend Harvey over here."

"Sorry about your stepdad, Ben," the man called Harvey said. "Terrible shame."

"She's not sorry; why should you be?" Benjamin said, cocking his head toward his mother.

"Benjamin! What's wrong with you? Have you been drinking?"

"Only a little bit." Benjamin held his thumb and forefinger a half inch apart. "To dull the pain, Mother."

Theodora walked across the room and pulled her son to his feet. "I think it would be wise to go upstairs and change for dinner, don't you?" she told him. "I'm sure you have some dress clothes in the closet."

"Yes, ma'am," he said, flinging an arm over her shoulder and taking her with him as he shuffled out of the room.

"And don't come down until you've had some coffee," Theodora said as she extricated herself from his embrace.

I saw her motion to someone in the hall before she rejoined us in the living room.

"He's so distraught," she said, sinking gracefully into the chair her son had just vacated. "He just hasn't been the same since he got home this afternoon."

"Losing two fathers will take its toll on a young man," Harvey said. "I'll invite him out on the boat next week. Perhaps that will take his mind off his troubles a bit."

"Thank you, Harvey," she said, reaching over to

pat his arm. "That's very kind." She gave him a weak smile and straightened in her seat. "Now, where were we?"

Before we were so rudely interrupted, my mind filled in.

"Oh, yes. James, I believe you were asking Mrs. Fletcher about the investigation."

"That's right. I was. How *are* the police coming along?" he asked, turning toward me.

The others in the room did the same.

"I'm really not privy to their investigation," I said, wishing the subject would change. Obviously, Theodora had invited me for precisely this reason, to offer insight into how the police were proceeding in trying to identify the person who'd poisoned her husband. I was annoyed with myself that this hadn't occurred to me earlier.

"At least it's now in the hands of professionals," Theodora said, her own hands neatly folded in her lap. "The detective on the train was a bumbler."

Had she come to that conclusion on her own, or had someone who'd continued on the Whistler Northwind fed her that negative evaluation of Detective Marshall? Did she consider the detective ineffective because no arrest had been made?

"Teddy was so shocked when the police informed her about the poison," Nancy Flowers confided when the conversation took a more general turn. "And the press has been so rude, camping out at the base of the driveway until the police insisted they move. It's so nice to have the police around when you need them."

I simply nodded. I was watching for Benjamin's return.

"All this must be fodder for your career, eh, Mrs. Fletcher?" Harvey said.

Usually, I'm hesitant to discuss my writing career,

especially with strangers. But when the conversation turned to questions of me on that subject, I was actually relieved to see the emphasis shift from Alvin Blevin's murder, and I happily answered their questions about how I create my plots, whether I know the ending before I begin, how extensive an outline I create before actually starting to write, and a dozen other areas of interest that invariably come up in such discussions. By the time we were summoned to the dining room, the topic of my writing habits had run its course, and I was happy to sit down at the elaborately set table.

A chastened Benjamin entered the room shortly after dinner began and took the seat opposite his mother, the one most likely occupied by Alvin Blevin when he was alive. He had scrubbed his face, the skin still red from the cold water and his sandy hair damp at the temples, and had donned a navy jacket and blue-and-white-striped shirt, but no tie, over his corduroy slacks. He took a gulp of the red wine that had been put at his place and said nothing.

Conversation over a dinner of Cornish hen and wild rice ran the gamut from politics to sports, the weather to the economy, fashion, and popular entertainment, every topic but the deceased. It was as if her friends were shielding Theodora from having to face the ugly reality of her husband's demise. But we were all aware of the tension between mother and son. The people across from me watched first one and then the other as if spectators at a soundless tennis match.

Benjamin sat silent throughout the meal, occasionally aiming scowls at Theodora. He barely ate and steadily drank one glass of wine after the other.

Just before dessert was served, Theodora stood and said, "I want to thank you all for being here tonight.

As you can imagine, the past week has been a night-
mare for me and for my family. That someone could
dislike my husband so intensely as to strike him down
in the prime of his life is beyond my comprehension.
I take great comfort in being at this table with each of
you, and I know how much Al would have enjoyed
being here, too." She raised her wineglass. "To Al
Blevin, and to the speedy apprehension of the monster who killed him."

As we all raised our glasses, I was aware that her
gaze was focused intently on me. I managed a smile,
which didn't entice a similar response from the lady of
the house.

Benjamin pushed himself out of his chair and
swayed on his feet. He raised a half-filled glass. "Oh,
yes. To Alvin, that paragon of virtue, the man who
managed to make my father disappear so he could bed
my mother."

There were gasps all around me.

"Really, Benjamin. Have a bit of sympathy for your
mother," James said.

"I have great sympathy for my mother." He took a
sip of his wine and then raised his glass in another
toast. "To my mother, who will live happily ever after.
Isn't that right, Teddy?" He sneered as he said her
name.

"That is so hurtful, Benjamin." Theodora, or Teddy,
dabbed at a tear I didn't see.

"Here, now, son," said Harvey, "this is neither the
time nor place."

Fury blazed in Benjamin's eyes. "Don't call me
'son,'" he ground out. "I'm not your son. I'm no one's
son." He glared at Theodora.

"What you are is rude and inappropriate,"
Theodora said. It was the first time I'd seen real emo-

tion mark her face. "I think you and I are overdue for a talk. I'm sure our guests will excuse our absence for a few minutes." She folded her napkin, laid it carefully next to her plate, and stood when James held her chair. Every action was controlled, but the turbulence in her eyes belied her restraint. She motioned to her son.

Benjamin, who seemed to realize he'd gone too far in baiting his mother, stumbled after her, wineglass in hand. "Guess I blew it this time," he said, flashing the guests a wobbly grin.

"That poor woman," said Erica, who sat to my right. "What a hellish thing to go through, seeing your husband murdered and then to have your son so disrespectful . . ."

"You have to give it to her," Harvey said. "She's made of steel."

"She'd have to be," said his wife. "First losing Elliott. And now Al."

"You all knew Mr. Vail?" I said.

"Oh, yes, very well," James, the Blevin family accountant replied. "You've heard, I assume, of the circumstances of his disappearance."

"Yes, I have," I confirmed.

"I expect to see his story on one of those TV shows that explore unsolved mysteries," Erica said. "It gives me the chills, thinking of poor Elliott falling from that train and being consumed by wild beasts."

"He was never found, though, was he?" I said.

"No, never." The accountant glanced at the door, lowered his voice, leaned into the table, and said, "Some people say he never died."

"Oh?"

He nodded. "They say—well, you know, they say he might have faked his death for the two and a half mil in insurance money."

"That's ridiculous," said Nancy Flowers, who sat across from me. "How would he collect?" She was a rail-thin woman I judged to be in her late forties or early fifties, someone who obviously spent a considerable amount of each day in a gym or spa. The skin was stretched taut across her cheekbones and forehead, and her bare arms were sinewy, slender but muscled.

"Make a good murder mystery plot for you, wouldn't it, Jessica?" said James.

"It would if the murderer were identified," I agreed. "The murderer is always revealed at the end of a good mystery."

"The one I feel sorry for is Benjamin," Nancy Flowers said.

"Does he live here with his mother?" I asked.

The accountant's laugh was smug and not especially pleasant. Again, he lowered his voice to a conspiratorial level as he said, "Ben moved out the day Teddy married Al. Has his own apartment in town."

"They didn't get along?" I asked, hoping I wasn't treading too deeply into forbidden territory.

"That's an understatement," Ms. Flowers said as Theodora suddenly reentered the dining room. I had the feeling she hadn't missed much during her absence.

"Benjamin is feeling a little under the weather," she announced. "He's lying down. He asked me to make his apologies for him." She surveyed the dishes on the table and rang a little bell that stood next to her water glass. "We'll have dessert now," she told the uniformed woman who responded to the signal.

We retired to the living room after a course of bread pudding and raspberry sauce. There was good-natured banter about the old tradition of cognac and cigars for the men, tea and inane talk for the ladies after a dinner, being a ritual no one missed. While the others settled on chairs and love seats that formed a conversation area in one corner of the large room, I ended up standing in front of the fireplace with Nancy Flowers.

"I love family photos," I said, slowly taking in each framed print. "It's too easy to lose touch with the past and the people from it."

Nancy agreed and moved along the elongated mantel with me, identifying people in the photos.

"That's Elliott in front of the locomotive," she said about one.

"Is it?"

I adjusted my glasses and looked closer at the man in the picture. He appeared to be shorter and not as broad-shouldered as Alvin Blevin, nor was he as classically handsome. His face was oblong, his hair a mousy brown, nose fairly prominent, the bones of his eyebrows jutting forward over eyes that were intense and surprisingly dark for a man who was fair-skinned. I must have fixated on it for too long because Nancy said, "Anything wrong?"

"What? Oh, no. It's just that after knowing the strange circumstances surrounding his disappearance, seeing him for the first time is compelling."

"Like an Elvis sighting?" she asked, adding a small laugh.

"Perhaps," I said. "Benjamin looks like him."

"Yes, he does, although Elliott never gave the kid the time of day," she said as we were invited to join the others.

The gathering broke up a half hour later. Theodora said she'd arrange for her driver to return me to downtown Vancouver, but Nancy Flowers insisted she'd drive me to the hotel. "I live downtown," she said. "It'll be my pleasure."

Nancy and I were the last to leave. As Theodora bade us good night, she held my hand for what seemed an unnecessarily long time and said, "You will keep in touch, Jessica. Somehow, I feel as though we've known each other a very long time."

"That's very kind of you," I said. "Thank you for including me tonight."

I walked down the steps to the gravel drive and turned to wait for Nancy, who was rummaging in her purse.

"I'll be right there, Jessica. I think I left my keys inside." She disappeared back into the house.

The sky was still light and I wandered toward the remaining car parked at the side of the house next to a line of cypress trees.

"Mrs. Fletcher?"

Benjamin's face was pale and perspiration sheened his brow. "I don't want her to see me," he said, moving back into the shadow of the trees.

He's suffering from his overindulgence, I thought. "You don't look very well, Benjamin."

"I—I—I need to tell you something."

"What is it?" I asked, taking a few steps toward him.

"It's all my fault. She didn't do it. She could never do something like that. I'm the bad one," he said in a raspy whisper. "You believe me, don't you? Tell the detective."

A noise distracted him and he glanced up the driveway toward the front door. Light reflected on the stairs indicated it was open. I followed his gaze.

"Good night!" Nancy called, descending the steps.

I turned back to Benjamin, but he had slipped away. What did he mean, it was all his fault? Was he admitting his complicity in the murder? Or was he regretting his dinnertime indiscretion, which implicated his mother? Unlike Theodora, Benjamin was only barely in control of his emotions. I had thought his brooding demeanor on the train was the immature role-playing of a young man determined to be dissatisfied with everything life had dealt him. Now I wondered if the weight of premeditated murder had shaped his disposition as well as his actions.

On the ride into Vancouver Nancy turned more talkative than she'd been at the dinner. She seemed anxious to have me know how close she was to "Teddy," how much she knew about the family, including Theodora's first marriage to Elliott Vail, his disappearance, and the events that led up to a court declaring Vail legally dead. I didn't say much in response. I took in what she said, interested of course, but not learning anything I hadn't already heard.

Until we pulled up beneath the canopy at the Sutton Place.

"Al wasn't the nicest of people, you know," she said.

I didn't react to her statement.

"I don't care how he dealt with adults in his life, but what he did to his child was, as far as I'm concerned, inexcusable."

"He had a child?"

"Sure. A little girl. You didn't know that?"

"No, I didn't. Where is she?"

She shrugged. "Nobody knows. He abandoned her when he divorced the mother, his first wife." She turned in her seat, smiled, and said, "I have a feeling you've already figured this out, Jessica."

"Pardon?"

"Figured it out. Al's murder."

I shook my head. "You give me more credit than I deserve," I said. "No, I haven't figured anything out. Care to be more specific?"

"I probably shouldn't, but I will. Don't misunderstand. Theodora has been a friend for many years, although it's been a friendship that's had its rocky moments. You know, a one-way friendship. Her way or the highway. She's a very calculating person, but I suppose you've already noticed that."

"She is sure of herself," I said. "Frankly, I was surprised to have been invited to the dinner and even more surprised she had such an evening so soon after her husband's death."

"Not unusual for Theodora. Most wives wouldn't even think of entertaining after the death of a beloved spouse."

"But?"

"But . . . Al wasn't a beloved spouse. He was a scoundrel. I doubt Theodora suffers even a twinge of regret that he's dead."

"How sad."

"And telling. Don't you agree?"

"Are you suggesting that—?"

"That she killed him? I'd never do that, not to a friend."

Some friend, I thought. *I'd hate to have you as an enemy.*

"Nice meeting you," she said. "I've never read any of your books, but I'll make a point of it now. Enjoy the rest of your stay in Vancouver."

I watched her drive away and turned to enter the hotel.

"Pleasant evening?" my favorite doorman asked.

"Well, it was interesting," I said.

I sat up and did what is second nature to me, made notes of what had been said during the evening, augmented with my own observations. I was about to stop and head for bed when what had been rattling around in my brain suddenly came to the forefront. The photo of Elliott Vail on the mantel. Although I couldn't pinpoint why or where, I had the nagging feeling I'd met him before.

Chapter Fifteen

" . . . And so between 1850 and 1860, there was enormous growth in the creation of railway networks within the United States. It was characterized by an expansion of east-west routes, rather than what had been an emphasis on north-south routes. But there were plenty of problems to be solved, particularly in the continuing development of the steam engine."

The speaker, a tall, gaunt man with horn-rimmed glasses and a tweed jacket with string tie and cowboy boots, was a history professor at the University of British Columbia. It was pointed out during his introduction that his area of historical expertise encompassed transportation in North America, particularly the advent of the railroads. His voice was pinched and he spoke in a slow monotone, which didn't help what appeared to be a drowsy audience that morning.

I'd taken an informal head count after settling into a seat in one of the hotel's smaller public meeting rooms. Everyone from the Whistler Northwind seemed to be accounted for, with the exception, of course, of Theodora Blevin and Benjamin Vail—and to my surprise, Hank Crocker. His wife, Deedee, was present, however, and sat in the back with Maeve Pinckney, whose husband, Junior, was in a front-row seat taking pictures of the professor's slides as they appeared on a screen.

I sat with Reggie Weems, who at breakfast that morning had expressed shock that I'd spent the previous night at a dinner party at Theodora Blevin's home.

"She called and invited you?" he asked, incredulous.

"Yes. I was as surprised as you are."

"Why did you go? I mean, didn't you feel awkward, a little strange?"

"Of course. I went because . . . I went because I was curious. After talking with the lead Vancouver detective, I—"

"You talked with the lead detective?"

"Yes."

"Why didn't you tell me you were going to do that?" I saw that my friend was hurt.

"I hadn't planned on it, Reggie. I received a call from him. What's wrong?"

"I just figured that since we worked together with Detective Marshall, we'd keep doing it."

Reggie felt as though I'd deliberately left him out of things. I hadn't realized how much he'd enjoyed being asked by Detective Marshall to participate in the investigation, if only tangentially.

"I'm sorry, Reggie," I said. "It never occurred to me that you'd be disappointed."

He gave me a wan smile. "I just liked being in on the action," he said. "It's not the usual kind of excitement I see in the insurance business."

"But you *are* in on the action."

"What do you mean?"

"We need insurance information. Have you heard back from your contact at Merit Life?"

"Not yet, but I should hear something later today,"

Reggie said, perking up. "So, what did the detective say?"

"He pretty much confirmed what Detective Marshall said, that he wanted, um, *us* to keep our eyes and ears open. They're under a lot of pressure because of Mr. Blevin's position in the Vancouver community."

"And last night?"

"What about it?"

"What did you pick up at Theodora's house? Was Benjamin there?"

I described the evening, including my reaction to the photograph of Elliott Vail on the mantel.

"You think you *knew* him, Jess?"

"I keep thinking I've seen him somewhere before."

"When could that have been?"

I'd asked myself the same question and found no answer. "It probably never happened. Just one of those strange moments, I suppose."

"I know what you mean. As I get older, all faces begin to look familiar. I see someone and think I graduated from high school with the guy, or I know him from somewhere else. I even stopped a man on the street once, sure I'd met him before. He had no idea who I was. I was really embarrassed. Maybe that's what you're experiencing."

"It could be," I said, "but I'm usually pretty good with faces."

"Who else was at the dinner?"

I described the guests and added, "One of the women at Theodora's drove me back to the hotel. Her name is Nancy Flowers."

"Never heard of her."

"She's no friend of Theodora, although she portrays herself as such."

I told him what Ms. Flowers had said about Theodora.

Reggie listened intently. "That wraps it up as far as I'm concerned," he said, slapping his hands together.

"What do you mean?"

"I've figured Theodora killed him all along, Jess. Al had a reputation as a womanizer, big-time. Theodora must have found out about one of his affairs and got even. You know, the woman scorned. *Cherchez la femme*. Look for the woman in the case. Right?"

"Sometimes," I said, "and maybe you're right in this case." I took a last sip of coffee, and we went together to the lecture room. "Oh, by the way," I said, "did you know that Blevin had a daughter from his first marriage?"

"No. Where is she?"

"That's what I asked Ms. Flowers. She said he walked away when he divorced her mother."

"What a lousy thing to do."

We took seats in the back of the lecture room.

Reggie leaned over to whisper in my ear. "You know that may change things."

"What things?" I whispered back.

"Depends on Blevin's will, of course, but there's always the possibility, if there's another heir, that we won't get to keep the rooms for our club."

Our lecturer finished his seminar with tales of the problems early steam engines presented, especially the tendency of their boilers to explode. "It happened with alarming frequency," he said, "mostly caused when the water level in the boiler dropped low enough to no longer cover the firebox, also known as the crown sheet. One of the more horrific examples happened in 1875 in a freight yard outside Boston. The force of the explosion was so great that a metal fragment weighing two hundred pounds was blown through the wall of the freight house more than twenty feet away. Another piece of the boiler, weighing more than thirty pounds, was found a quarter mile away. Of course, things got safer as engines were refined and heavier-duty materials were used.

"Thank you for your kind attention. I'll entertain questions now."

Junior Pinckney jumped to his feet and asked a highly technical question that the professor answered in numbing detail.

Winston Rendell, who had been taking notes during the lecture, raised his pencil in the air. "Professor, we all know that passenger trains are going out of business left and right. In fact, there are rumors that we may have been on one of the last passenger trips offered by BC Rail on the Whistler Northwind. What's your prognosis for rail travel in North America?"

"With the exception of local commuter trains, passenger rail service has been shrinking for many years, and the reasons are many," he replied. "During the Second World War, there was an urgent need for rolling stock and lots of it. Since the whole system was built for steam, the U.S. government froze construction of diesels—except by General Motors—lest companies abandon manufacturing steam engines before they were proficient at building diesel ones. However, after the war, instead of bankrolling diesel development, federal money was dumped into the interstate highway system spearheaded by President Eisenhower. Plus, the advent of jet aircraft certainly contributed to the decline. And, of course, railroad companies found that hauling freight was considerably more profitable than hauling passengers. I'm sure, as railroad passengers,

you've all been on a train shunted to a siding to wait
while a freight train with priority was allowed to take
over the main track. Sadly, I don't see much of a future
for passenger rail travel. Next?"

Reggie and I left the meeting room together and
were headed for the lobby when Maeve intercepted us.

"I'll catch up with you in a minute," I told Reggie.

"Now that we're not seatmates, ah miss seeing you,"
she told me. "It was exciting sitting with a celebrity.
Oh, doesn't that sound terrible? Of course, that's not
important. I just enjoyed your company."

"Thank you, Maeve. I enjoyed yours as well."

"Will I see you at the club this afternoon? Junior's
going to the board of directors' meeting, and I thought
I'd go and see this famous train layout they're always
arguing about. It must be impressive since Alvin spent
so much money on it."

"Reggie hasn't mentioned it, but I'd like to see it,
too. I'll ask him about it. See you later."

I started to walk away, but she pulled me back.

"Jessica, ah know ah'm bein' nosy, but have you
heard any more about the murder investigation? Just
this morning, Junior was saying that he saw a photograph of Theodora Blevin in the paper and read that
the police are looking into her husband's death. I said
to him, I'll ask Jessica what she knows because, of
course, you and the detective on the train might have
solved the case by now."

"Unfortunately, it's not quite that easy," I said. "I
hope you'll excuse me. Reggie is waiting."

She started to object when Winston Rendell interrupted us. "A moment of your time, Mrs. Fletcher?"

Maeve flashed Rendell a look of annoyance and
quickly fled.

"May I offer you a drink?" Rendell asked.

"Much too early for me," I said.

"Not even a Bloody Mary?"

"Maybe another time," I said, starting to see this wasn't going to be a friendly chat. "My friend is waiting for me, Mr. Rendell."

"I won't be but a moment." He'd been leading me through the Fleuri Restaurant toward the Gerard lounge, but we stopped where the lunch buffet would be set up in a couple of hours, and the chocolate buffet later that evening.

"I probably shouldn't feel the need to bring this up to you, Mrs. Fletcher, but circumstances compel me."

I waited for him to explain.

"I was contacted yesterday afternoon by members of the Vancouver police department," he said, his voice mirroring the gravity he was assigning to the event. "A persistent bloke, a detective from the homicide division."

"I'm not surprised," I said. "The investigation into Mr. Blevin's murder is now in their hands."

"That may be, but you see, I didn't appreciate the tone the detective took with me."

"I'm sorry to hear that."

"To be direct, Mrs. Fletcher, he referred to certain circumstances that the detective on the train told him I was involved in."

"Oh?"

"That unfortunate incident where you almost lost your life when the vestibule door swung open. Did you tell him about that?"

"I don't see why I shouldn't have mentioned it," I said. "But I had nothing to do with that—did I?"

"I certainly hope not."

"And then there was that phone call you eavesdropped on," he said.

"I beg your pardon?"

"When I was on the phone with a business associate back in London. I saw you listening."

"I think a correction is in order here," I said. "I didn't eavesdrop on you, Mr. Rendell. You were speaking loudly, and I happened to be standing nearby. If you don't want people to hear your conversations, you should find a more private location in which to conduct your calls."

"But you reported my phone conversation to that detective, Marshall."

"Yes, I did. I thought it was relevant."

He'd been relatively pleasant until that moment. Now he turned nasty, his face reflecting his antagonism. "Mind your own bloody business, Mrs. Fletcher. Blevin might have been a conniving bastard who buggered me in our business deal, but I don't need some fantasy-loving novelist pointing fingers at me." He turned and stomped off before I could respond to his insult.

I felt my face reddening and took a deep breath to calm myself. I was halfway to where Reggie waited for me in the lobby when Martin and Gail Goldfinch, walking in the opposite direction, stopped me. "We were hoping we'd find you. Time for a cup of coffee?" Martin asked

"No, I'm sorry. I'm already late for an appointment."

"We'd really like a word with you," Gail added.

"Another time, please," I said, and continued on my way.

I hated to be short with them, but I was still fuming at Winston Rendell's arrogance and wasn't in the mood to speak with anyone at that moment, especially a member of the Track and Rail Club. It seemed that half the people in the group had decided that if they convinced me of their innocence in the murder of Alvin Blevin, they wouldn't have to worry, while others wanted to gossip about the details.

Reggie saw the tension in my face. "What's wrong, Jess? What did they say to you?"

I repeated the conversation with Rendell and told Reggie what I'd been thinking as we waited for the elevators to take us upstairs.

"I know some of them can be a little difficult," he said, "but most of the members of the Track and Rail Club are really nice. Besides, you have to take into consideration that being there when Al Blevin was poisoned was pretty upsetting to just about everyone."

"I know that," I said, taking a deep breath, "and I also realize that by allowing myself to be singled out by Detective Marshall, my original intent of just wanting to help has ballooned into a larger role. Unfortunately, I seem to be a target for attack by those who resent my involvement and a center of attention for the curious. Rendell has been particularly unpleasant. I'm still shaking my head over the fact that he had the temerity to follow us from the restaurant in Prince George. I hope he's not planning to do it again here in Vancouver."

Reggie laughed. "Winston certainly turned out to be a blowhard, Jess, but I'll bet he's all bark and no bite." He paused and his eyes grew wide. "You don't think he's the killer, do you?"

"Reggie, not right now, please."

He smiled sheepishly. "I suppose we're all caught up in the mysterious aspect of Al's death. We want to find out what's going to happen next."

"I understand the interest, Reggie, but it's not a game. A man was murdered. The person who killed him had no compunctions about taking a life and might not be averse to killing someone else if he or she got in his way."

"Are you in danger, Jess?"

"Now, don't you worry about me. I'll take care. The best thing for all of us is to see that the killer is apprehended."

Chapter Sixteen

During my previous visit to Vancouver, I'd spent an idyllic day at famed Stanley Park and had taken a boat to Victoria, where I'd basked in the beauty of that city and its harbor, the lights of the Empress Hotel and the legislative buildings reflected in the water. I'd also ridden the Skyride, an aerial tram, up Grouse Mountain, from which the panoramic views of the city and surrounding mountains and sea were breathtaking. There were other sights to be enjoyed to be sure, but the one place I'd missed, and wanted to see, was the Capilano Suspension Bridge. Others who'd experienced the popular tourist attraction had waxed poetic about the thrill of crossing the narrow, swaying, wood-and-wire footbridge, the Capilano River and gorge twenty-five stories below.

The Track and Rail Club had arranged for a van to take interested parties over to North Vancouver and up the mountain to the bridge. Initially, I'd been eager to sign on, but considering my irritation with the club's members, I briefly debated skipping the tour. *But Reggie was right,* I told myself, *these people were nice—well, possibly Mr. Rendell was an exception—and their curiosity was understandable.*

I went to my suite, where I packed a few things into a fanny pack and pulled a slicker and hat from the closet. It had turned rainy, par for the course, I was told. We'd been lucky with our sunny days as the more common forecast for this time of year was for wet weather.

At the entrance to the hotel, the doorman pointed me to the club's hired van. I climbed aboard and was surprised to find I was the sole occupant.

"Must be the rain," the driver said, checking his watch. "We'll give it another few minutes, if you don't mind, to see if anyone else wants to come."

I was beginning to think I might have a private ride to the bridge—and was not unhappy at that prospect—when, at the last minute, Marilyn and Samantha Whitmore joined me in the van.

Our trip took us on what was by now a familiar route, through Stanley Park and over Lions Gate Bridge, into North and West Vancouver, and past the station from which the Whistler Northwind had departed and where we would board the Pacific Starlight Dinner Train that evening.

Although I wouldn't characterize the Whitmores as being chatty during the ride, Marilyn commented on how the rain never stopped her from doing what she wanted, and raved about last night's dinner at the Blue Water Café—"It was always one of my husband's favorite places"—and Samantha managed to add that the Capilano Bridge was *her* favorite place in Vancouver and that her mother should try walking across it once. Marilyn shuddered at the thought. Before we knew it, we were paying our admission to the park.

The bridge was part of Capilano Park, a wilderness area marked by hiking trails that wound through a misty rain forest, a salmon enhancement facility below Cleveland Dam, and the home of 500-year-old Douglas fir trees and abundant wildlife.

"The conditions are pretty nasty today," the attendant at the entrance told us. "They may decide to close the bridge."

"We came all this way," Samantha told her sternly. "I'm not turning around now."

"Just letting you know."

Once inside, we followed signs through exhibits on early settlers and their Indian neighbors and wandered past colorful examples of totem poles, more correctly called story poles these days, to the platform leading to the suspension bridge. Marilyn left us to go talk with the carvers of the story poles, with whom she had arranged a memorial carving for her husband.

Samantha and I stood at the top of a short staircase anchored to the hill and looked down. A heavy mist had formed below in the gorge and had risen above the decking of the bridge, obscuring portions of it for moments at a time until a breeze dissipated the wispy haze. I felt a chill and ran the zipper of my yellow rain slicker up to my neck and tugged down on my hat. The rain and wind had kept tourists away; Samantha and I were among only a handful of visitors. We could hear a few people on the bridge, a couple of boisterous teenagers and a young couple whose laughter echoed back to us from the center of the span. I half expected the park's management to close the bridge at any moment, at least until the weather improved, but that didn't happen. We were free to go down the steps and cross to the other side.

"Are you ready?" Samantha asked.

"I'm not sure," I said. Although I don't suffer from a classic fear of heights of the sort Samantha's mother admitted to, I'm not insensitive to danger. Crossing a wobbly footbridge in the fog where you can't see your next step—a situation of that sort might make me uncomfortable. This, I realized, could be one of those times. The slender bridge swung in the wind, which seemed to have picked up.

"Come on," Samantha said, starting down the steps. "It'll be fine."

I took tentative steps down and stood on the first plank of the bridge, feeling the pulsation caused by the steps of other people walking. The teens reached our side and headed up the stairs toward a concession stand. The voices of the young couple grew fainter as they made their way to the other end, and the vibrations from their footfalls faded.

Samantha stepped onto the bridge, creating a strong throb of the decking under my shoes. She held on to one of the thick steel cables that ran along the top of a side barrier made of metal mesh, and moved forward with determination. The bridge swayed in the wind and she yelled, "Wheee!" She looked back at me. "Come on," she said. "It's great."

With her a few paces ahead of me, I started across, gripping the steel cable tightly, at times with both hands when a gust caused an especially rough movement of the bridge. I looked back; no one had joined us from that direction. I looked ahead. The bridge seemed interminable, stretching into an ever-narrowing strip, encased in mist and floating above the deep gorge and the raging river I could only hear below.

I felt more than saw someone in the distance step onto the bridge from the opposite end and was glad of another person nearby. Samantha had continued walking while I stopped and caught my breath and refueled my resolve to complete the crossing. I moved, one step at a time, hand wrapped around the cable, the rain and wind stinging my eyes and dripping from the top of my hat onto my nose. Samantha had stopped at midspan and was leaning over the cable. I reached her and stood at her side.

"It's beautiful," she said in a strangely disconcerting voice.

"Beautiful, yes," I agreed, "but also treacherous." The wind caught my words and my rain hat, carrying them into the atmosphere.

The boardwalk bounced as a park attendant who'd come from the other side paused near us. "Better head back, ladies. The wind is increasing. We're going to close the bridge soon."

"In a minute," Samantha said.

He nodded and continued walking. I held tight to the cable as he passed, and gave a little sigh of relief when he gained the stairs and the shudder of the planks under my feet stopped.

"You know what this reminds me of?" Samantha whispered.

"What?"

"Elliott Vail falling off the train into Fraser Canyon."

"What makes you think of that?" I asked.

"I just wonder what it's like. To let yourself go and *fling* yourself into the air," she sang out, her arms held wide as she turned slowly in a circle, "falling, twisting, spinning, maybe shouting, knowing you're seconds away from oblivion. Do you think that's what he was feeling?" She sat down in the middle of the bridge, breathing heavily.

Her words were more chilling than the weather. It was impossible not to imagine the scene she'd described, whether it was Elliott Vail or—or me. And I was reminded vividly of the desperation I'd experienced, hanging from the train's vestibule door as it swung out over the void.

There was a break in the mist, and I poked my head

over the steel cable and peered down into the sort of wildness that only nature can provide. The rain had caused the normally placid river to churn with white water, spume rising where the waves crashed into jagged rocks. I felt Samantha stand, sensed her presence next to me, and turned. She was staring at me. What had been a docile, pleasant expression was now stone-hard, the same threatening demeanor I'd seen in the pool at 100 Mile House.

"Thinking about falling?" she asked, and flung her body against the opposite side of the bridge, causing it to rattle and groan as the force of her action made the suspended walkway swing violently.

"It would be so easy, wouldn't it?" she said in a singsong, little girl's voice. "Just let the bridge dump you over into the abyss."

"Cut it out, Samantha," I said. "This is not funny. You're endangering others as well as ourselves."

"Scared? Don't you like the feeling? I let you ride once before."

So it was Samantha. "*You* released the latch on the train door. You might have killed me."

She shrugged. "I saved you, didn't I? Swinging is fun. Daddy used to like to go on the swings with me," she said, bending her knees and pushing up, as if she were pumping on a swing in a playground. "Daddy? Wanna go on the swings again?"

"Samantha, stop fooling around." I used my sternest tone. "We have to go now."

"Up we go. Down we go."

"Samantha!" Marilyn's voice, calling from the end of the bridge, held a note of panic.

"Look down, Jessica. See the rocks? If we jumped down there we'd be dead, just like my daddy. Then I could see him again." Although she was losing her hold on sanity, she looked at me with such sadness in her eyes, it broke my heart.

"Samantha, you couldn't have saved him. His heart wasn't strong. It wasn't your fault."

"I should have been there," she wailed. "I could have helped him."

"Please, Samantha," I said, holding out my hand. "Come back with me. Hurting yourself is not the solution. Come on now."

She started to sob; then abruptly, her misery became rage. "I could have helped Blevin, too, but I didn't want to. He killed my father. Let him die."

"Did you poison Alvin Blevin?" I asked.

A hysterical laugh erupted from her lips. She rocked the bridge again, hurling herself against the metal barrier, cackling and hooting. The violence of her action and its reverberation through the footbridge threw us both down on the wooden boards. Samantha panted, holding her side. "Oh, I wish I had," she said fervently. "Thank you. Thank you, whoever killed him."

On the cliff, Marilyn's pleas to her daughter were faint over the rising wind.

Samantha collapsed against the mesh sidewall, tears and rain dripping down her cheeks, but the mad look was gone from her eyes.

I appealed to her. "Your mother is calling for you. It's time we went back."

She pouted like a petulant child and folded her arms. "Tell her to come and get me."

"You know she can't. She won't walk on the bridge. She's terrified of heights."

"I don't care."

"Well, I do," I said, refusing to let her play out her misbehavior. "I'm tired of your games, and I'm tired of getting wet out here." Maybe without an audience

Samantha would pull herself together, I thought. If I didn't indulge her theatrics, she might stop acting out and follow me back to where her mother was waiting.

It was a calculated move. As wretched and sick as she was, I was betting that Samantha didn't really want to die. She was distraught and irrational. She had wanted to save her father and in her mind's eye had failed. Now she grasped at ways to control the world around her—and I might have died when she'd played out that need on the train. She was desperate for help. And she wouldn't get it until we were both off the bridge.

Struggling to my feet, I prayed it was the right decision. "I'm leaving now. I think you should come, too," I said, walking away from her as quickly as I dared. She rose and followed me, but with little grace. My arms snapped out to grab the cable as I lurched to one side of the narrow bridge, then to the other, my hair flying in the whipping wind and my knees buckling every time Samantha purposely stomped on the suspended walkway. I made it back to the side of the bridge we'd started from and was relieved to climb onto the fixed steps to the platform, and from there to solid ground.

Marilyn's face was wet with tears, but she didn't look at me as I passed her. Instead, her eyes were fixed on her child. She held out her arms and Samantha fell into them.

I went to the concession stand and bought a cup of tea. All I knew at that moment was that I was more than happy to be off the Capilano Suspension Bridge. I was still unsteady on my feet and my hand shook as I brought the Styrofoam cup to my lips.

Samantha Whitmore was a mentally deranged woman. I hoped Marilyn would get her daughter immediate medical attention. As a loving mother, it would be painful for her to admit her child to a mental institution, but Samantha needed treatment urgently, and putting it off might imperil others. Samantha had come close to killing us both today and had been the author of my harrowing experience on the train. When might she cross the line again? And would her next victim emerge unscathed?

I remembered the scene in the club car before Alvin Blevin succumbed to the poison. I had thought to hold Samantha back from giving him mouth-to-mouth resuscitation but realized now that that had never been her intent. She'd wanted to see Blevin die, certain he was responsible for her father's death. But I believed her when she said she hadn't poisoned him. She might have withheld her assistance, but she wasn't his murderer. Now I had to find out who was.

Chapter Seventeen

I bumped into Reggie on the elevator and we rode down together, hurried across the lobby, and climbed into the back of a taxi hailed by the doorman. Reggie gave the driver the address of the office building owned by Alvin Blevin, headquarters for the Track and Rail Club.

"Can't believe you went to the bridge," Reggie said. "Most people who'd signed up opted out because of the weather."

"They were wise," I said, and gave him a capsule history of what had occurred.

"Now I understand why she's on a medical leave. You're okay, right?"

I assured him I was. It might be a while before I stepped onto any suspension bridges again, but the incident was in the past, and we had a lot to do going forward.

We were on our way to the board of directors' meeting that Maeve had mentioned. It had been shoehorned in before our final evening aboard the Pacific Starlight Dinner Train. Reggie had explained that it was imperative to elect new officers, in light of Blevin's death. I had given him more to think about when I'd told him Blevin had a daughter. He was worried that the club would lose its headquarters as well as its president.

As we headed across town, my thoughts went to the model railroad setup Blevin had built at club headquarters. I'd seen Reggie's layout back in Cabot Cove and had been impressed with its size and attention to detail. But the way others had described Blevin's model, it would put Reggie's to shame. I was eager to see it.

"You never gave me the details of your conversation with the reporter from the *Vancouver Sun*," he said. "How did that come about?"

"He tracked me down at the hotel. Did you know that Benjamin was arrested a few years ago for attacking his new stepfather?"

"No. The reporter told you that?"

"Yes. But we talked mostly about Elliott Vail and his disappearance."

"Why?"

"This reporter—his name is Driscoll, Gene Driscoll—is convinced that Vail's disappearance and Blevin's murder are connected."

"Why would he think that? Both men were members of the Track and Rail, yes. And they both died on the Whistler Northwind. But the tragedies occurred years apart, and they died under very different circumstances. Where's the connection?"

"That's what I'm trying to figure out. Did you get hold of anyone at Merit Life?"

"Yes, an old friend who's pretty high up there. He didn't seem keen on talking to me about an ongoing investigation, but he said he'd get back to me with what information he could release. He'll call me at the hotel. Why do you want to know the name of the investigators, Jess?"

"Just to fill in some pieces. Do you have your cell phone with you?"

"Sure."

"May I?"

I took the phone from him and dialed the number on the card Gene Driscoll had left with me. I caught him as he walked into the newsroom.

"Mr. Driscoll, Jessica Fletcher. I was wondering if you've done any background checks on Al Blevin's former marriages."

"No, I haven't. Why?"

"It occurs to me that any of his former wives or children might be able to shed light on Mr. Blevin, the way he lived, his business dealings, things like that. I'd also like to know what sort of settlements he made with them."

Driscoll paused before asking, "Are you suggesting that one of his ex-wives might have killed him?"

"It never crossed my mind," I answered. "Can you get me that information?"

"Sure. Marriages, births, and divorces are all public record—unless you've got a judge in your pocket who closes the records. How soon do you need the information?"

"Whenever you can do it. I'm on my way to a meeting, but I should be back at the hotel by five." I glanced at Reggie, who nodded. "I have a dinner this evening, but that's not until—"

Another glance at Reggie, who held up his hands, five fingers extended on one, one on the other.

"The dinner is at six. I'll be in my room until I leave for it."

I clicked off the phone and handed it back to Reggie.

"So," he said, "what's this sudden new interest in Al's previous marriages?"

"I told you the woman who drove me home from Theodora's said he had a daughter from his first marriage."

"Yes. And I know why that information is important to the club, but why is it important to you?"

"I'd just like to know how old the daughter is and where she's living now."

He started to ask questions, but I held up my hand. "That's all I know at this point, Reggie. Let's wait until I hear back from the reporter and you hear from your contact at Merit Life. Right now everything is pure speculation."

"Knowing you, Jess, I doubt that, but I'll follow your lead."

We pulled up in front of a sleek modern office building, its walls reflective glass that mirrored the buildings across the street and anyone walking by. A sign above the revolving doors said BLEVIN BUILDING.

"Here we are," Reggie said as he paid the driver and held the door for me. The rain was coming down hard now, and we raced for the cover of the building's overhang. As we pushed through the revolving doors, we saw Deedee Crocker and Junior and Maeve Pinckney waiting for the elevator.

In the marble lobby was a newsstand, behind which an elderly Asian man prepared to close up. A store specializing in travel items occupied another space. And there was a small luncheonette behind floor-to-ceiling windows and an open glass door. A few people sat at the counter.

A chime indicated the elevator had arrived, and I entered the cab and faced forward. As the doors closed, I looked across the lobby through the windows of the luncheonette. There was a familiar figure sitting at the lunch counter—Detective Christian Marshall of the RCMP. Was he there because of interest in the Track and Rail board meeting, or was the luncheonette a favorite spot of his? I didn't know where he lived, but I did know his office was on the other side of the city. Was it a coincidence that he was there on that particular afternoon? I doubted it.

People milled about the fourth floor as we exited the elevator. Directly across from us was an open door leading to a small boardroom in which some people were seated around a table. Another open door at the far end afforded a distant view of the club's controversial model railroad layout. Reggie saw me straining to see it and suggested I take a close-up look before the meeting started. Junior had already preceded us into the room.

What I was able to see from my vantage point near the elevators represented only a small portion of the room. Once inside, its enormous size became obvious. The room was almost completely consumed by the model railroad.

"This is remarkable," I said, walking slowly into a maze of narrow passages between scenic mock-ups, over which ran a variety of trains.

"If you come over here," Junior called out, "you'll see the Whistler Northwind."

I followed his voice till I came to the part of the setup that reproduced our trip.

"Watch this," Reggie said. He stationed himself at an elaborate control panel connected to a maze of wires running up to a series of beams that provided conduits for the wires. He flipped some switches and pushed some buttons, and soon sounds erupted from the layout in front of me: "All aboard!" A yard-long steam engine began pulling away from the model of Vancouver station. Steam belched from its smokestack as it started up an incline.

"See the firebox," Reggie said, pointing to a red glow inside the engine. "Just like the real thing," he said proudly.

"I'm impressed," I said. "Al Blevin built this himself?"

Reggie laughed. "No. He brought in a company that specializes in building high-end layouts. There's hundreds of thousands of dollars in this benchwork, Jess. The engine alone cost two thousand. There's fifty thousand in the model trees. There's over a thousand feet of track; you can run fifteen trains at the same time."

I couldn't help but smile at the sheer pleasure written all over my friend's face as he manipulated the trains. I'd seen the delighted faces of children on Christmas mornings when they came down to see a small layout beneath the Christmas tree, and Reggie's expression was no different.

"Hey, come on," Hank Crocker said from the doorway. "Let's get the meeting started."

Reggie closed the switches and we went to the boardroom. The walls of the room were covered in what appeared to be brown leather; chairs were upholstered in the same masculine material. A large plasma-screen TV and assorted audiovisual equipment occupied one end of the room. Another wall held framed photographs of Blevin with politicians and entertainers, all of them signed to him. Opposite the door was a curtain glass wall affording a view of Vancouver's impressive harbor, where cruise ships awaited their Alaska-bound passengers.

There were several seats available on the long sides of the table, and one at the head. Crocker immediately took the head chair, leaving Junior Pinckney fuming. He and Reggie sat in vacant chairs. Folding chairs had been lined up beneath the framed photos, and the wives had gravitated to them. I sat down next to Deedee and looked at the faces around the table. I recognized almost everyone from the three-day train trip—they were obviously members of the club's board—but there were some I'd only spoken to briefly. Marilyn Whitmore, however, was not present, and I assumed that she was taking care of Samantha, hopefully getting her daughter the medical attention she needed.

"All right," Crocker announced, "let's get started. I'll be chairing the meeting as vice president. That's the way the bylaws read."

"Hold on a second," Junior Pinckney said. "I'm a vice president, too, and so is Reggie."

"Second vice presidents," Crocker said. "I'm first vice president."

I glanced at the Goldfinches, who sat to my left, and saw Martin roll his eyes at the debate that had erupted. Reggie shook his head and fiddled with a pen he'd taken from his pocket.

"Look," Crocker said, "we won't get anywhere if we get bogged down in this sort of garbage. We have bylaws, and we're going to follow them. If we don't, we—"

The opening of the door cut off conversation, and all eyes went to the new arrival. If I'd been surprised at seeing Detective Marshall downstairs, the sudden presence of Theodora Blevin in the boardroom was even more unexpected. The quizzical looks on the faces of the others in the room matched mine.

"Sorry to be late," she said, not unpleasantly. She circumvented the table and stood behind Crocker. "Well, here we are on a rainy day," she said. "The weather reflects, I suppose, the sadness we all feel that Al isn't present to occupy his customary chair at the head of the table, but—"

If she expected Crocker to offer her his chair, she

was to be disappointed. He sat rigidly, a scowl on his face.

Theodora smiled and said, "As you all may have surmised, I now own this building, including the Track and Rail Club's space."

"Give her your seat, Hank," his wife said.

Crocker's only move was to turn in his chair and look up at her. "You may own the building, Theodora, but you don't have any official role in the club. The by-laws state that as vice president, I'm in charge until a new election is held."

"Are you going to run for president, Theodora?" Reggie asked.

She started to respond, but Junior Pinckney cut her off. "Hank's right," he said. "You're not even a dues-paying member of the club."

The attack on Theodora caused a visible reaction. Her face turned hard, and her lips retreated into a harsh slash. "You would all do well to remember that Al *donated* this space to the club. You and the others who constantly criticized him seem to ignore that fact. Of course, if you wish, you can go out and find your own space for the club. I'm sure I can rent this floor for a lot more than the dollar a year Al asked for."

"And do what with the model layout, Theodora?" Hank asked. "Does that come with the space?"

"That model layout belonged to Al," she snapped.

"Built with club dues," Hank said. "Using other people's money for personal gain was always Al's way, wasn't it?"

Junior stood as he spoke. "Al told me he was leaving the model layout to the club in his will, Theodora. What about his will?"

"The contents of the will haven't been made public yet," she said.

"But you know what's in it," Junior said. "Did he leave anything to the club, or are you the only one to benefit?"

"I think I've had just about enough of your selfishness and insults," Theodora said, fire in her eyes. "I should have known there isn't one of you capable of demonstrating the thanks and gratitude Al deserved. This meeting is over. You can all leave now."

Theodora took a step away from the table. Hank jumped up and appeared to be ready to physically attack her, but Deedee had flown from her chair and grabbed her husband's arm. All eyes were on Theodora as she made for the door. But someone beat her to it. Winston Rendell came through it, almost knocking Theodora from her feet. They glared at each other before she vanished from sight.

"Sorry I'm late," he announced. "I see the dragon lady has taken her leave."

Hank's dour persona changed at seeing Rendell. "Hello, Winston," he said, sinking back into his chair. "Please, grab a seat. Good to see you again."

"Take mine," Reggie said. "The meeting is over."

"The hell it is," Hank Crocker said. "It's just starting."

"Ya'll're actin' like children," Maeve said. She'd grabbed her coat and handbag and appeared ready to leave.

"Sit down, Maeve," Junior commanded. "We're not going anywhere yet."

"I'm calling for a special election right now," Hank said.

"You can't do that," Junior objected. "The membership has to vote."

"Not according to the bylaws," Hank said, a smug smile on his face. "A special election can be called any time there's an emergency. This is obviously an emergency."

Reggie spoke up: "May I suggest that emotions are running too high for a really useful meeting. Why don't we adjourn and meet again tomorrow morning?"

I hoped his suggestion would be taken seriously. I'd found the atmosphere to be stifling, at best. My full attention wasn't on the machinations in the boardroom, however. I kept thinking of Detective Marshall sitting downstairs in the luncheonette and wondering why he was there.

"That's just like you, Reggie," Hank snarled. "Walk away from anything unpleasant. Go on, leave. I don't need your vote anyway."

"If that's the way you feel about it," Reggie said. To me he added, "Coming, Jess?"

"Yes, I—"

The Goldfinches hadn't said anything to this point, but Martin spoke: "Mr. Weems is right. I know, I know, Gail and I don't have any official capacity here, but it seems to me that—"

"If you don't have any official capacity, then I suggest you keep quiet," Hank said.

The exodus was swift and spontaneous. Reggie and I followed the Goldfinches out the door.

"The nerve," Reggie mumbled.

"Is he always like that?" Gail asked as we headed toward the elevators.

"Sometimes he's worse," Reggie said. "I heard he was searching Al's files all day looking for the bylaws. I think he's pushing hard because he's already been giving interviews as the new president."

Reggie went to push the elevator button, but Gail stopped him.

"What's the matter?" he asked.

"I'd love to see the infamous model railroad layout before we leave," she said. "Is that possible?"

"Sure," Reggie said. "The room is open. I just hope Theodora's not in there."

Reggie started leading them away from the elevators but turned to see that I hadn't moved. "Coming, Jess?" he asked.

"You go ahead," I said as the elevator doors opened. "I've already seen it. Besides, I'd like a cold drink. I'll meet you downstairs."

"I can get you something—"

I stepped into the open elevator before Reggie could continue his offer and watched the doors slide shut. When I stepped out into the lobby, I saw that Detective Marshall was still at the counter, a cup of coffee in front of him.

"We'll be closing in a few minutes," the woman behind the counter told me when I entered.

"I won't be staying long."

"Hello, Mrs. Fletcher," Marshall said.

"Hello," I said, sliding onto the stool next to him. "Just happen to be here?"

He laughed. "Actually, I thought you might just happen to be here. How did the meeting go?"

"Unfortunately, just another opportunity for everyone to vent their dislike for Al Blevin—and, I think, for each other. You're here because of the meeting?"

"In a manner of speaking. I had a feeling you'd be here. Thought I'd stick around to see. Anything new you can give me?"

I told him about my encounter with Samantha at the Capilano Suspension Bridge.

"She's a very sick young woman," I said, "but I don't think she's a murderer."

"So I can cross one off my list."

"I would say so. Now, turnabout is fair play. Do you have anything new you can share with me?"

"Well, we've got patrols keeping an eye on the Blevin house. But then you would know that since you were there for dinner last night."

"My goodness, your network is efficient," I said. It made sense to me. The police always look first at the spouse when there's a murder. I had suspected that her phone was tapped when the Vancouver police contacted me. "You're very clever, you know. Theodora's friends think she has the police guarding her house to keep away the press."

He smiled.

"Oh, so that's why you're here. It has nothing to do with me, really. Theodora just came here for the meeting and you're tailing her, aren't you?"

"Got to close up," the waitress said.

Marshall dropped money on the counter and picked up his hat from the stool next to him. "Going back to your hotel?" he asked as we walked into the lobby.

"I see you don't want to answer my question."

He winked and put on his hat.

The elevator doors opened, and Reggie, the Goldfinches, and Winston Rendell appeared. Detective Marshall walked away without saying a word and left the building.

"Share a cab back to the hotel?" Reggie asked the Goldfinches.

"Thanks, no," Martin said. "We have another appointment. Hell of a board meeting." He laughed. "Is it always like that?"

"Fortunately, no," Reggie said.

The Goldfinches started to leave but stopped when I asked Reggie, "Was Elliott Vail active in the club?"

"Yes, he was," Reggie said.

"He was on the board, wasn't he?" Gail said.

"That's right," Reggie confirmed.

Winston Rendell joined the Goldfinches as they left the building. "Care to make a comment for the record? I've already interviewed the new president."

Reggie and I stood under the building's overhang as we waited for a taxi.

"What was Detective Marshall doing here?"

"I think he's keeping tabs on Theodora."

"No kidding. What did I say to you this morning? It's got to be her. Do you think—"

"What I think is that we don't really need your friend at Merit Life to reveal the name of the investigators looking into Elliott Vail's disappearance."

"Oh? Why?"

"Because I think they've been traveling with us ever since the Whistler Northwind left Vancouver."

"What do you mean?"

"The newcomers, Gail and Martin Goldfinch. If I'm not reading the signs wrong, I'd say they have an interest far beyond old trains."

Chapter Eighteen

The light on my phone was flashing when I walked into my suite at the Sutton Place. The first message was from the reporter, Gene Driscoll, and I returned his call immediately.

"Hi, Mrs. Fletcher. I got the info you asked for."

"Good. What did you come up with?"

He sounded as though he was reading from a list. "Blevin was married three times before his marriage to Theodora Vail. The first one was twenty-two years ago. Number two was twenty years ago. His third wife was the one he divorced to marry Mrs. Vail. That marriage took place nine years ago."

"Were they all amicable divorces?" I asked

"Except for the last one. They really fought it out in court. She—his wife at the time—she went after everything he had. They eventually settled out of court, the terms sealed."

"What about children?" I asked, making my own notes.

"There was that kid from the short-lived first marriage."

"And?"

"His first wife didn't contest the divorce. They were young; the marriage only lasted two years. He signed over rights to the kid, no visitation, no involvement with her at all."

"It was a girl?"

"Yeah. Her name was Tiffany. I looked her up on the Internet. No luck."

"What was the mother's maiden name? Maybe she took it back and gave it to her daughter."

"Never thought of that. You'd make a good investigative reporter, Mrs. Fletcher."

"Thank you."

"I might have that information here. Let me see."

I heard the rustle of papers on the other end of the line.

"Yes, her maiden name was Carroll. I'll try inputting Tiffany Carroll into the Internet and let you know."

"See if there are any pictures of her, too," I said.

He laughed. "You want a lot, Mrs. Fletcher. A picture? I'll see what I run across."

"I'm sorry," I said. "I suppose I was reaching."

"That's okay. I understand. Anything else I can do for you, Mrs. Fletcher?"

His question sounded snide, and I couldn't blame him. I'd taken advantage of him in a sense; I'd turned his visit to me into a one-way street that benefited me more than him. On the other hand, I didn't have much to offer him in the way of the quotable comment he'd sought but had promised to call him first should I come up with anything newsworthy.

"Have you looked into Blevin's will yet?" I asked.

He laughed again. "Have you been talking with my editor?"

I could picture him shaking his head. "I really appreciate all your efforts, Gene. You've been very helpful."

"I'll be back in touch," he said, and hung up.

I sat on the couch and looked at the notes I'd made

during the conversation. I'd written "Tiffany Blevin" and crossed it out and substituted "Tiffany Carroll." Not that seeing the name in black and white provided me with any insight or corroborated a potential theory I'd conjured. But at least I'd confirmed that Blevin had had a daughter, who would be about twenty-two years old. I was now regretting that I hadn't brought my computer along. But when I wasn't working, my laptop was not a customary part of my luggage, which meant finding someone who did carry such things.

That person was Reggie, who never traveled anywhere without his computer. I called his room.

"I was just about to call you," he said. "My buddy at Merit Life just got back to me."

"And?"

"He wouldn't give me any names. All he'd say was that the guy was—"

"*Guy?* The investigator is a man?"

"Well, now that you ask, I'm not sure if he specified whether the investigator was a man or a woman."

"I was expecting the investigator to be a woman."

"Gail Goldfinch."

"That's right. I was certain she was investigating Vail's disappearance for the insurance company. But I could be wrong. It could be Martin. It makes sense. They could have paired up a male investigator, Martin, with a woman who happens to know a lot about trains. Pretty clever, if my assumption is correct."

"I bet you've put your finger on it. But what led you to the conclusion that they're insurance investigators, Jess?"

"More a hunch than a conclusion, Reggie. There's just something askew with them."

"I remember you told Detective Marshall that they didn't act like a married couple."

"Exactly. And she casually tossed out the two-and-a-half-million-dollar figure as the payout to Theodora Blevin, as though she knew precisely what it was. And she was right. At dinner last night, one of Theodora's friends said she was the beneficiary of two and a half million dollars. And today, Gail knew Elliott had been on the club's board."

"But how does knowing this help solve Blevin's murder?"

"It may not, but I'm always more comfortable knowing the true identities of people around me. Reggie, you have your laptop with you, don't you?"

"Sure, my ink-jet printer, too. I've been checking and printing out my e-mail."

"A favor?"

"Of course."

"Does the Track and Rail Club have a Web site?"

"Of course. We've got our meeting schedule up there and minutes of the board meetings, although I think we may have to edit the latest ones. We've got photos of the members' model train layouts, the history of the club, lots of things."

"Any old photos of club members?"

"Probably. Who are you looking for?"

"I'd love a couple of pictures of Elliott Vail and, ideally, some older shots of Alvin Blevin."

"If they're up there, I can get 'em for you. I'll do my best. By the way, Jess, I've been thinking about Marshall shadowing Theodora."

"Yes?"

"Do you think maybe the police have been following everyone, including you and me? I'll bet they have the whole TRC under surveillance."

"Perhaps," I said, amused by Reggie's enthusiasm for being an object of police scrutiny.

Reggie hesitated. "Um, there's something else I wanted to say to you."

"What's that? Is something wrong?"

"I'm sorry you had to witness that scene at our board meeting. It was embarrassing. A lot of us foamers are just big kids at heart. I guess that's both good and bad."

"Well, the bad was certainly on display today, but that doesn't include you, Reggie. You are always a gentleman. Oh, my goodness, look at the time. I have to get ready for dinner."

I'd just finished dressing when the phone rang.

"Mrs. Fletcher, it's Gene Driscoll again."

"Yes, Gene."

"I did a little further checking on what we discussed and on that daughter Blevin had with his first wife."

"Tiffany Carroll?" I said.

"I actually found someone by that name, but she lives in Ontario, not BC—at least she graduated from high school there. But Carroll's a much more common name than Blevin, so she may not be who you're looking for. Anyway, I don't know why she's of such interest to you, but I figured I'd pass along what else I learned."

"I appreciate that," I said, sitting at the desk and uncapping a pen. "Go ahead. I'm listening."

Once that call was completed, I dug out of my purse the card Detective Marshall had given me and dialed his direct line. He answered on the first ring.

"Jessica Fletcher, Detective," I said. "I think you might be interested in some conclusions I've come to, and I've been told the Pacific Starlight Dinner Train serves an excellent dinner."

Chapter Nineteen

The heralded Pacific Starlight Dinner Train operated by BC Rail, which also ran the Whistler Northwind, was the final event of the Track and Rail Club's annual meeting. The next morning, everyone would be heading for Vancouver Airport and flights to various parts of Canada and the U.S. or, in Winston Rendell's case, to London.

Our arrival at the train station was festive. A nine-piece swing band called Night Train led by a baritone saxophone player and featuring an attractive female singer played popular standards such as "Night and Day," "Cheek to Cheek," and "Take the A Train." A few couples started dancing on the platform, and others clapped their hands in tempo with the infectious music. A photographer snapped photos of each person or couple as they entered the station house; it had all the trappings of boarding a luxury cruise ship. The pictures would be developed and for sale at the conclusion of the three-hour trip.

We were assigned tables in the various dining cars that made up the train. Our car, the Apollo, was attractively decorated in orange tones. The drapes had a fruit design, the chairs were brown with tiny orange dots, and the carpeting was also brown. The tables were covered with crisp white linen and set with heavy silver-plate utensils. A small vase with fresh yellow flowers sat in the middle of each table. The lights were dimmed, casting a flattering glow over everyone as we took our seats.

My table had evidently been designated for the single members of the party. I sat with Marilyn Whitmore, Reggie Weems, and Winston Rendell. I'd been surprised to see Marilyn there. She looked haggard, and I was sure she had had a difficult afternoon, but I wouldn't ask her about Samantha while others were present. The table across from us held the Crockers and the Goldfinches. Behind me were the Pinckneys. Their tablemates had not shown up yet.

I looked out my window and saw Bruce make a hurry-up gesture to unseen people. The engineer gave three short blasts of the train whistle and we started to move. As we did, the car door opened and Theodora Blevin entered, followed by Benjamin.

I had to hand it to Theodora. She was dressed immaculately and made her entrance as though arriving for an awards show. None of the rancor of the past week, or the cloud of her husband's murder, seemed capable of dampening her composure. There was also, I acknowledged to myself, a hefty dose of arrogance involved. She greeted everyone as she passed, and she and her son took the two empty chairs at the Pinckneys' table.

Benjamin Vail wore a black suit, black shirt, and white tie, something one might have expected John Travolta to wear in a gangster movie. His hair was wet and slicked back, darkening the sandy strands and completing the dramatic brooding image he was so obviously trying to project.

But Theodora and Benjamin weren't the only unexpected arrivals that evening. Callie, our bartender on the Whistler Northwind, appeared through a door that led to the train's kitchen. She was carrying a small pad and pen and had a serving tray tucked beneath her arm. As she made her way through the car taking drink orders, passengers warmly welcomed her. Callie, more than anyone else on the staff, had reason to suffer as the maker of the fatal Bloody Mary someone had spiked with strychnine. She arrived at our table as the train gained speed leaving the station, gave us a pleasant hello, and wrote down our orders. At the same time, Bruce's voice came over the PA: "Welcome aboard the Pacific Starlight Dinner Train, ladies and gentlemen. Our travel time each way will be approximately an hour and a half. We'll enjoy dinner on our way up the coast, spend forty-five minutes at the turnaround, where there'll be dancing, and then have our dessert, coffee, and after-dinner drinks on the return trip to Vancouver. Settle back, relax, and enjoy the scenery."

Hearing Bruce's voice over the intercom brought me back to the Whistler Northwind, where Jenna had made most of the PA announcements. She lived in Vancouver, according to Detective Marshall. If Callie was working the dinner train, was Jenna scheduled to work, too?

My question was answered when our drinks were served. Instead of Callie delivering them, Jenna appeared carrying a tray. The smile that had greeted us on the first day of the Whistler Northwind trip, which had vanished following Alvin Blevin's poisoning, had not returned. She looked as though she would rather be anywhere but on that train. She managed a hello as she served our drinks, but I was aware that her attention was focused beyond me, on Benjamin. There was apprehension in her wide blue eyes, and I wouldn't have been surprised if she'd dropped the tray and bolted. Where she would have gone was another matter. We'd left North Vancouver and were now moving along West Vancouver's Gold Coast, albeit slowly. I assumed we'd be passing Theodora Blevin's house, although I doubted I'd be able to identify it from this vantage point.

Jenna finished serving the drinks and left the Apollo car.

"To the Whistler Northwind and to the continuation of passenger rail travel in North America," Reggie said, raising his glass.

We followed suit.

"To the end of an incredible week. I'm glad it's over," Hank Crocker said in his familiar growl.

His comment prompted discussion of the week and whether others agreed with him. I took in the comments while looking to the door through which Jenna had exited. She'd left it open, affording a view of the kitchen, where two men in chefs' whites, one of them Karl from the Northwind, labored over dinner.

My focus was drawn back to the dining car when Theodora stood and asked for everyone's attention.

"I know this has been a stressful week for all of you. It certainly has been for me. But I've always been a person who looks for good to come from evil. I suppose you could say I live a glass-half-full philosophy. I know how much the Track and Rail Club means to all of you, as it did to Al, rest his soul. He would be very proud to be here and see the looks of gratitude on your faces at what I have to announce."

I took a quick survey of the others' faces and saw puzzlement mixed with disdain. Hank Crocker scowled, eyebrows tightly knit, fists clenched on the tabletop. Winston Rendell had taken his unlit pipe from his breast pocket and chewed on its mouthpiece. Marilyn sat stoically, eyes fixed on the drink in front of her. There was silence inside the car as Theodora continued.

"I was hoping the lawyers would allow me to say what I wish to say this evening, and they have. What a perfect setting for the announcement I'm pleased to make. As many of you know, Al was an extremely successful businessman."

A soft, involuntary groan escaped from Marilyn Whitmore.

"And he was a generous man, too. For years the club has benefited from his donation of space in the building that bears his name. Well, I am pleased to announce that Al has left to the Track and Rail Club one million dollars."

The silence was broken by a few surprised gasps and other expressions of pleasure. I knew about the million-dollar bequest to the Track and Rail Club because during one of our phone conversations, Gene Driscoll had told me the beneficiaries of Blevin's will, thanks to someone he termed "a good source inside the probate court." My only question was whether Theodora would go on and name the other beneficiaries. I doubted she would.

She read from a card: "Al specified in his will that the money be used to further the appreciation of railroads and the role they've played in opening up the vast North American continent to exploration and development."

She looked up from the card and took us in. When no one made a move, she said, "I'm sure we'd all like to thank Al for his generosity." There was a smattering of polite clapping.

"That's really great," Reggie said after Theodora had resumed her seat and Jenna and another server brought us our appetizer, smoked salmon with avocado and vodka mousse, accompanied by dark bread and a sun-dried tomato spread. "Who ever figured he'd leave a million to the club?"

"A guilty conscience," Marilyn said under her breath.

"I suppose he left the grieving widow the rest," Rendell said, almost loud enough for Theodora to overhear. "Or her kid."

"You should join the club, Jessica," Theodora called to me from where she sat. "Al would be so pleased to have a famous writer as a member."

"Good idea," said Reggie. "I'll sign you up."

"I'll have to think about that," I said, my eyes again on the open door to the kitchen, where I could see Jenna helping prepare salad plates.

We'd been given a choice upon boarding of salmon or beef Wellington as a main course. I chose the beef, and it was as good as I'd anticipated. As cynically as Theodora's announcement had initially been received, it did serve—along with a tasty dinner, it seemed—to lighten spirits. Callie kept our wineglasses filled, and a general sense of celebration set in, enhanced by music coming through the speakers—oldies sung by Eddie Fisher, Frank Sinatra, Peggy Lee, Sammy Davis, Jr., Doris Day, and others of that musical era. We enjoyed our dinners, and conversation became lively. Before I knew it, we were slowing down as we approached the place where the train would be turned for the trip back to Vancouver. The tables had been cleared, and the staff was off getting dessert ready. As we pulled into the small station known as Porteau Cove, the sounds of the band that had played for us in Vancouver wafted into the Apollo dining car. I asked Bruce how they got there before us: "They pile into cars and drive up here in time to greet us," he replied. "They can drive a lot faster than the train goes."

I joined everyone on the station platform, where a joyous atmosphere prevailed. The band provided toe-tapping music, which had couples up dancing. The attractive blonde singer had been given names of couples celebrating anniversaries or individuals with birthdays and announced them to applause.

"Isn't this wonderful," a woman said to me. "Like a big party."

"Yes. Everyone seems to be enjoying themselves."

I looked across the makeshift dance floor and saw Callie standing near the idling train with Jenna and Bruce. And then I saw another familiar face standing on the fringe of the dance floor, Detective Marshall. My initial instinct was to acknowledge having seen him, but I realized that was exactly what he wouldn't want to happen.

"Excuse me," I said to the woman, and meandered toward Callie, Jenna, and Bruce. As I approached, Jenna moved away from the others and walked down the platform toward the engine and a path that crossed the tracks and led to a concrete walkway overlooking a body of water. I followed. She eventually stopped at a railing, leaned on it, and appeared to be deep in thought. I came to her side and said, "It's good seeing you again, Jenna. Or should I call you Tiffany, Tiffany Jennifer Carroll?"

She reacted as if I'd physically struck her and jerked her head in my direction. "How—? What? What is it you want?" she said. She looked terrified.

"I want to talk to you."

"About what?"

"About your father, Alvin Blevin."

She turned back to the water but not before I saw tears well in her eyes.

"I know this is painful, Jenna," I said, "but I have a feeling you'd just as soon have it off your chest."

I waited for a response. When she finally faced me again, her demeanor had changed. There was pleading written all over her face.

"Why are you doing this?" she asked. Before I could respond, she added, "Please, please, just leave me alone."

"I can do that, Jenna, but others won't. Others can't."

"What others?"

"The police."

"You don't think—"

"It isn't a matter of what I think, Jenna, it's what others will know."

"Because you tell them?"

"It would be better if *you* told them."

"Told them what? That Alvin Blevin was my father? What does that prove?"

"Nothing in and of itself, Jenna. But they'll come to their own conclusions. They'll want to know if the money your father left you motivated you to—well, I might as well be direct. Motivated you to kill him."

"What money?"

"In his will. The million dollars he left to you."

Her mouth dropped open and her eyes widened. "I didn't know," she said, more to herself than to me.

"You didn't?"

"No. He did that? Left me money?"

As I looked into her pretty face, I was certain she was being truthful, that she didn't know of her late father's bequest.

"How did you find out?" she asked. "About me and my father?"

"I know a little of the circumstances surrounding your birth, Jenna. Oh, and once I was told that Tiffany's middle name was Jennifer, I was more than confident that you were the daughter he abandoned at birth. That must have been a painful burden to carry all these years."

She nodded.

"Do you know you resemble him?"

"I do?"

"I think so."

I opened my purse and drew out photos Reggie had downloaded from the club Web site for me. In one, a picture of a younger Alvin Blevin, the resemblance was clear, even down to the twinkling blue eyes and dimpled chin.

Jenna studied the photo. "May I keep this?" she asked.

"Of course," I said.

"But you couldn't have known from this alone, could you?"

"No. There was more," I said. "I questioned the intensity of your reaction to his murder. Your demeanor, everything about you, changed so dramatically after he died in the bar car." I paused before asking, "Did he know you were his daughter? I mean, did he know you were on the train with him?"

She shook her head; silent tears now erupted into overt sobbing. "I was waiting for the right time, and now he'll never know."

I rubbed her arm in sympathy. She was so young and had seen such unhappiness in her life.

"He just walked away, Mrs. Fletcher," she said

plaintively, bringing her crying under control. "How could a father do that, just walk away?"

"I don't have an answer for that," I said. "Your mother took you away from Vancouver. To Ontario?"

She nodded.

"Where were you brought up?"

"Toronto," she said.

"When did you come back to Vancouver?"

"A year ago."

"You never attempted to contact your father?"

"I thought about it, lots of times. But I didn't want to—" A whimper swallowed her words.

"Didn't want to be rejected again," I said.

She nodded.

I looked back to where the rest of the group was enjoying the music. The strains of "All The Things You Are" reached us. I saw Detective Marshall, who'd come halfway toward Jenna and me and pretended to be examining the train's engine.

"Jenna," I said, "when the bequest is made public, the police are going to ask you if you poisoned your father."

Had I been a prosecutor and asked her that question when she was on the witness stand, her response wouldn't have convinced a jury. "I didn't do it," she said weakly, wiping her wet cheeks.

"Do you have any idea who did?"

She shook her head.

"Did you know your father would be on the Whistler Northwind that day?"

"Yes."

"Did you intend to confront him on that trip?"

"Mrs. Fletcher," she said, "I've intended to confront him a hundred times since I moved back to Vancouver. But I never had the courage."

"I understand," I said. "Does Theodora know?"

"No."

"But Benjamin does," I said.

"Please leave him out of this."

"If he knows," I said, ignoring her warning, "it's logical to assume Theodora knows it, too. And if you're to collect what your father left you, she'll have to know who you are."

She sighed. "It doesn't matter anymore, does it?" she said. "It doesn't matter who knows now. If the money is mine, I'll take it and that's the end of it." She looked past me down the platform. "I have to get back and help set up for the return trip. Thanks for the picture and the news about the money, Mrs. Fletcher."

I watched her walk back to the train platform, passing Detective Marshall as she went. He casually observed her and came to where I stood.

"Did she acknowledge being his daughter?" the detective asked me.

"Yes."

"Did you discuss the murder with her?"

"Yes, I did."

"And?"

"And I believed her when she said she didn't kill her father."

"Based upon what?"

"A gut feeling."

"Gut feelings don't hold up in court, Mrs. Fletcher."

"I know that. But she was a daughter yearning to make contact with the father who'd deserted her. His death kept her from doing that, which is why she mourned him so noticeably. Even if she had hated him, had harbored resentment over the abandonment and wanted to kill him, it makes more sense that she would have revealed herself to him beforehand."

"And she never did."

"No. She was too timid, and I think she'll regret that all her life."

"How did you make this connection?"

"How are you at remembering faces?"

"I suspect I'm not as good as you are."

"She looks like her father," I said. "That was the first inkling I had that she might be his daughter. But it took the other information to confirm it in my mind. I was right, and I think I might be right about my other gut instinct, another answer to one of my 'what if' questions."

He looked at me quizzically.

The loud blast of the diesel engine's whistle announced we were about to leave for the dessert and coffee portion of the trip.

"Are you alone?" I asked.

"No. Detective Jillian and I are in a car up front with the general population, people not involved with your group. A couple of anniversaries, a young guy proposing to his girlfriend."

"Did she accept?" I asked as we walked together back to the train.

"Yeah. Very touching. Would have been awkward if she'd said no."

The festive atmosphere on the platform carried over into the Apollo dining car as we chugged out of the station and headed back to Vancouver. Some people had changed tables: Reggie had joined Theodora, Benjamin, and the Pinckneys. Marilyn Whitmore had taken a seat at a table occupied by Winston Rendell, and the Goldfinches asked if they could sit with me, which I readily agreed to.

Jenna avoided me as she, Callie, and another young woman started serving dessert and coffee and took after-dinner drink orders. I heard Theodora order a Brandy Alexander, and Benjamin, who hadn't said much the entire trip, opted for Kahlúa.

The door to the kitchen remained open, giving me and others facing in that direction a view of the preparations going on in there. The chef, Karl, who'd delivered the vodka to Callie the day Blevin died, faced me as he worked behind a stainless steel table. He was wearing a chef's toque today instead of the white bandana he'd worn on the Northwind. I watched him take off the hat and wipe his brow with his sleeve.

Winston Rendell left Marilyn at the table and bumped into me as he made his way toward the kitchen. "Excuse me," he said. "Have to order another drink." The writer and businessman claimed not to have suffered at Blevin's hands in their business deal to manufacture new steam engines, but I'd learned differently from my old friend George Sutherland of London's Scotland Yard.

My mind raced, and I closed my eyes to better focus on the visuals that came and went.

"Sleepy?" Gail Goldfinch asked.

I opened my eyes and smiled. "No, no, just daydreaming."

My thoughts went back to my first day in Vancouver this trip, when I had been jostled by a man in a hurry. He'd been watching the arrival of a couple in a limousine. The Blevins. I saw his face clearly, as though it had just happened. And I was mentally transported to the dinner party at Theodora Blevin's home when her friend Nancy Flowers identified people in photographs strung along the fireplace mantel. I saw only one face at that moment of reverie on the Pacific Starlight: Elliott Vail, who'd disappeared under mysterious circumstances and whose body had never been found.

Callie was preparing the after-dinner drinks that had been ordered. She mixed the drinks and poured them into glasses on the steel table, coming into view as she did, and disappearing from my sight when she returned the bottles to wherever they were stored. Rendell had his back to me.

I turned to Martin Goldfinch. "Find him yet?" I asked.

"Pardon?"

"Have you found Elliott Vail yet?"

"I'm not sure what you're referring to," he said.

I kept my voice low. "I know you want to keep it a secret," I said, "but I've come to learn that you and your wife—if she is your wife—aren't along on the trip because you love old trains, and I'm sure Merit Life isn't interested in them, either."

Martin smiled. "We were afraid you'd find out. How did you know?"

"I'd love to say that the proverbial little bird told me, but that wouldn't be true. And it isn't important. What *is* important is that you determine whether he actually died in a fall from the Whistler Northwind."

He, too, spoke in a low, conspiratorial voice. "You're absolutely right, Mrs. Fletcher. Any ideas that would help me?"

We were interrupted by the arrival of Bruce, Callie, and the third server carrying trays with our desserts. Jenna brought up the rear with another tray on which our drink orders rested. She followed her colleagues as they placed the dessert plates in front of each person, and consulted a slip of paper on which table and chair numbers were paired with drink orders. She started behind me, at the table where Theodora and Benjamin sat. I turned and saw Theodora lift her brandy snifter in preparation to offer a toast.

I stood. "I wouldn't drink that if I were you."

Her puzzled expression testified to what she was thinking.

Reggie came to me. "What's going on?" he asked.

"Reggie, please get Detective Marshall. He's with Detective Jillian in the next car down. Ask them to come back here."

"I thought I saw him," he whispered to me. "I figured he was following Theodora again."

"Reggie? Please, just do it."

As Reggie left the Apollo car, Benjamin said to me, "This is ridiculous. Are you still playing amateur detective, sticking your nose into everybody's business?"

"I plead guilty," I said. "And what I'm attempting to do now is keep someone else from being poisoned."

My statement brought about the expected reaction from others in the car. "Oh, no," I heard Marilyn say.

"Another murder?" someone else said.

"Please," I told Theodora. "Just put your drink down until the detectives arrive."

"Detectives?" Rendell said.

"Not again," was another comment.

Reggie returned with Detectives Marshall and Jillian.

"I think you'll want to check that brandy snifter," I said to them.

Jenna, who'd stood motionless, still holding the tray, paled and started for the door leading to the kitchen. I stepped in her path. "I think you should stay," I said. Detective Jillian quickly came to my side and replaced me, preventing Jenna's departure.

I looked into the kitchen, where Karl, who'd now removed his tall white chef's hat, was packing up to leave. I turned to Martin Goldfinch: "I think you might find Elliott Vail in the kitchen," I said. "He looks very different from when he disappeared, but there's still enough similarity. Plastic surgery and hair dye can change many things, but not the eyes."

Goldfinch jumped up and joined Detective Marshall in a dash for the kitchen.

Benjamin stood. "Dad? Where?"

"*Elliott?*" Theodora exclaimed. "He's here?"

"Yes, he is," I said, "and this time he wanted to kill the right person. *You!*"

Karl burst through the door before the two men could catch him and made for the vestibule leading from the Apollo to the next car, which had the same sort of half-doors as the Whistler Northwind. Reggie and I followed and reached the vestibule in time to see Marshall and Goldfinch wrestling Elliott Vail back over the bottom half of the door he'd tried to climb. They pulled him to the floor. Vail kicked at them and swore, but they managed to subdue him by yanking his hands behind his back. Marshall pulled a set of cuffs from his belt and snapped them on Vail's wrists.

Bruce joined us. "This is just terrible," he said. "This has never happened before. People are upset. Can't you—?"

"We'll keep him out of your way," Marshall said, yanking Vail to his feet and pushing him up against the vestibule wall. To Bruce he said, "How much longer to Vancouver?"

"Fifteen, twenty minutes."

"We'll hold him here until we arrive."

Bruce thanked him and started back into the Apollo. He stopped, turned, and said to me, "Coming, Mrs. Fletcher?"

I looked back at the members of the Track and Rail Club, who were shouting at each other. Detective Jillian had his hands in the air, trying to calm everyone down. "If it's all the same to you," I said, "I'd just as soon spend the rest of the trip someplace else."

"Sure," he replied. "Go on up to the next car."

"I'll stay with you," Reggie said.

"Thanks," I said. "I appreciate that."

"We did good, Jess, didn't we?"

I smiled. "Yes, Reggie. We did good."

Chapter Twenty

Reggie and I stayed in the other car until Vail had been led away and the others had exited the train and were on the bus back to the Sutton Place Hotel. When Bruce escorted us down to the platform, Detective Christian Marshall was waiting. "Need a ride to the hotel?"

"That would be nice," I said.

When we arrived at Sutton Place, a television van was already parked in front. I suggested we enter through a door leading into the Gerard Lounge, where we would be less likely to run into the press or members of the Track and Rail Club. The room was relatively empty and we settled in a corner booth as far removed from the bar and main entrance as possible.

"Will you join us for a drink?" Reggie asked Marshall.

The detective checked his watch. "I'm officially off duty now, so a drink would seem to be in order."

Once we'd been served and I'd relaxed a bit, Marshall raised his glass of Canadian Club on the rocks and said, "Well done, Mrs. Fletcher."

"I'll drink to that," Reggie said, "only you've got to tell me how you knew that the chef they called Karl was really Elliott Vail."

Marshall nodded that he, too, wanted an answer.

"It never made sense to me that Elliott Vail had disappeared and that his remains had never been found," I said. "A view obviously shared by the Merit Life Insurance Company. That led me to wondering why he would fake his death."

"Money," Reggie said.

"That's the usual motivation," I agreed. "Vail's life was heavily insured, it's true, but he wouldn't have been able to collect, would he? After all, presumably he was dead. Unless—"

"Unless he had an accomplice," Marshall put in.

"Yes. His wife was the one who would benefit, so he needed her cooperation if they were going to be rich. It wouldn't be the first time something like this has happened," I said. "A husband with a big insurance policy conspires with a wife, his beneficiary, to fake his death, goes into hiding, waits it out until she collects from the insurance company, and they meet up somewhere far away, Europe, South America, wherever, to enjoy the spoils of their scheme."

"But Theodora married Blevin," Reggie said.

"Exactly," I said. "Theodora double-crossed her husband. She seduced Blevin and convinced him to use his influence to persuade a judge to declare Vail dead. Blevin was so besotted, he divorced his wife and married Theodora, leaving Vail high and dry."

"Boy," Reggie said, "that must have really ticked Vail off."

"Enough to want to kill," I said.

"To kill Blevin," Reggie said. "To get even."

"I don't think so, Reggie," I said. "I believe Vail intended the poisoned drink for Theodora. When he served the drinks at the club reception, he turned the tray so the Bloody Mary was in front of her, but Blevin took it instead. Vail, masquerading as Karl, couldn't grab it away without raising suspicion. It wasn't what he intended, but I don't think he was sorry. He left the car immediately after that and never returned."

"I see," Reggie said. "Sure, that makes sense. But you still haven't said how you knew Vail was on the train, pretending to be a chef."

"I wasn't positive—until I saw him again on the Pacific Starlight Dinner Train. There was something familiar about Karl, but I didn't realize what it was until I saw the man in the photos—Elliott Vail—at Theodora's house, and the photos you downloaded on your computer from the club's Web site. A man can change his features with plastic surgery, but facial expressions, the eyes, and the way he stands are habits of a lifetime. What convinced me that Vail was indeed alive was remembering the face of a man who bumped into me on my first day here. The photos, together with a vivid recollection of that man's face, tipped the scales. When I saw him again tonight, he took off his hat, revealing the light roots of his dyed hair, and I put it all together. I realized he wasn't going to settle for his failed attempt to kill Theodora on the Whistler Northwind. He was determined to make a second attempt on his double-dealing wife."

"I'll be interested to see BC Rail's report on his background, as bogus as it might come up," Marshall said.

"Bruce told me that 'Karl' signed on just before the trip," I said.

"Vail must have known Blevin couldn't resist a T and R Club trip on the last run of the Whistler Northwind," said Marshall.

Reggie and I both gasped. "Oh my," I said. "The last run. What a shame."

"I was afraid of that," Reggie said. "They've been

losing money on passenger trains. Freight is much more profitable. How did you find out?"

"Driscoll wrote about it in this morning's paper," Marshall said.

"Driscoll!" I said. "I owe that young man a telephone call."

Reggie sat back in the leather booth and fingered the silver souvenir pin we'd all been given at the start of our three-day trip. "Hang on to your pin, Jessica," he said. "Looks like it just became a real collector's item. Might be worth a lot of money someday. Speaking of which—money, that is—I was sure Theodora had killed Elliott. But then I thought she might've killed Blevin, too."

"Which wasn't a bad supposition, Reggie," I said. "Until I was confident in my own mind that the chef, Karl, was actually Elliott Vail, I suspected several others, too."

"Who? Jenna?" Marshall asked.

"Why would she suspect Jenna?" Reggie asked.

"Because she's Blevin's daughter by his first marriage."

Reggie shot forward in his seat.

"I know," I said, "it surprised me, too."

"Did Benjamin know?" Reggie asked. "Junior said they were an item."

"I believe she told him," I said. "It must have been difficult for him to know. He was never happy with his mother's marriage to Alvin Blevin. He must have felt torn when Jenna revealed her secret."

"So, who *did* you suspect?"

"Winston Rendell was at the top of my list, but I must admit that his rudeness to me may have influenced that placement. According to my friend George Sutherland of Scotland Yard, Rendell's position as a writer for the most popular magazine of train enthusiasts brought him into contact with a lot of wealthy people. He began to present himself as someone with insider knowledge, a real wheeler-dealer. As a result, he hooked a lot of investors into the scheme of refurbishing old steam engines and consequently lost a lot of money when Blevin, who'd apparently agreed to go into business with him, backed out. When Blevin reneged, it left Rendell with tons of inventory in the form of rundown steam engines and no way to pay for them." I looked at Reggie. "I hope his book is a success, because he needs the money to repay his debts."

Reggie laughed. "You're a very generous woman, Jessica."

"And now, gentlemen, I trust you will excuse me," I said, struggling to stifle a yawn. "This lady is very tired. I would like to go up to my suite and soak in a hot tub."

"I'd say you deserve that soak, Mrs. Fletcher," Marshall said, motioning for a check.

I promised to keep in touch with Detective Marshall, and we parted at the door to the lounge.

"I really like him," Reggie said as he escorted me to the elevator.

"So do I," I said. "A good man."

"You know, Jess, I'm really happy that I helped bring a murderer to justice."

I smiled and patted his arm. "As well you should be."

A week after returning to Cabot Cove, I received a call from Detective Marshall. Elliott Vail had confessed to everything: his staged death from the Whistler Northwind, his attempt on Theodora's life that misfired, and his second attempt to kill her on the Pacific Starlight

Dinner Train. The Brandy Alexander she almost drank was laced with strychnine, from the same type of rat poison that Elliott, a.k.a. Karl the chef, had hidden on the train.

"The 'suicide' was planned," Marshall said. "He made his jump when the train slowed down just before crossing Fraser Canyon and had a car, clothing, documents, and whatever else he needed stashed at one of the ginseng fields nearby. He made his way to Chile, where a plastic surgeon altered his appearance, and he settled down to wait. And you were right. The scheme was for him to hook up with Theodora in Chile once the two and a half million in insurance had been paid and establish a life together again. Theodora threw him a big curve by marrying Blevin and pocketing the insurance when it finally came through. When Vail realized what she'd done, he had to find a new identity and a way to support himself. He dyed his hair, took a job as a chef—and plotted his revenge."

"Will Theodora face charges for her involvement in the attempted fraud?" I asked. "Are there grounds to prosecute her?"

"We have only Vail's accusation that they planned it together," he responded. "Had she gone through with meeting up with him, that would have linked her to the scam. As it stands, everything is circumstantial, probably not enough to bring charges. But we continue to explore it."

"If she'd gone through with the plan and met Vail in Chile, Blevin would be alive today," I said.

"Yes, bad luck for Mr. Blevin. Mr. Vail is one very angry man, as you can imagine. If he hadn't been driven by that anger to make the second attempt on his former wife, he could have gone back to Chile, or anywhere else for that matter, and we might never have known who poisoned Blevin."

"What about Benjamin?" I asked. "Didn't he recognize his own father despite the plastic surgery?"

"He claims he didn't know anything about his father's presence on the train, or if his mother knew the suicide was faked. Frankly, I'm not sure whether I believe him, but there's little to go on. He was protecting his mother before and he's still protecting her. If I might be allowed to indulge in your 'what if' game, I can't help but wonder whether it was Benjamin who switched glasses and saw to it that Blevin drank the poison, not his mother."

"Interesting," I said. "You may be right. He certainly hated his stepfather."

"And I may be wrong. That's the problem with your 'what if' game. It's useful if it pans out, as it did with Mr. Vail. Otherwise, it remains a game, albeit an enjoyable one. Are you working on a new book?"

"I'm about to be," I said. "I've already started playing my game."

"Well, I hope it leads you to a smashing plot and a satisfactory ending. And by the way, I've got regards for you."

"From whom?"

"Gene Driscoll. He says he's up for an award for his front-page series on the Blevin murder, and he credits you with helping to make it so good."

"He's a talented young man," I said. "Please return the greetings and say hello to Detective Jillian as well."

Fall arrived in Cabot Cove, and then winter, an especially harsh one. I settled in to write my next novel, taking time off only for an enjoyable holiday season with my good friends. But I often thought about those members of the Track and Rail Club I'd met, and wondered how they were doing. Reggie continued his involvement in the club and was elected president, defeating Hank Crocker by a landslide. We met for lunch one day in February, and I got to ask about some of them.

"Samantha Whitmore?" he said when I raised her name. "Marilyn had her admitted to a mental hospital, I'm told. I guess she was sicker than anyone realized."

"I'm not surprised," I said, "but I'm sorry for both of them. Do you ever hear from the Pinckneys?"

"Yes. You won't believe this. Maeve got tired of Junior's accusations of infidelity and divorced him. He's given up the auto parts business and is hiring himself out as a photographer and consultant on model train layouts."

"The scale police at work."

"Exactly. And how about this?" Reggie said, relishing having juicy gossip to pass on to me. "The judge who declared Elliott Vail dead after only three years was indicted for bribery. Blevin had paid him off to hasten the process. Merit Life has sued Theodora for the two and a half million they paid her. Oh, and I brought this for you."

He handed me a copy of the magazine in which Winston Rendell had written an article about the BC Rail trip. It was filled with the murder, of course, as well as observations about the rancor and divisions within the Track and Rail Club, the allegation about Blevin having misused club funds, and the fight over his model railroad layout. According to Rendell's piece, which I read at home later that afternoon, the club had moved out of Blevin's building and used most of the million he'd left it to buy a modest building of its own in Minneapolis. The model layout was dismantled and housed in crates in the event it would be dispatched for display at club chapters around North America. To date, according to Reggie, it hadn't been. Rendell subtly hinted that he'd figured out who'd killed Al Blevin before anyone else had and had been instrumental in breaking the case. He never mentioned my name.

As Reggie and I were getting ready to leave the restaurant after lunch, he handed me something else, a manila envelope.

"What's this?" I asked.

"All the information on this year's Track and Rail trip. The Orient Express. I know you've always wanted to take that trip, and here's your chance. It'll be great, Jess. The plans are really falling into place, and as club president, I've been able to . . ."

I let him finish and took the envelope home with me, promising to seriously consider accompanying him on the junket. But I knew I wouldn't. I'd had enough excitement during the Vancouver trip to last me a lifetime—Alvin Blevin's gruesome death, hanging over the door on the Whistler Northwind while crossing the Fraser Canyon, and getting away from the demented Samantha on the Capilano Suspension Bridge. At this juncture in my life, I was perfectly content having the characters in my novels face danger, suffer death at the hands of murderers, and wrack their brains trying to solve those murders.

Still, it was tempting. Maybe I'd feel differently about it in a month or so, when the book was done and the urge to travel bubbled up in me. What if I were to go on the Orient Express and—? What if that trip were to—?

"What if I make myself a cup of tea and forget about such things for now," I said aloud as I headed for the kitchen.

Which was exactly what I did.

Turn the page for a preview of

another of Jessica Fletcher's adventures

A VOTE FOR MURDER

Available from Signet

"The White House?"

"Yes. A reception there."

I was enjoying breakfast at Mara's Waterfront Luncheonette with my friends Dr. Seth Hazlitt, and Cabot Cove's sheriff, Mort Metzger. It was a gloomy early August day, thick gray clouds hovering low over the dock, the humidity having risen overnight to an uncomfortable level.

"When are you leaving?" Seth asked after taking the last bite of his blueberry pancakes, Mara's signature breakfast dish at her popular eatery.

"Day after tomorrow," I said.

"I don't envy you, Mrs. F," said Mort.

"Why?"

"August in Washington, D.C.? Maureen and I were there about this time last year. Never been so hot in my life."

I laughed and sipped my tea. "I'm sure the air-conditioning will be working just fine," I said.

"Ayuh," Seth said. "I don't expect they let the president sweat a whole lot. Or U.S. senators for that matter."

Warren Nebel, Maine's junior senator, had arranged for my trip to Washington. He'd invited me to join three other writers in our nation's capital to help celebrate a national literacy program at the Library of Congress. I'd eagerly accepted, of course. And when Senator Nebel included a reception at the White House on our first evening there, my heart raced a little with anticipation.

I don't believe that anyone, no matter how sophisticated, worldly, well connected, or wealthy, doesn't feel at least a twinge of excitement when invited to the White House to meet the president of the United States. I am certainly no exception. It wouldn't be my first time at the People's House, although it had been a few years since my last visit. Adding to the excitement were the writers with whom I'd be spending the week, distinguished authors all, some of whom I'd been reading and enjoying for years, and I looked forward to actually shaking hands and chatting with them. Writers, with some notable exceptions, tend to be solitary creatures, not especially comfortable in social situations. I suppose it has a lot to do with the private nature of how we work, sitting alone for months at a time, sometimes years, working on a book, with only spasmodic human interaction. Those who break out and become public personalities often end up so enamored of the experience that writing goes by the boards. I've always tried to balance my life between the necessary hibernation to get a book done, and joining the rest of the world when between writing projects. That was my situation when I received the invitation from Senator Nebel—a book recently completed and off to the publisher, and free time on my hands. Perfect timing.

Our little breakfast confab ended suddenly when both Seth and Mort received calls on their cells phones, prompting them to leave in a hurry, Seth to the hospital for an emergency admission, Mort to the scene of an auto accident on the highway outside of town. Seth tried to grab the bill from the table, but I was quicker.

"Please," I said. "It's my treat. Go on now. Emergencies can't wait."

I wasn't alone at the table very long because Mara, the luncheonette's gregarious proprietor, joined me.

"Hear you're going to Washington to give the president some good advice," she said, blowing away a wisp of hair from her forehead. She'd come from the kitchen; a sheen of perspiration covered her face.

"I'm sure he doesn't need any advice from me," I said.

"Not so sure about that," she said. "Going alone?"

"To Washington? Yes."

"Thought you might be taking Doc Hazlitt with you."

"I'd love to have him accompany me, but—"

"Shame you won't have a companion to share it with you, Jess."

"Oh, I really won't be alone. I. . . ."

Mara's cocked head, and her narrowed eyes said she expected more from me. Besides being a wonderful cook and hostess at her establishment, she's Cabot Cove's primary conduit of gossipy information. She not only knows everyone in town; she seems to be privy to their most private thoughts and activities.

"I'll be meeting George," I said casually, making a point of picking up the bill and scrutinizing it.

"George?"

"Yes," I said, pulling cash from my purse. "George Sutherland."

"That Scotland Yard fella you met in London years ago?"

"That's right," I replied, standing and brushing crumbs from my skirt. "He'll be there attending an international conference on terrorism. Just a coincidence. Breakfast was great, Mara. Bye-bye."

The last words I hard from Mara as I pushed open

the door—and she headed back to the kitchen—were "You are a sly one, Jessica Fletcher."

I chided myself on my walk home from having mentioned George Sutherland. Knowing Mara, half the town would have heard about it by noon, the other half by dinnertime. Mara didn't mean any harm with her penchant for gossip, nor was she the only one. Charlene Sassi's bakery is another source of juicy scuttlebutt. (What is it about places with food that seem to spawn hearsay?) Small towns like my beloved Cabot Cove thrive on rumors, and in almost every case they're utterly harmless. As far as George Sutherland was concerned, there had been plenty of speculation that he and I had become romantically involved since meeting during a murder investigation in England. There was no basis to those rumors, although he'd expressed interest in advancing our relationship to another level, and I'd not found the contemplation unpleasant. But after some serious talks during those times when we managed to be together, we decided that neither this handsome Scottish widower, nor this Cabot Cove widow were ready for a more intimate involvement, and contented ourselves with frequent letters, occasional long-distance phone calls, and chance meetings when our schedules brought us together.

The rain started just as I reached my house. I picked up the local newspaper that had been delivered while I was gone, ducked inside, closed some windows, made myself a cup of tea, and reviewed the package of information Senator Nebel's office had sent, accompanied by a letter from the senator.

It promised to be a whirlwind week in Washington, and I added to my packing list an extra pair of comfortable walking shoes. The reception at the White House was scheduled for five o'clock the day I arrived. Following it, Senator Nebel would host a dinner at his home. The ensuing days were chockablock with meetings and seminars at the Library of Congress, luncheons and dinners with notables from government and the publishing industry, and other assorted official and social affairs. Why event planners think they must fill every waking moment has always escaped me; everyone appreciates a little downtime in the midst of a hectic week. My concern, however, was that I wouldn't find time to enjoy again being in George Sutherland's company. It had been a long while since we'd last seen each other, our schedules making it difficult for him to come to the States from London, where he was a senior Scotland Yard inspector, or for me to cross the Atlantic in the opposite direction. It had been *too* long, and I didn't want to squander the opportunity of being in the same city at the same time.

When I picked up the newspaper, a headline on the front page caught my eye: NEBEL'S VOTE ON POWER PLANT STILL UNCERTAIN.

The battle within the Senate over the establishment of a new, massive nuclear power plant in Maine, only twenty miles outside Cabot Cove, had been in the news for weeks. From what I'd read, the Senate was almost equally split between those in favor of the plant, and those opposed. Its proponents claimed it was vitally necessary to avoid the sort of widespread blackouts the East Coast had experienced since the late fifties, five of them since 1959, including the biggest of them all in 2003. Senator Nebel, who'd pledged to fight the plant during his most recent campaign, had pointed to the enormous cost, not to mention the ecological threat the plant posed to our scenic state, and further condemned the lobbyists behind the project and their clients, large multistate electric power companies that would benefit handsomely from the plant's construction. Some members of President David Dimond's cabinet had enjoyed strong ties to those companies prior to entering public service.

But the article claimed that Nebel's opposition to the plant could no longer be taken for granted, according to unnamed Washington insiders. The piece ended with: *Reports that Senator Nebel has recently received death threats are unconfirmed, although unnamed sources close to the senator say that security has been beefed up for him, both on Capital Hill and at his home.*

Death threats! Usually they came from demented people who had no intention of carrying through on them. But you can never take that for granted, and every such threat must be taken seriously. I knew one thing: Our junior senator had chosen a contentious time to be hosting a literacy program at the Library of Congress. Was there ever a time when something important, something potentially earth-shattering, wasn't going on somewhere in the world, and by extension in Washington, D.C.? I doubted it.

I replaced that weighty thought with a more pleasant one: visiting the White House and meeting the president, spending time with some of my fellow writers, and, of course, touching base in person with George Sutherland.